NEITHER MAN NOR DOG

GERALD KERSH was born in Teddington-on-Thames, near London, in 1911. He left school and took on a series of jobs—salesman, baker, fish-and-chips cook, nightclub bouncer, freelance newspaper reporter—and at the same time was writing his first two novels. His career began inauspiciously with the release of his first novel, *Jews Without Jehovah*, published when Kersh was 23: the book was withdrawn after only 80 copies were sold when Kersh's relatives brought a libel suit against him and his publisher. He gained notice with his third novel, *Night and the City* (1938) and for the next thirty years published numerous novels and short story collections, including the comic masterpiece *Fowlers End* (1957), which some critics, including Harlan Ellison, believe to be his best.

Kersh fought in the Second World War as a member of the Coldstream Guards before being discharged in 1943 after having both his legs broken in a bombing raid. He traveled widely before moving to the United States and becoming an American citizen, because "the Welfare State and confiscatory taxation make it impossible to work [in Great Britain], if you're a writer."

Kersh was a larger than life figure, a big, heavy-set man with piercing black eyes and a fierce black beard, which led him to describe himself proudly as "villainous-looking." His obituary recounts some of his eccentricities, such as tearing telephone books in two, uncapping beer bottles with his fingernails, bending dimes with his teeth, and ordering strange meals, like "anchovies and figs doused in brandy" for breakfast. Kersh lived the last several years of his life in the mountain community of Cragsmoor, in New York, and died at age 57 in 1968 of cancer of the throat.

By Gerald Kersh

NOVELS

Jews Without Jehovah
Men Are So Ardent
Night and the City
The Nine Lives of Bill Nelson
They Die with Their Boots Clean
Brain and Ten Fingers
The Dead Look On
Faces in a Dusty Picture
The Weak and the Strong
An Ape, a Dog and a Serpent
Sergeant Nelson of the Guards
The Song of the Flea
The Thousand Deaths of Mr. Small
Prelude to a Certain Midnight
*The Great Wash**
*Fowlers End**
The Implacable Hunter
A Long Cool Day in Hell
The Angel and the Cuckoo
Brock

STORY COLLECTIONS

I Got References
The Horrible Dummy and Other Stories
Clean, Bright and Slightly Oiled
*Neither Man nor Dog**
Sad Road to the Sea
*Clock Without Hands**
The Brighton Monster and Other Stories
The Brazen Bull
Guttersnipe
Men Without Bones
*On an Odd Note**
The Ugly Face of Love and Other Stories
More Than Once Upon a Time
The Hospitality of Miss Tolliver
*Nightshade and Damnations**

* Available from Valancourt Books

NEITHER MAN NOR DOG

by

GERALD KERSH

VALANCOURT BOOKS

Dedication: For Ann Dvorak

First published in Great Britain by Heinemann in 1946
First Valancourt Books edition 2015

Published by Valancourt Books, Richmond, Virginia
http://www.valancourtbooks.com

ISBN 978-1-941147-72-6 (*trade paper*)
Also available as an electronic book.

Cover design by Lorenzo Princi/lorenzoprinci.com
Set in Adobe Caslon

CONTENTS

Neither Man Nor Dog

One day I asked Adze if he had ever known what it feels like to have a friend. "I have had a friend; one friend, once," he replied.

"Whom you loved?"

"Loved?" He paused. "Well, yes: whom I loved."

"A woman?"

Adze sneered. "A woman!"

"A man, then."

"Man? *Tfoo!* Men are dust and ashes."

"Not a child, I suppose?"

"Children! *Ptoo!*" He spat. "People are weeds, and children are the seeds of weeds."

"I should have guessed," I said. "Horse or a dog."

"Horses and dogs are as bad as men. They *like* men! They *admire* men! Fools! *Ketcha!*" He seemed about to burst with pent-up scorn.

He was silent for a while; for as long as it takes to smoke a cigarette he said nothing. There was always an oppressive and threatening quality about the silences of Adze. They made you think of lifeless wildernesses of broken stones: there was death and desolation in them. Then he laughed, and his laughter was short and harsh, like something splitting in a bitter frost. "Friend!" he said. . . .

Friends are for cowards. You have friends because you are afraid to be alone. You value your friends because they are a kind of mirror in which you see reflected the best-looking aspects of yourself. Friends! And as for women, bah! What is there in a woman that a man should lose his head over her? A woman is impossible to live with. She is always talking. You support her, and she expects you to be devoted to her body and soul. She smells. She gets fat. She whimpers like a pup, that she is all yours . . . and the moment your back is turned her lover comes out from under the bed. Listen to me. I am a very old man. I have known a lot of men and women, but never any to whom I could

7

offer either love or friendship. No, I am alone, me! Yes, I have known everybody, high and low, in all parts of the world ... in fine houses and in gutters, on mountains and plains, in forests and on the sea, but I have always been alone, alone with myself.

Always, except just once. This was more than fifty years ago. I left Russia from Vladivostok, working on a stinking ship that sailed for the South Seas down past the Sea of Japan and the Riu-Kiu Islands. The name of the ship was *The Varvara*. The captain was a pig, and the crew also were pigs. The purpose of the voyage was to trade among the Islands. We had tobacco, beads, hatchets that would not cut, and some barrels of alcohol. This rubbish we intended to exchange for such things as pearls —because our white women loved to hang their necks with these little white sicknesses out of the bellies of oysters, and the South Seas are full of pearls and other nonsense.

Well, it was an unlucky voyage. Before we were out of the Sea of Japan we hit a storm, and the ship was rotten and the cargo was badly stowed, so that we were in a bad way when the winds died down. Everybody said that it was madness to go on, but the Captain swore that he would put a bullet into the guts of the first man who might dare raise a voice. I did not care. I had a feeling that, whoever died, I should live. So we repaired the *Varvara* as best we could and went on. And so we came to grief. Do not ask me where we were, because I do not know. Another wind came, howling like a devil out of hell, and it seemed to smash us like a bomb. The end of the matter was, that the crew, pigs and fools that they were, gave up hope. They cracked one of the bottles of vodka, and drank it out of their cupped hands, as the ship foundered. They died singing of sweet kisses, blue-eyed maidens, and love in the meadows, while the sharks were crowding round them like Society ladies around a millionaire. That was the end of them. Good. But the Captain, as I foresaw, had taken care of himself. He and the first mate got into the one remaining boat. Needless to say, I got in with them. They had half a mind to toss me out, only there has always been something in my face which makes men think twice before playing such games with me. The sea was heaving, but growing still now. Our little boat went up in the air like a cork and then down again between cliffs of green water. Yes, the sea is very powerful. The last I saw of our ship was a kind of scum of bits of wood. Good. Then I was alone with the other two men in the boat, and they were fast asleep exhausted. So I slept too. That was just before dawn. I awoke with the sun on my face. It was like the open door of a blast furnace when they let out the molten iron. The Captain awoke too, and said: "Open that locker behind you and pass me the water."

I did so; that is to say, I passed him one of two water-kegs in the locker, and also took out a little barrel of biscuits. He and the mate drank like fishes, and then handed me the keg. I also drank. Then we ate some biscuits. The sun rose higher. We lay and gasped. There was only half a gallon of water left in the keg, and the devil knew where we were. I said nothing. The day passed, and then the night, and then another day. The keg was drier than bones in a desert.

"The other keg," the Captain said.

I looked at him, and said: "There is no other keg."

At that, they looked at each other like criminals in a cellar when they hear the police kicking down the door, and a sort of despair came down upon the mate, and he put his face between his hands and wept—only he was too dry to have any tears left. The night was a hundred years long, and the next day came like a flame-thrower, and the mate went mad, and jumped overboard, and the sharks were very pleased to see him. And the Captain raved and gasped and, for the first time in his life, cried for water. Then he too went. He thought, all of a sudden, that this blue sea was some stream or other where the women of his village used to go and do their washing, and leaned over the side of the boat. Sharks have a habit of leaping up and snatching. They leapt up. They snapped. His name, if I remember rightly, was Avertchenko. But who cares?

So I was alone in the boat. I used the keg of water that I had hidden, sip by sip, and ate the biscuits. I do not mind being alone. I do not enjoy company. But then being imprisoned in that little boat, rising and falling and rising and falling, with nothing left but a sky like a house on fire, and a sea that covered the whole world ... why, then, suddenly it seemed to me that I wanted company. I never felt like that before, and perhaps it was the sun that made me feel so. I kept looking out of my burnt-up eyes, and seeing nothing but this damned emptiness everywhere, this rotten emptiness for fire and salt . . . and it seemed to me that a hole had been bored in my chest, and some of this silence and emptiness had leaked into me.

I lay like this for days, drinking my water drip by drip. And then I was down to the last pint of water and the last biscuit, and also the last thread that held me to the world. In one day I knew that I also would start singing and babbling about snow and grass and trees. But I broke this last biscuit, determined to keep alive as long as I could, for it is a man's duty to save himself. I broke this biscuit, I say, and a cockroach crawled out. I watched it. It ran across my hand, dropped to the bottom of the boat and tried to find a place to hide. I followed it with my eyes, put out a finger and headed it off. It crawled up my finger, ran up into my palm, and stayed there, doing something or other with its feet. I put up my other hand to shelter it from the sun, and there it stayed. I made crumbs of a little biscuit and—devil take it—I actually moistened these crumbs with a finger dipped in water. I wanted that cockroach to stay with me. I wanted it to stay alive. Yes, of all created things, that thing is the only one which I wanted to live with me! It made me feel that the whole world was not dead, and that, somehow, there was land beyond the sea, the salty and murderous sea.

So the madness that was coming on me went away, and the night came with cooler air; and still the cockroach rested on my hand, which I did not dare to move for fear of frightening it away; and that night passed quickly until it cracked—my last night—cracked like my last biscuit and let in the dawn. And for the one time in my life, just for an instant, I felt that I also was small and resting as it were in the palm of some hand powerful enough to crush me.

I looked over the water; it was calm as glass, and saw a sail. It belonged to a Norwegian clipper-ship, but I was too weak to signal. My head went round and the darkness fell down, and I knew nothing more until I tasted water, and found myself lying on a deck looking up into the face as round and red as the sun, the face of a man with a yellow beard. There were men all around me, all offering me clothes, blankets, food, drink, sympathy. But I looked at the palm of my hand. The cockroach was gone. I had been lost and alone on an empty sea in an empty boat for forty days and forty nights. But when I saw that my cockroach was gone, then, for the first time in my life, I felt lonely.

Uncle Kuzma

When I think of Uncle Kuzma I feel somehow, a sense of loss. He came from the land of the plains, down by the Black Sea. He was a fine, hospitable, generous man.

He had a way of talking that made things seem fresh and clear. He hated little, evasive people and things.

"What!" he would say. "Do I put spectacles on to look at an elephant? Whatever is worth seeing makes itself seen. What! Is anything that is beautiful ashamed to be seen? Does that which is good disguise itself? A tiger makes itself look like grass. An insect makes itself look like a leaf. Bah! Tigers! *Tjooptchah!* Insects! *Ptchut!*

"Nice clean things are to be seen and known. Take them or leave them, there they are. Does good grass try to look like tigers? Do nice leaves try to look like bugs and flies? Thus are men, boychik."

Boychik was his way of saying *Little Boy*. He would call a doctor a *Doctchik*. Everything was little to him; he was a vast man, and a simple one. He knew only two symbolic colours: black and white. He would never compromise between good and evil—as he saw good and evil.

Bad was black. To him all criminals were Black Criminals, and I have heard him call a red rose a White Rose. White, to him, was the same as Good. He always wore a white hat and white trousers.

"They tell you when they are dirty," he said. "Roll in mud," he would tell me, "swim in mud, go to bed in the dustbin. But *know* that there is mud and dust, and afterwards wash it away in nice white water. Grey is a bad colour because it is mediocre. Grey is the colour of compromise. It is neither here nor there. It is made to hide dirt. There are many men whose minds and souls are grey. Be careful of grey. It always looks respectable. But shake it! Shake it and see ..."

He could fight like a terrier, drink like a fish, and sleep like a bear. He bought himself a bit of landed property in Hampshire, some half-dozen acres of useless, ragged wilderness overlooking a stretch of lifeless beach and shadowy sea.

The local peasantry never knew what to make of him, but the children followed him.

He was the grave of God knows what dead romance; worshipped women from afar, behaved in their presence like an old-fashioned serving man with a repressed adoration, but never (as far as I know) had a love affair.

He remained faithful to a ghost enclosed in a gold locket which he wore round his neck. I opened it once. He had fallen asleep and I knew, somehow, that he would not wake up for an hour or so.

In a thin gold case there lay the likeness of a young woman who was neither ugly nor beautiful, a dark-haired woman smiling into a camera.

I clipped the locket shut and replaced it on his chest, where it had lain by the second button of his open flannel shirt. This happened when I spent a holiday with him.

My holiday with Uncle Kuzma was the finest I ever spent. I was a timorous child then, having recently recovered from a long illness. Uncle Kuzma taught me to fear no man, devil or beast.

He loved running for the sake of running, and made me run with him over the grass: taught me the technique of a knockout punch. Whenever I hit him in the right place he fell down: this gave me confidence.

He told me that he, also, had been a sick child, but that he had become a strong man by wrestling with a tree. First he tried to pull it over, then he tried to push it over, and in five years he developed the torso of a wrestler.

I wish I knew more about him. I only know what I saw, and what I saw I loved. When I went away from him I kissed him. I never even kissed my mother: kissing people embarrassed me.

But kissing Uncle Kuzma gave me a certain sense of exaltation. It was all I could do to thank him, and I felt he—who had claimed that everything good was comprehensible—he, Kuzma the giant, understood and was pleased.

My departure, if I remember rightly, was on a Friday. In that case, the Banquet must have taken place on the previous Monday.

Uncle Kuzma had been invited to some dinner. Never ask me what it was: I never knew, and even if I did know I should have forgotten the ins and outs of it.

He met thirty or forty local gentlemen, and had a pleasant evening. They asked him to speak. If there lives, now, any ancient gentleman of Hampshire who was present at that dinner, and happens to remember a white-headed man who had to squeeze himself through most doors—a phenomenally immense man of about sixty-eight, with a flaming face and a heavy white moustache, who talked queer English in a queer staccato singsong and beat tables with his fists when he talked—if anybody lives who was there, I should be glad to know what he said.

It is certain that he ended by inviting everybody present to eat with him on a certain Monday. This is the Monday of which I want to tell you.

Uncle Kuzma had about ten dozen of a very fine old Burgundy, and some bottles of exceedingly ancient brandy. There had been a time when he used to drink wine and judge it with the best.

He devised a magnificent meal. The weather was hot, so he hired a marquee, and borrowed a table—or series of tables on trestles—about twenty feet long.

Places were laid for more than thirty people. A cook was found. Waiters—one for every three guests—were brought from the nearest town. He even had a major-domo in a pink coat.

You understand that he assumed that everybody would come, since he had invited everybody. Uncle Kuzma was a man of simple instincts and plain mind. The food was superb.

I remember the ices most clearly; there were five different kinds. He had arranged a menu of ten courses—he was a hospitable soul who loved a lavish spread and the sight of people enjoying themselves. As if all this were not enough, he hired a band at awful expense—a seven-piece band to play while the meal was being eaten.

And for the occasion he dressed himself all in white. It was summer. I thought that Uncle Kuzma looked astonishingly beautiful, with his white clothes and his scarlet face and white hair and moustache.

The band came, the waiters came, and everything was made ready for the Banquet at midday. Twelve struck. The guests had been invited to take luncheon at twelve.

But no guest appeared. I don't think that his invitation had been taken seriously. They were ceremonious folk: Uncle Kuzma came from a desolation dotted with farmhouses, where a word was enough.

I watched his face. I had a habit of watching faces even when I was a child.

One o'clock struck. The cook came out gesticulating.

Nobody was coming.

Uncle Kuzma laughed, asked me to wait—as ceremoniously as if I had been an honoured guest—and went away. Fifteen minutes or so passed and he returned, but not alone.

He had about twelve men and women with him, but they were people such as I had never seen before. Some were in rags.

Most of the men were bearded; but I remember at least one who had a moustache and no beard—a superb moustache, nearly a foot and a half long, redder than fire.

Uncle Kuzma, roaring like a lion, drove these people before him like sheep. I seem to recollect a woman there whose face made me think of a witch in a fairy tale ... she had a beard on her chin and a man's billycock hat, dreadfully battered, on her head.

As soon as they were in sight, Uncle Kuzma stopped shouting. He conducted them to the table under the marquee. And then he told the waiters to sit down, and called out the cook and made him sit at the head of the table.

The table was nearly full. He made the major-domo take his place. And he himself served the meal, with my help. And at the end of it—I saw him counting on his fingers and nodding—he placed a bottle of brandy before each person sitting there, and made a speech.

I don't exactly remember what he said; but while most of his words have run through my mind, some have stuck there. He said:

"Ladies and Gentlemen! Servants of God! Honoured friends! You have honoured my humble table with your presence and I am deeply grateful ..."

At this word, I remember distinctly seeing a man with a carbuncle on his neck putting a fork in his pocket.

"... I have not for a very long time had the honour of your acquaintance. But brief as our friendship is, it is I who am flattered by it ..."

The woman with the beard carefully folded ten serviettes, counted them, re-counted them, and thrust them into the mysterious interior of her blouse.

At this point, just as Uncle Kuzma was saying: "You and I are all sons of men and women and children of God——" I burst into tears. I don't know why—probably because I felt that the kindness of Uncle Kuzma was meeting with such a scurvy return ... that his generous hand was being bitten by the wretches it was feeding. I felt sorry for everybody, especially Uncle Kuzma.

I rushed to his side, leaving a superb fruit-ice, and wept. I could not have known that he had picked up gipsies, tramps and beggars from an encampment in the woods to fill the table: I only knew that something was wrong and he was hurt.

He laid an immense red hand on my head and finished his speech. I never heard any more, except the words *fellows on earth, brothers in exile, and creatures not forgotten of God crying for human comfort in the dark.*

I only knew that at the end of it everybody banged the table. And then Uncle Kuzma went into the house and came back with a pale, flabby leather bag of money. He opened it and emptied it into one of his great hands.

He went round the table, giving one golden pound to everybody there. Then he threw the empty purse over his shoulder—I picked it up later and kept it for years—and then he said: "Go." And everybody went away.

And he put his hands on my shoulder and said: "Was that

nice ice? ... Fool! Why cry?" And I cried again. I was sorry because I knew that this beautiful banquet, of which I had eaten so heartily, had gone wrong for him.

My most treasured possession at that time was a live stag-beetle in a box. I gave it to Uncle Kuzma.

He was a great man—he took it and gave me a little dagger, the hilt of which was a cloven chamois foot.

But he insisted that I must give him a coin. I gave him a farthing. "We must not break our friendship," he said.

I left on the Friday—I cannot be certain—and did not see him again until just before his death. He was lying very still. His face was no longer scarlet, but dead grey. There were folds in it.

He looked thin and small. "How big you have grown," he said to me. I was only thirteen then. "You are going to grow into a strong man, with a fine chest and a great back. But run, run! Run a long way every day, because if you don't your legs will be short ..."

It seems to me that everything he ever said was right. If Uncle Kuzma could have been my comrade-in-arms! What pleasure we could have found, fighting and surviving together!

In a Room Without Walls

"If it could only be like this for ever!" said the quiet girl called Linda, looking over Jimmy's shoulder at the dim grey face of the clock. "Oh, Jimmy, this is heaven! How happy I am! What can I have done, to deserve such happiness?"

She felt Jimmy smiling. "Are you happy too?" she asked Jimmy. He nodded, observing the reflection of the clock face in the long mirror on the wardrobe door. He had been grimacing.

Last year, he thought chafing and trying not to fidget, *I made a hundred and four thousand five hundred pounds. All that money in three hundred and sixty-five days. It works out at ... what? ... Twelve-pound-ten an hour. I have given this girl twenty-five pounds' worth of my time, at that rate. Four shillings and twopence a minute—nearly a penny a second. I've thrown away twenty-five pounds, being gracious to Linda for two hours. And she talks of this*

*going on for ever—for ever, at a penny a second! There isn't that
much money in the world!*

Linda, with a luminous glory behind her somewhat faded
face, closed her eyes and, resting her chin upon his shoulder and
caressing his cheek with her forehead, said: "How sweet, Jimmy!
How sweet! How can I ever tell you how grateful I am to you for
making me so happy? Ah, my dear darling—now, just now, do
you know what? I'm so full of love and happiness that another
tiny bit would be too much ... I'd die. But this is Heaven: I'll
never want any Heaven but this—to be here, with you, exactly
like this, loving you as I do and knowing that you love me. You
do love me?"

Jimmy was inclined to say: "Oh, nonsense! Love? Ha! You?
Bah! What, *me?* Love *you?* Who are you? A laundress. I am
Jimmy—you know who I am—Jimmy the Star. I could have
world-famous actresses, take my choice of the beauties of five
continents. The world is mine, and all the women in it. Titled
women, even. Because a whim takes hold of me, and I beckon
to a poor pale creature in a clutching crowd of infatuated fans—
because I, like a god, confer upon you the glory of my intimacy for
a moment you talk of love? Love? My love? For you? At four-and-
twopence a second, do you realise what a lingering look is worth?"

But he said: "Of course I love you," and he looked at the
reversed reflection of the clock that told the time.

"All my life," said Linda, "all my life I've dreamt of such a
moment. Don't laugh—I felt somehow that it *might* happen to
me. I never dared to say to anybody that I had a dream of love.
They would have laughed; I'm so plain and ordinary. Oh, dear
God, but I love you, Jimmy! You're too good for me!"

In spite of his seething distaste, Jimmy muttered: "Nothing of
the sort. Charming girl!"

"Ah, my own dear love! My dream-come-true! Do you know
what? I believe you if you say so. I believe! I believe! I believe in
you. This morning I was washing sheets, and you were only a
picture, a splendid vision. And now I'm here, with you, in your
arms, hearing you telling me you love me. There *is* a God! Where
is yesterday? Where is the grey when the sunlight bleaches it
away? *Why* do you love me?"

"Sweet," said Jimmy, with his eye on the time. The movement of the big hand was worth thirty-four shillings an inch.

He was in an ecstasy of boredom and visitation. *Oh, to be rid of this ridiculously happy woman!* he thought. *Why did I do it? Why? Why?*

"Tell me why you love me," she said. "No, never mind. Just say it again."

What was Jimmy to say? If he could have said: "I only said so to please you. It tickled my vanity to beckon you out of the mob around the stage door. You helped me to condescend, you made me feel greater"—then he would have been talking like an honest man. If he had had the courage to say: "You were such a whole-hearted worshipper that I wanted to be a god," then he would not have been where he was at that moment. If he could have told the truth he would have been an honest man—not a man in anguish, caressing a woman with his hand while he gritted his teeth and watched the clock.

But he said: "Of course I love you!"

There was a silence: it seemed to cling to his ears for a lifetime. Then it came away with a sort of thick sucking noise, and he heard the sharp tick of the round white clock. His face looked drawn in the darkening mirror. He had a desperate yearning to speak a little truth.

"And you promise to stay with me always?" Linda asked.

He had meant to say "No," but heard himself muttering: "Mm."

"Jimmy! Hold me!"

Although he had intended to get up and go away, Jimmy found himself embracing Linda and looking into her eyes.

"Always?" she whispered.

He answered: "Always." Candour stuck in his throat.

"Oh, Jimmy, if this could go on and on for ever!"

Unutterably weary, he muttered: "Uh-uh; sure!" He was sick, sick to the heart, of pent-up truth.

"Did you say 'sure'? Do you mean it?"

"Yes."

"If you say you mean it, I know you mean it," said Linda. "Dearest, there *is* a God. There *is* a Heaven!"

"Oh yes, yes. Sure, sure," said Jimmy, with a half-laugh. "This *is* Heaven, isn't it?"

He shifted, meaning to pull himself away from her. Something happened; he moved in the wrong direction. Linda was in his arms.

"It is! It is!" she whispered.

He sneered. "And hell? Where's hell?"

Something comparable to a bladder, a grey strained veinous membrane, seemed to burst in a splash of pure, cold light. Out of the indefinable centre of this light a grave, clear voice said: "Think!"

Jimmy looked at the clock. Its hands still marked seven minutes to four of a drizzling February afternoon.

He remembered that there had been a judgment, a hundred thousand years ago. Linda, on his shoulder, had achieved paradise; and he was damned. And for all eternity the clock had stopped.

The Last Battle

Ali was preparing for the fight. Ali was fat, fantastically fat. When he was naked, one could see how malevolently time had dealt with him; blowing him up like a balloon, and dragging him down like a bursting sack. His pectorals hung flabbily, like the breasts of an old woman. His belly sagged!

He brushed his moustache, pinched out a length of Hungarian Pomade, and moulded the ends to needle-points with a dexterous twirl.

"Kration'll try and grab that," said Adam, "just to give the lads a laugh."

"Let him try!"

"Ali, why not trim it down?"

Ali swore that he would as soon trim down another essentially masculine attribute. He put on a curious belt, nearly a foot wide, made of canvas and rubber. "Pull this tight, please; as tight as you can," he said; and muttered with an apologetic look: "I do not want the people to be under an impression that I have been getting a leetle bit fat . . ."

Adam pulled at the straps, and, like toothpaste in a tube, soft fat oozed up above Ali's waistline.

"Ali, is this wise? This belt squeezes your guts together. If Kration hits you, or kicks you there——"

"Let him try." Ali writhed into a set of long black tights, and pulled over them a pair of red silk shorts. "Now, help me with this sash." He held up a long band of frayed red satin, embroidered with Arabic characters. "This was a present from Abdul Hamid..."

"Ali, you're crazy to press your belly in like that!"

"Ptah!" Ali drew himself up, and stood with folded arms. "Tell me, do I look good?"

Adam felt an impulse to shed tears.

"Listen, Ali; be cautious, for heaven's sake."

"My little friend, you forget that I have won hundreds of fights—that I never have been beaten!"

"I know. But I should hate like hell to see you hurt."

Ali laughed. "Professor Frochner tore one of my ribs right out of the skin, but I beat him; and I fought again next day. In all my life, nobody ever heard me cry out! Nobody ever saw me tap the mat. Leblond had me by the foot in a ju-jitsu hold. 'Give in or I break your ankle,' he said. I said: 'Break on, Leblond: Ali never gives in.' And he broke my ankle, and I got up on one foot, and pinned him. I said: 'You cannot hurt Ali. But he whom Ali grips, God forgets!' That is me!"

"Oh, I'm sure you'll win. I've betted on you."

"Good boy! What odds did they lay against me?"

"Very small."

"You're lying. They think I'm an old man. They laugh. Good, let them. And in the end, when they laugh on the other side of the face, I shall laugh, too—I shall laugh right into their eyes, and say: 'The old wolf still has teeth.' Do I look good?"

"You look like a champion, Ali, you really do."

Ali laughed, until the fat on his stomach bounced like a cat in a sack. "Ha-ha-ha! I surprised you, eh? ... They think I'm going to fool about with this Greek, this Cypriot. No. I shall walk in— one, two, three; up with the legs, back with the head—dash him down, pick him up like a child, shake him like a kitten; then over my head, bim-bam, and pin him. Back again—forward with his head, under my arm with it, and *khaaa* my old stranglehold, until his eyes pop out. Then I shall pick him up like a dumb-bell, and hold him above my head, and say to the crowd: 'This is the man who thought he could beat Ali the Turk!' Then——"

An open door let in the shouting of a crowd. An attendant came in, and said:

"*Ali!*"

Ali put on a dressing-gown of quilted red silk, thirty years old, and eroded by moths. "Smart, eh? A woman gave me this in Vienna, in ... I forget the date ..."

Adam whispered: "Give me your glass eye: it's madness to wrestle in one of those things."

"Rubbish! And let him see I have a blind side?"

"Give it to me, I tell you!"

"If you insist, then, take it." Ali slid out his left eye, and gave it to Adam, who put it in his waistcoat pocket. Then he strode, with slow dignity, out to the ringside, while through his head ran the cheerful rhythm of the March of the Gladiators, the tune to which the old wrestlers at the International Tournament had strutted in glory round the arenas.

There was a roar of applause. Ali raised his hands to acknowledge it, when he saw Kration, already in the ring, bowing and smiling. Ali grasped the ropes and swung himself up. There was a pause. A little trickle of clapping broke out; then laughter, which rose and swelled, pierced by high cat-calls and shrill whistles....

"Hoooi! Laurel and 'Ardy!"

"Where did you get them trousis?"

"Take yer whiskers orf! We can't see yer!"

Somebody began to sing, in a good tenor voice: "It happened on the beach at Belly-Belly!"

Figler's friend, Lew, rose and shouted, in a voice trained in the market-places of the earth: "Good old Ali! We remember you!"

Ali tore off his dressing-gown and threw it to Adam.

"Go on, laugh!" he cried.

They laughed.

Fabian shrieked into a megaphone: "Ladies and gentlemen! On my right, two hundred and forty pounds of bone, muscle, brain and nerve, Kration of Cyprus, contender for championship honours!...On my left——"

"Father Christmas!" said a voice; and there was another shout of laughter——

"Ali the Terrible Turk, ex-heavyweight champion of the world, now making a sensational come-back——"

"Champion of wot world?" yelled a thin, Cockney voice.

"Ladeez and gentlemen! The name of Ali the Terrible Turk was a household word at the beginning of the century——"

"Wot century?"

("That's what you get, if you get old without any money," said Lew to Figler.)

Fabian stepped back. Kration and Ali went to their corners. Kration still smiled. It was best, he decided, to let it seem that this affair was an elaborate joke. Ali was as grim as death.

"Now don't forget—take it easy!" whispered Adam.

Ali replied: "I shall have pinned him within twenty seconds. Count twenty, slowly——"

The gong clanged.

The wrestlers went out into the ring.

* * * * *

Kration advanced with the grace of a dancer. Ali moved slowly, jaws clamped, chin down. They circled about each other, feinting. Then there was a sound like the crack of a whip. Before Ali's fat-clogged, time-laden muscles could co-ordinate in a counter-attack, Kration had slapped him on the buttocks.

"Get him by the 'orns!" somebody shouted.

"Right," said Kration, and grabbed at Ali's moustache. But next moment, a grip like pincers closed on his wrist, a force like an earthquake twirled him round, and his hand went back over his head towards his shoulder-blades.

Kration broke out into a sweat. It occurred to him that Ali was in savage earnest. He had not sufficient skill to break the hold. Resisting Ali's pressure with all his strength, he butted backwards with his head. The hard, round skull, padded with kinky black hair, jolted against Ali's jaw. The Turk snarled, and tried to knock Kration's feet from under him; but between himself and his opponent, his vast abdomen stood like a wall. Kration's head jerked back again. In Ali's nose something like a lever in a pump, and bright red blood began to run on to his moustache.

Kration broke away, whirled round, and, in turning, struck Ali on the jaw with his forearm. It seemed to Ali that the Cypriot was swimming in a sea of red water reticulated with a network of dazzling light; and that the voice of this sea was laughter. But even as his brain wavered, his ancient instincts were sending him lumbering after Kration, while his consciousness automatically juggled with the logic of a hundred different forms of attack. . . .

"*He's too fast! Waste no strength chasing! Get close and crush!*" His huge right hand hooked Kration's neck. Kration's fingers, forked like a snake's tongue, flickered towards his eyes. Ali ducked. Kration's nails scratched his forehead. Then Ali had his right hand in an irresistible grip. Adam saw his back quiver.

"Flying mare!" screamed a woman's voice.

Ali heaved Kration off his feet by his right arm; stooped to throw him over his shoulder; then stopped. The edge of his belt had cut him short. They stayed, for a moment, in this ignominious posture. Then Kration, wriggling like a python, caught Ali's throat between his biceps and forearm, twisted a leg between Ali's thighs, grunted, tugged; then writhed away as they fell. The Turk's body struck the mat with the dead thud of a falling tree. Something snapped; his belt had burst. Kration uttered a triumphant yell, and pulled it away; leapt back, and held it over his head.

Laughter roared through the spectators like a wind through trees. Ali was up, growling. Fabian took the belt from Kration's hands, muttering, as he did so: "Liven it up a bit, can't you, you two? Don't play about like kids in a bloody nursery! Come on, now!"

Kration evaded Ali's slashing right hand, threw himself back against the ropes, and fired himself across the ring like a stone from a catapult. His right shoulder struck Ali in the abdomen.

Ali fell backwards, with a tremendous gasp, but even as he fell, rolled over with a grunt and caught Kration below the ribs in a scissors-hold.

Kration felt like a man in a train smash, pinned by a fallen ceiling. He writhed, but Ali held fast. The crowd screamed. Kration breathed in short coughs: "*Assss ... Assss ... Assss....*" He tensed all the iron muscles of his stomach. Ali still struggled for breath: every exhalation, blowing through the blood which still ran from his nose, spattered the mat with red drops: "*Prupaghhh ... prup-aghhh ...*" He realised that he could not hold Kration for more than another ten seconds. Cramp crawled in the muscles of his thighs.

Kration ground the heel of his hand into Ali's mouth, and broke loose; leapt high in the air, and came down backside first. Ali saw him coming, but could not move quickly enough. Kration's fifteen stone dropped, like a flour-sack falling from a loft, on to Ali's chest. Wind rushed out—"Affffffffff!"—with a fine spray of blood. Darkness descended on the Turk; for perhaps one second he became unconscious. His mind floundered up out of a darkness as deep and cold as Siberian midnight. He found himself struggling to his feet.

Adam's voice reached his ears as from an immense distance: "Careful, Ali, careful!" Kration was upon him again, on his blind side, and had caught him in a wrist-lock.

Ali's brain flickered and wavered like a candle-flame in a draught. There was a counter-move; something ... something ... he could not remember. He put out all his might, and caught one of the Cypriot's wrists; grunted: "Hup!" like a coal-heaver and used his tremendous weight to spin Kration round and swing him off his feet. As Kration staggered, Ali caught one of his ankles; twirled him round, six inches off the mat, in the manner of an acrobatic dancer, then let go. The Cypriot fell on his face, kicking and heaving like a wounded leopard. Ahai! yelled Ali, springing forward as Kration rose to his hands and knees. "Waho!"

"Nice work!" screamed Adam.

Ali had Kration in a headlock. Kration crouched, gathering his strength; then began to strain left and right, in spasmodic jerks. Blood from Ali's nose fell like rain on Kration's back. Both men were red to the waist, slippery with blood. Ali's grip was slipping: Kration was as hard to hold as a flapping sail in a raging wind.... Kration's head was free. Ali caught a glimpse of his face, purple, swollen, split by a grin of anger that displayed all his teeth, white as peeled almonds. Then Kration swung his left arm. His hard, flat palm struck Ali in the face: one of his nails scraped the surface of Ali's eye.

A blank, bleak horror came into the heart of the Turk. "*My eye! My last eye! If I lose this eye, too!*" Then he roared like a maddened lion, buried his fingers in the softer flesh above Kration's hips, lifted him above his head by sheer force, threw him across the ring, and followed him, growling unintelligible insults and spitting blood——

Clang! went the gong.

Ali groped his way back to his corner, and sat limply. Adam sponged him with cold water, adjusted his sash, and wiped the blood from his face.

"My eye," said Ali, "my eye!"

"It's badly scratched," said Adam.

Ali's eye was closing. The lids, dark and swollen, were creeping together to cover the blood-coloured eyeball.

The crowd shouted. One voice screamed: "Carm on, Nelson! Carm on, whiskers!"

Ali sucked up a mouthful of water and, like a spouting whale, sprayed it towards the crowd. "Cowards!" he shouted. "Cowards!"

Figler muttered: "This is disgusting. Let's go."

Lew, shaken by emotion, did not answer, but raised his piercing voice and called to Ali: "Good work, Ali. I've not seen anything better since you beat Red Shreckhorn in Manchester."

Ali called back: "Thank you for that!"

"Go easy, for God's sake go easy," said Adam.

The gong sounded, Kration advanced, smiling. To Ali, he looked like a man half-formed out of red mist. He thought: "*If I do not get him within five minutes, this eye will close, and then I shall be a man fighting in the dark!*"

This thought was indescribably terrifying. The curtain of

mist was darkening. Now, by straining the muscles of his fore-head and cheeks, and holding his mouth wide open, he could barely manage to see.

A voice cried: "Look out, Kration! He's going to swallow you!" Another shouted: "Oo-er! Look at 'is whiskers! They're coming unstuck!"

Ali's moustache had, indeed, fallen into a ludicrous Nietz-schean droop, matted to a spiky fringe with congealing blood. Kration snarled, leapt in, struck Ali across the neck with a flailing arm, and seized his moustache. He tugged. If the hair had not been slippery with the blood from Ali's nose, Kration might have pulled it out. But it slid through his fingers. Ali, weeping huge tears of pain, grasped blindly, and caught the Cypriot by the biceps of his right arm. The darkness had come. He knew that if he relaxed that grip he was lost. As Kration jerked back, Ali followed. The Cypriot began to gasp with pain: "Esss-ha; esss-ha ..." Everything in Ali's body and soul focused in the five small points of his finger-tips. He was blind, now, utterly blind, lost in a roaring, spinning ring, dumb with agony, choked with blood, deafened with howls of derision and encour-agement which seemed to have no end—and in this world of sickening pain there was only one real thing, and that was the arm of his enemy, in which he was burying his fingers.... They clung together, spinning round and round like two twigs in a whirlpool; the Cypriot groaning, now; Ali silent. He felt cold. A ring-post ground into his back. He groped with his other hand, and found nothing. The noise of the crowd was becoming fainter, his face seemed to be swelling and swelling, while in his breast his heart thundered like horses galloping over a wooden bridge. Something knocked his feet from the mat. He fell, still clutching Kration's arm. The Cypriot said: "For Christ's sake!" Ali replied: "You feel my grip, eh?"

Voices were shouting: "Stop the fight! Stop it!"

Out of his midnight, Ali roared: "Stop nothing! Ali never stops!"

Suddenly he released Kration's biceps, slid his hand down until it reached the wrist, where it shut like a bear-trap; swung his other hand to the elbow. The Cypriot's arm broke. Ali heard his scream of pain, but still held on. Kration became limp. Ali held his eye open, with the first and second fingers of his free hand. He could see nothing except an interminable, fiery redness. Somebody tried to prise open his fingers, which still gripped Kration's wrist. Ali struck out blindly. A voice said: "Stop! You've won! It's me, Adam!"

"By God," said Ali, "that Greek went down like bricks."

The crowd was delirious. Fabian said: "You certainly gave those sons of bitches their money's worth."

Adam led him back to the dressing-room.

Ali found his voice: "Did you see how I beat him? Did you see how I broke him up? Did you see how I pulled him down? Did you see how his arm went? Did you see my grip? I could have beaten him in the first ten seconds, only I wanted the public to see a *fight*. Did you see my grip? What Ali grips, God forgets!"

"You were great, Ali."

"Now am I fat?"

"No, Ali."

"Now am I old?"

"No, Ali."

"Now have I no teeth?"

"Teeth like a tiger."

"Now can I wrestle?"

"Better than ever, Ali."

"Now am I undefeated?"

"Still undefeated, Ali."

Ali raised his head, brushed back his moustache, twirled it again to fine points, and said: "Nobody on God's earth ever beat me. Nobody ever will. Look at me. If he hadn't scratched my eye, I should be as right as rain."

"Have a rest, Ali."

"Close the windows," said Ali, "there's a devil of a cold wind."

The windows were already closed.

Ali muttered: "I wonder if my eye is badly damaged? Get me some boracic acid crystals and a little warm water——" He stopped abruptly and said: "Put your hand on my chest!"

Adam did so. In Ali's chest, he felt something rattling, like a loose plate in a racing engine.

Ali exclaimed, with an astounded expression: "The clock's stopping!"

"Nonsense, Ali! Rest."

Ali struck his vast belly with a colossal fist, and murmured: "What a meal for the worms!"

Those were the last words he ever uttered.

That night he died.

An Undistinguished Boy

"It's potato soup," the mother said. "You like potato soup. Be a good boy, now, Dolfie, and eat it all up."

The boy shook his head.

"Aren't you well?"

He shook his head again: then nodded, swallowed and managed to say: "Yes, I'm all right."

"Then why don't you eat?"

The boy said nothing.

"It's getting cold. Come on now, eat your nice soup, Dolfie."

"Stop calling me Dolfie!"

"Adolf, then. A lot of boys would be glad of nice soup like that in times like these."

Little Adolf shrugged.

"Has somebody been upsetting you, then?"

"Oh, leave me alone!"

The father folded his paper and said: "That's what it is. They've been on at the kid again. Why can't they leave him alone?"

The mother sighed and left the dining-room. The father rose, and laid a big, gentle hand on his son's head. "Come on, son, what's the trouble?"

"Nothing."

"Anybody been bullying you? You tell your Pa."

"I'm all right, I tell you."

"I know. You came low in the class this term. Is that it?"

Adolf did not answer.

"Ah, I guessed it. Well, now, you eat your soup and don't you care. Keep your chin up like a Brit—I mean, you keep your chin up like a man, and keep smiling. You'll do better next term. Why, when I was your age——"

"It isn't that."

"Bad conduct? Well ..."

"No."

"Attendance? Been playing hookey? Say if you have. I won't punish you, son. So long as you tell the truth, I shan't mind. Every boy plays hookey once in a while. It's natural."

"It isn't that either."

"What is it, then? Tell your old man."

"Nearly everybody's getting a State Service Medal on Speech Day."

"Ah. And you're not getting a State Service Medal?"

"No."

There was something like elation in the man's voice as he said: "To hell with their silly little tin medal, and eat your dinner."

"It isn't tin. It's solid nickel. And it isn't silly. Everybody's getting one, almost, except me."

"Well, Dolfie, you're only eleven. Maybe you'll get one next year."

"Hermann Macdonald's only eight, and he's getting one."

"What for?"

"He caught a spy."

The father frowned. "I'll tell you what, son. What say we go fishing on Sunday?"

"Don't want to go fishing."

The man looked down at the red cropped head which seemed too heavy for the thin white neck. Something in his breast seemed to swell and grow taut; something oppressive, where his ribs parted and the strong pulse throbbed. "Poor old fellow," he said, and took out his watch. "Did I tell you I had a watch for you?"

The boy looked up. "A watch?"

"Uh-huh."

"But that's your watch."

"It was. It's yours now. So stick it in your pocket and eat up like a good fellow."

"Coo ... thanks."

"Your soup's got cold. I'd better get your Ma to warm it up for you."

The father carried the plate out to the kitchen. The boy sat looking at the watch. It was a handsome one, many years old, with a silver case and heavy black numbers. There was an extra hand which jerked in a fascinating way as it went from second to second ... 15 ... 30 ... 45 ... 60 ... When his father returned, the boy Adolf asked: "Honest? Can I really?"

"Certainly. It's yours now. But take care of it. Your grandpa gave me that for my twenty-first birthday. Solid silver. They don't make 'em like that any more. You don't find watches like that every day. That's better than your silly old medal, isn't it?"

The boy, eating, said nothing.

"Gah! You and your old State Service!"

Adolf sat silent.

The mother, returning, said: "What's the matter with him, George?"

"He's upset because he isn't going to get a State Service Medal this year."

"Oh dear. What a shame!"

The father rose suddenly. His face was red. He cried out, striking the air in a furious gesture: "Shame! Shame! Shame! What the hell should we care about their damned tinpot medals? To hell with their State Service! And their State! Are we British? Or are we damned Ger——"

"George!"

"All right," said the man, and went out.

The mother said, nervously: "Your daddy doesn't mean it, Dolfie. It's only his way of talking."

Adolf shrugged. The mother, passing her hand over the bristles on his bony skull, felt a sudden pang of pity, of pity so overwhelming that she fell on her knees and clasped the boy in a desperate embrace.

"Oh, Dolfie!" she said. "My poor darling Dolfie!"

"Adolf," said the boy, and writhed away.

She saw him put on his little white cap. "I'm going to school," he said. "Heil Hitler, mother."

"Mind how you cross the roads."

He nodded and strode out. His bony little legs kicked out in an absurd caricature of a military strut.

* * * * *

Three boys were waiting for him. The biggest of them stepped forward to meet him. "Cry-baby!" he said, and struck Adolf in the face.

Another asked: "Who came last in the hundred yards?"

The others replied, in chorus: "Cry-baby Adolf Robinson!"

"Who got nought per cent for gymnastics?"

"Cry-baby Adolf Robinson!"

"Who howled like a baby when he got walloped for clumsy saluting?"

"Cry-baby Adolf Robinson!"

"Who swats books and reads poetry?"

"Cry-baby Adolf Robinson!"

"*Who isn't going to get a State Service Medal?*"

"*Yah! Cry-baby Adolf Robinson!*"

"Leave me alone," said Adolf.

"Look out, he's going to cry!"

"I'm not," said Adolf, and burst into tears.

They followed him, hooting. At the school gate a very small boy accosted him and said: "I'm down for a medal!"

"What for?"

"I reported a Liberal. I'm going to get a medal. You're not. I am. Cry-baby Robinson, Cry-baby Robinson!"

Another boy said: "We ought to beat him up, just to give him something to cry for."

The leader of the three who had followed Adolf to school said: "Young Robinson is letting the class down. If we all had medals, we'd break the school record. We'd get a Special Mention. Last year, Class Three was congratulated by the Gauleiter in person, for getting twenty-nine State Service Medals out of thirty-five. D'you hear, cry-baby?"

Adolf broke away from the group and ran into the school. One of his class-mates, passing, kicked him with considerable skill on the ankle, and pretended to apologise.

Adolf Robinson paused. His eyes were wet, and at the back of his throat there was something big and round, which he could not swallow. A bell began to ring. He stood, trembling, thinking of the coming afternoon; the ferocious scorn of the boys, and the savage contempt of the master, Old Josef Goebbels Edwards, who called him an "undistinguished boy", and a "snivelling pup". He bit his lip, wiped his eyes, and knocked at a door marked HEADMASTER.

"Come in!"

The boy stood stiffly on the harsh fibre carpet. "Sir, I beg to report."

"You are permitted to speak."

"I have information."

"What information?"

"I have information relative to an enemy of the Reich, and beg to apply for a State Service Medal."

"Is there something the matter with your throat? Speak up!"

"A man said: 'To hell with the State' . . ."

"Proceed, Robinson!"

That afternoon, the Headmaster issued a special announcement.

"Adolf Robinson is to be awarded a State Service Medal of the First Class, together with a Dagger of Honour, for an act of patriotism worthy of a Brutus. His class, therefore, has broken the State Service Record for the entire school. Three cheers for Adolf Robinson!"

Heil! . . . Heil! . . . Heil!

One of the masters said: "Good for him: I never thought he had it in him."

*   *   *   *   *

Adolf was the last to leave school that evening. Ten of his classmates accompanied him, vociferously cheering. At the bottom of his street he stopped, and said: "Let's go for a walk." It was good to see how the rest agreed with him, and walked where he walked.

But night came. One by one the boys went away. Adolf went

home. There was a smell of burned food. His mother was sitting in his father's chair. Her hair and dress were torn. Her face was bruised. She looked old, white, still, and lonely, like a stone.

His father was not there.

She raised her head. Adolf saw, in her eyes, a horror as at a nightmare or a monster. She said only one word: "Adolf."

Adolf threw down his books and ran away. He was found in a doorway at three o'clock in the morning. The little boy was weeping with dreadful bitterness, occasionally raising his head to listen to the heavy, steady ticking of a big old silver watch.

An SS man took him home.

Hero-Worship

"How many hours to dawn?" asked the thin boy.

"Scared, eh?" said the man with the battered face, laughing. "Don't feel so sure of yourself now, do you, eh?"

"I'm not scared," said the thin boy; but his voice was much too loud. "I don't care. A short life and a merry one. What's the odds?"

"Tough, eh?" said the other, and curled a cruel lip.

"My name's Tito, see? I ran with Three-Finger Casca's mob. See? They wouldn't have got me alive, only I was drunk at Red Hannah's place."

The man with the battered face laughed again, and said: "Never heard of you. Tito, eh? Wipe the milk off your lip, baby-face! Do you know who I am?"

"I don't know and I don't care, see?"

"Did you ever hear of a man called Kamzan—Johnny-the-Tongs. Shall I show you my grip, eh?"

"I'm sorry, sir, I didn't know. I heard a lot about you, sir. They say you once broke a bullock's neck with your hands. I heard—"

"That was nothing—just a little friendly bet, kid."

"I didn't know you'd been caught, sir. They must be getting pretty good if they can catch a man like you."

"Somebody turned me in. I wish I had him here! It took twelve of 'em to hold me: they broke three clubs over my head.

Ah well, I'm not the first good man that came to a bad end on account of a woman, and I won't be the last. It'll be dawn soon, kid; and then up we go."

The boy licked dry lips. "Does it hurt as much as people say?" he asked.

"What the hell?" said Kamzan, shrugging his immense shoulders. "It happens to us all sooner or later. I'd sooner have gone down fighting. Women! Women are bad luck. I ought to have learned my lesson. But there it is. Why, when I was your age —you're about twenty, aren't you?—didn't I see what happened to Little Mannie and Davie the Schemer?"

"Did you *know* Little Mannie?" asked the boy, with awe.

"Know him? He was my pal. So was Davie."

"Lord, I wish I'd known you then, sir! Why, Little Mannie's famous, all over the world."

"The cleverest thief *I* ever knew, son."

"And you're famous, too, aren't you?"

"They won't forget *me* in a hurry," said the man known as Johnny-the-Tongs, with a satisfied grunt.

"Were you always as strong as they said you were, sir?"

"Son, when I was your age I could break a man's back with one hand. I got my living that way."

"Was it sheer strength, or a knack?"

"Both, *plus* speed. Why, once a royal mob sent a Greek wrestler against me, a real all-in Pankration-grappler. The idea was, that this fellow was to get me to wrestle for a friendly bet, and then crack my neck. I cracked his, in fifteen seconds, without knowing the first thing about wrestling either. That was down in Alexandria. A decent sort of town, Alexandria."

"Lots of nice girls, eh?"

"Much good *they* did me. Women! Pah! They were the ruin of me, the same as Little Mannie and Davie."

"They were . . ." The boy choked on the word.

"Sure they were," said Kamzan. "Twenty years ago. And they died the same way as they lived—hard. And game, too. They never yelled for mercy, like some I've known. They bawled each other out—blinding and cursing and shouting dirty names at each other to the bitter end. And all for a flat-faced Gippo girl, a black-eyed Gippo dancer. Two men like that! I worshipped the ground they trod on, especially Little Mannie. And I was never afraid of any man in my life, except Davie the Schemer. I could have killed him with a finger and a thumb, easy as putting out a light; but I was scared of him—you just had to do what Davie said. Everybody was afraid of Davie. And then this girl beats him in the end! My mother always warned me against women. Ah, *she* was a woman, if you like! I wish there were more like her. She used to run a House on the waterfront: they called her Mary the Battering-Ram. Whenever there was a rough house she'd butt with her head—she could knock two strong men stone cold with a kind of left-right jerk, so fast your eye couldn't follow it. She was a fine woman. But that Gippo girl . . ."

"What happened to her in the end?" asked Tito.

Kamzan uttered a wordless growl. There was silence for a few seconds. Then the boy murmured: "It must be getting near dawn. . . . I'm glad we're together: I always wanted to meet you. Can I call you Johnny?"

"Sure you can, kid, sure you can. Don't let it get you down. Little Mannie always used to say to me: 'Kamzan,' he used to say, 'mark my words, it's easier to die than to live.' What a man he was! He taught me all I ever knew."

"How did he come to get caught?"

"Why, like I told you; he went silly on this Gippo girl. Picked her up off the wharf. She'd been knocked about by some Italian sailors. Mannie took her in, got her a doctor, gave her food and clothes free of charge. When she got better she followed Mannie about like a dog. He couldn't bear the sight of her at first; kicked her out more than once, but she always came back, begging to be allowed to stay as a servant. Then Davie took a fancy to her, and so she and he got together. She was clever, sharp as a needle; not pretty, but she had a way with her. Most men came running when she lifted an eyelid. Yes, she was smart, that Gippo girl; she could twist men round her finger. She could take a watchman's mind off his job while the mob got to work on a house. She could do anything she liked with most men. But she was no good.

"As soon as she got thick with Davie—that's the way things

are—Mannie sort of decided that he'd wanted her all the time. Said he'd found her in the first place. There wasn't much ill-feeling at first, but later it turned out that she was carrying on with Mannie and Davie at the same time. Then there was nearly murder. The knives were out, when Davie—he had the coolest head of the lot of us—Davie said: 'What the hell is the use of letting a skirt interfere with business? Let's throw dice for her.' Mannie agreed to that. They got out the dice, and threw. Davie won the first game of the three: he was using loaded dice. Mannie guessed what he was up to, and changed dice: he was the cleverest man with his fingers in the whole world. He could distract your attention just for one split second, no matter what you were doing, while he got at your valuables. He could steal the liquor out of your mug or the rings off your fingers, and you'd never know. So he got Davie's dice and won the game. Davie saw what had happened when it was too late, and he went white as ashes, but never said a word. Only from that time on, there was bad blood between them.

"Then a rich young fellow, a Greek who'd just come into his father's money, he fell in love with this Gippo girl. Mannie let her go to him, the idea being that one nice dark night she was to let us into the house. There was a ton of money in a strong-box, and any amount of other stuff worth picking up—jewels and what not. There was a fortune in it. She was willing to work with us on the job. She was all sorts of things, but she'd never let us down in a matter of business.

"So the job was organised, and it was only a matter of waiting for the right time to do it. Do you follow me?"

The thin boy, Tito, said "Yes."

Kamzan took a drink of water and looked towards the narrow barred window of the cell.

"Getting near daylight," he said. "To cut a long story short, Mannie and Davie and me, with three others, went into the house at the time the Gippo girl had arranged, and when we got inside the big gate slammed and was bolted behind us, and all of a sudden, from nowhere as you might say, twenty or thirty armed men jumped out on us. Mannie and Davie were taken, the other three were killed, and I smashed my way out by brute force with a cut in my head that you could have laid three fingers in. And the last thing I saw in that house was the Gippo girl, laughing like a devil, and screaming: 'Tie them tight! Bind them fast!' She'd double-crossed us. She'd got rid of the whole mob, so as to be free with her rich Greek. And he actually married her: he owned the biggest perfumery business in the world, and was worth millions. But Mannie and Davie were sentenced to death as common thieves. Little Mannie and Davie the Schemer! It nearly broke my heart. That's what women do for you."

Tito sighed. Kamzan grunted: "Trust a woman!"

"And so they died," said Tito, "the same way as you and I are going to die."

"I hope you and I die as game," said Kamzan. "They argued to the last. Davie blamed Mannie, Mannie said it was all Davie's fault: they'd have torn each other to pieces, given half a chance. What men they were! And to think that I've got to hang next to such as you! Oh well ... what's the odds? Yes, like brothers one day, and at loggerheads the next; that's how it was. There was a chance that one of them, either Davie or Mannie, might get a pardon. There was a religious ceremony going on about that time of the year. 'I'll see you hanging yet,' Mannie said. And Davie said: 'Yes? Don't be too sure. I'll be on the ground when you're up there in the air.' But they were both wrong. It was a stroke of bad luck: everything turned unlucky after that Gippo girl came on the scene. Some dirty politician was under sentence, some politician with influence in the City. He got let off scot-free, and Davie the Schemer and Little Mannie and some other bloke went up the Hill to die."

"Who was the other one?" asked Tito. "One of the mob?"

"Nobody in particular," said Kamzan, "a tub-thumper or a preacher of some sort. Davie the Schemer cracked jokes about him while he was hanging there—Davie had guts, son; he was a man!—and Mannie, even in his agony, answered back. But the other fellow just took it and said nothing. I don't know who he was. The bloke that got reprieved at the last moment, *he* was the lucky one. They made a sort of hero out of him—a big bragger, a loose-mouthed geezer with a loud voice. He was in the crowd next to me. 'See what it means, to be highly regarded by a discriminating public,' he said to me. And I said to him: 'You?' I said, 'who are you compared with Mannie?' And he said: 'I, my good fellow, I am Barabbas.' And I said——"

Footsteps sounded. Armour clanked and a bolt rattled. The door opened. A black figure appeared against an oblong of grey half-light, and a voice said:

"Dawn. Get outside, you two."

Wolf! Wolf!

"A wolf is nothing," said Adze; "I could kill one wolf myself with a stick."

I believed him. Adze feared nothing, and, in spite of his seventy-five years, he was as strong as a lion. His real name, I think, was something like Khakabadze, but the abbreviation was remarkably apt. He must have been forged on an anvil, not born. I have never seen a man with a more impregnable air of cold, tempered hardness. Look for comfort in the rocks and warmth in the snow—then expect kindness from Adze. There was no pity in his bleak black eyes, and under his heavy white moustache, harsh as an iron-wire pot-scourer, his mouth was merciless like a rat-trap.

His face might have been cut out of white stone. Life had finished with him; Death did not want him, but still he spat in the face of time and sneered at human virtues. Caring nothing for your good opinion, Adze never lied; but in his bitter and contemptuous veracity, he demonstrated how the truth can be more barren than Siberia. Adze told me this story. I cannot convey the offhand, brusque way in which he muttered it at me, but I believe it—every word of it.

* * * * *

"I fear nothing. Nothing in the world but wolves," said Adze. "Not one wolf. Not two wolves. I mean a pack of wolves in the winter, five hundred of them, all hungry. Nothing can stand against them. They are as strong as the devil. Writers say that one wolf alone is a coward. That is a lie. A wolf is not a coward, only cautious.

"You think a fox is cunning? Then you do not know wolves. The wolf is clever. Watch a wolf hunt a stag. He wastes no effort. No theatricals like a lion; no boasting, like a bear. One jump—one bite through the big vein in the thigh—then, trot-trot-trot after the trail of blood till the stag falls down from weakness.

"This is science. Or else he jumps, and twists in mid-air as he jumps, the same way as a shark turns; opens the stag's belly, and clings. A wolf is clever and brave. He never gets tired. Good horses move fast with a good sledge over frozen snow, and when horses smell wolf, they don't run, they fly. But a wolf can run down the fastest horses.

"Listen. I was going between home and Bakay. It was deep winter, frozen hard. Wolves were out. We had a heavy load: me, my father, and three Tckerkess girls—very good-looking girls, sixteen years old. We were taking them eastward."

"What for?" I asked.

"What do you think? For sale. What else should they be for? Tcherkess girls are plump. There used to be a big demand for them in the harems. These girls had nice figures; but no light weight to carry. We had a fast sledge and three fast horses—a real Russian troika.

"We left early. We wanted all the daylight. We took good care to arm ourselves well. My father and I each had two American revolvers and a Turkish rifle. We got well out. It was good running. We covered twenty miles. Then the old man turned to me and said: 'Boy, I smell wolves.'

"I said: 'What do you mean, you smell wolves? Leave it to the horses. They don't smell them.' The old man said: 'No, but I do.' I said: 'Nonsense. Anyway, we have fifteen miles start of them, and the horses are as fresh as a daisy.' 'There's another sixty miles to go; maybe seventy,' the old man said, 'and I know wolves. This is the pack that ate up a company of soldiers last week: nothing was left but their buttons and their guns. So you see that the rifles are loaded.'

"I broke open the revolvers. They were all right. So were the rifles. I said: 'All right. Now you'd better hand me the ammunition.' 'What do you mean, hand you the ammunition?' 'The cartridges,' I said, 'two boxes full of cartridges.' The old man swore: 'You this, and you that; I gave them to you—one box of Colt's revolver, and a bag full of German cartridges for the rifles!'

"I felt in all my pockets. Only a dozen loose rifle cartridges. 'No,' I said, 'you had them.' My father felt in all his pockets. Nine or ten revolver cartridges, but no boxes or bags. 'You lie, you son of a dog,' he said, 'I gave them to you.'

"But all the same, they weren't there. 'When we get to town,' the old man said, 'I'll take the skin off your back for this!' And just as he said this, the horses threw back their heads and began to whinny. 'If we get to town,' he added. I listened. Miles and miles away I could hear a noise, very, very faint, like wind in an empty house: *Whaaaaaaaaa*—like that.

" 'Wind,' I said. 'Wolves!' said my father, and slashed at the horses. But they didn't need the whip. They could smell wolf; that was enough. In the distance I could see a black patch moving: on that flat snow you can see miles. It was moving fast, like the shadow of a cloud on a wind. The old man said: 'The moment they get within range, let them have it. Waste one bullet, and I'll tear your heart out.'

"Then the girls started to get close together and whimper. 'Stop that,' I told them, 'or I'll kick you all out.'

"The wolves came on. We flew and slashed the snow to ribbons; but they cover the country like ghosts. The old man held the reins loose and got his revolvers ready. I got the rifles ready. Me, I used to hunt wild geese in half-light with an old muzzle-loading carbine, and hardly ever missed a shot. Hah! What Adze aims at, God forgets!

"At four hundred yards I opened fire. Bang! Down went the old leader of the pack, and turned a somersault like an acrobat; then another. Crack-crack went the whip over the horses. They ran like mad. Foam flew out of their mouths like snow; and as they ran they screamed. Fools to waste breath! The wolves came nearer.

"They ate the fallen ones without stopping. They scooped them up as an express train scoops up water. Then the old man opened fire with a Colt over my shoulder. Boum-boum! I still have the scars of the powder-burns—look at my neck. I used up the cartridges. I didn't waste one. Sixteen wolves in sixteen rifle-shots. Good, eh? The old man got six. Still the rest came on. 'Take these revolvers,' he said, 'I'll handle the horses.'

"I was good with a pistol, too. I gave the empty gun to one of the girls—'Anna, load!' She was a nice girl. She loaded. I fired. I killed thirty-two wolves with the Colts alone. I dropped them like skittles, boum-boum-boum! 'Used up,' I said, 'but it holds them back.'

"The old man laughed: 'That won't hold them back. But whether we get out of this alive or not, with my dying breath I'll say that there never was such shooting from a moving sledge.'

"He was a tough handful, the old one.

"Well, the wolves had fallen back a bit. They had a little meat. Crack-crack went the whip; but in five minutes they were after us again. They were within two hundred yards, and still gaining. The old man said: 'Only one thing for it, loose a horse.' I said: 'What? And trust to two horses to drag this load?'

"The old man said: 'All right. Chuck 'em a girl.' I got hold of one of the heaviest girls and chucked her out. You never saw anything like. Hai, the Tcherkess woman! Give her sharp teeth and she would be equal to any wolf! She ran, then she realised that running was no good; turned round and caught the first wolf by the legs with her hands. But what was the use of that? *Pfaff!* Gone, as if she had fallen into a pit! gone from sight. The sledge rushed on. We got away. But a few minutes later the wolves came back.

" 'Another,' said the old man. But this time I said to him: 'And where do all our profits go? Do we make this trip for fun? Loose a horse!' 'All right. Cut one loose.' I loosed one of the horses. She rushed off screaming, and the pack swerved after it. There were tears in the old man's eyes. He said: 'That was a lovely grey, a jewel of a horse.' 'But we're saved,' I said. 'No, not yet,' said the old man; then *whaaaaaaaaa!* the pack came back. 'Hell's fire!' I said, and lashed the horses until they dripped blood.

"Then Anna spoke to me. 'I saved this in case I might need it,' she said; 'but you take it, it means two more wolves.' And she took out a little brass pistol with two barrels. She was a nice girl. *Bing-bing!* Not bad, this toy pistol! Two more wolves went down.

"But the rest poured over them like water, and the horses were labouring, dead tired. 'Another girl,' the old man shouted. Anna was the heavier of the two left, but I liked her. Did I mention it? She was my cousin.

"I said to the other: 'Out you go.' She was too scared to move. I dropped her out. She just lay still. No nerve, no fire! The sledge was lightened. It went faster. So did the wolves. In five more miles they caught up with us again. The old man sighed, and said: 'Nothing for it; better live penniless than die rich.... Chuck out the last one.' I looked at Anna, and Anna looked at me. 'Well?' I said. 'Anna, you're a nice girl, and I'm sorry. But what would be the sense of your staying here and killing us all? Will you jump, or shall I push you?' She covered her eyes and jumped. The sledge almost left the ground. Aha, the good troika!

"But the horses were beat, finished, and there was still a long way to go. They were almost on the back of the sledge. I was beating them back with the butt of a rifle. 'Can't loose any more horses,' the old man said. I said: 'No, and there are no more girls to shove out.' Sweat started dripping off the old man's face. He said: 'Nothing for it.... Unless one of us jumps. No, damn it, loose another horse, and chance it!' I said to him: 'It wouldn't be a chance, it'd be a certainty. We'd both be finished. What for? One or the other, but not both.'

" 'You're right,' he said, 'I'm an old man. My life's finished. I'll jump.' 'All right,' I said, 'but there's no time to lose. Take a rifle and at least smash a few before they get you. Don't worry. I'll take a good revenge on these damned animals.'

" 'That's the style,' said the old man. He kissed me on both cheeks.

"Then he stopped and said: 'These are new boots I've got on. Why waste new boots? I asked the bootmaker to make me a pair to last seven years. Wait a moment while I get them off. But don't wear them; sell them. Dead men's boots are unlucky.'

"He pulled off his boots, covered his throat with his sleeve, took his knife in his hand, got a rifle by the barrel, and jumped right into the middle of the pack smashing them right and left like a whirlwind. I didn't look round. I heard him yell: 'Take that, you lousy wolf!' Then, yelp-yelp-yelp. I beat the pack into town by a matter of minutes."

* * * * *

Adze sneered at the look of horror on my face.

"What's the matter? If we had all died, would that have been more practical? Yes? Bah. Well, that winter I had revenge. I went into the forests, wolf-hunting. I shot them, I trapped them, I gave them what for. I wiped out the rest of the pack. I made nine hundred roubles on the skins."

"Fratricide!" I muttered.

Reflections in a Tablespoon

I remembered all this in a grim, cold, northern restaurant.

A sour waiter, twisting his face in a pale sneer, banged down a plateful of something flabby floating in grey water and, snarling over his shoulder, said that I could have Spam or boiled salt cod and brussels sprouts to follow. I replied that in the meantime I needed a spoon, so he brought one, wiped it on his trousers, and let it fall with a clang. Then he went away with a shrug of despair.

It was a magnificent tablespoon, weighing several ounces; heavily plated and monogrammed—a relic of old, good, solid days. Turning it over I saw the autograph of Gino engraved on the handle. Gino's name, scrawled with a flourish, looked remarkably like Gino himself. The big loop and the fine curly tail of the G were the nose and the moustache, the ino recklessly sprawling downwards were the pendulous lower lip and the three fat chins of that noble restaurateur.

His silverware had gone under the hammer, I supposed; and I wondered what had happened to the bold brass fittings and the honest round mirrors that used to look so massive and gay in Gino's Long Bar. Gino, I knew, had turned to dust, which he hated, and to flowers, which he loved—he was always beating away dust or arranging flowers. But his place had been built to last a thousand years. All the same, it began to die when Gino died of an enlarged heart in 1923—I always thought that his heart was dangerously big for a man who owned a restaurant. Yes, the place went into a decline and sank from owner to owner until a bomb closed its eyes in 1940. It had been beloved for Gino's sake. He was a good man, bright and kind; people in trouble found their way to Gino as lost dogs find their way to a watchman's fire in the cold, inhospitable night.

Things pass: they break, or they wear away.... "You don't like?" grunted the waiter, jerking a contemptuous thumb towards my soup.

I said: "I see that you have some of poor old Gino's silverware here."

"You knew him?"

"He was my friend," I said, "he gave me credit."

The waiter changed. He stood up and grew taller; he smiled and became friendly. "In a minute I get you two nice little lamb cutlets," he whispered.

We smiled at each other. I was moved. Although Gino was dead and the dust carts had dragged away the rubble that had been his house, by God's grace his generous heart had not stopped beating.

The waiter said: "He was patient. My goodness, what would have drove me mad, so it only made Monsieur Gino say *Well!* My Gawd, you remember that yellow woman what she called herself. The Countess? With the scar on her face?"

"Gino was very patient with her." I said, "Poor woman."

The waiter winked and said: "Don't drink that muck: I get you two nice little lamb cutlets—they do you more good, yes?"

"Yes," I said and he went away, flapping like a seal on his big flat feet in his shiny black coat.

*   *   *   *   *

The Countess had been a beautiful lady, but when I knew her she was nothing but an attenuated shadow in a late afternoon. Her scar, a small one over her left cheek-bone, made her face arresting. She was reminiscent of beauty, as an echo is like a voice.

Yet in spite of her wild yellow hair, nobody denied that she was a lady. Have you ever come upon a ruin left tottering after a raid —some bit of bedroom wall, for example, broken beyond repair, still retaining a few strips of carefully-chosen wall-paper? You know that although blast has .opened it to the rain and that it is pitiful in its exposure, it has, in its day, been beloved: it has witnessed certain glorious moments. The Countess was such a ruin. She always had a little money on the first of every month —about eight pounds. Then she was a great lady, ready to carry the weight of all the troubles of the world. For about two days she gave drinks to strangers and money to beggars. On the fifth day, she would be alone, twitching, with the Black Dog looking over her shoulder into the small glass which she was trying to keep half-full until somebody happened to offer her something. It was awful to see her on the edge of the twenty-one arid deserts of her next three weeks.

Then Gino would catch the barman's eye and nod, looking tired and sick. His nod said: *Let her have credit.* He insisted only that she ate something. Sometimes he would coax:

"Madame la Comtesse, for you especially I make a little something. Not for anybody, not for everybody, but for *you*."

She was always contemptuous, and said: "It doesn't concern me. I am not interested in your little something."

"If I have make it, could Madame la Comtesse not be gracious and say: 'I will taste'?"

"Very well, only you must cash me a cheque."

"First, you must give me your opinion. There is an entrecôte. Nobody could tell, nobody could judge—only you. We beg your opinion."

And so she ate. As for her bill, Gino "charged it to expenses", as the saying goes; he chalked it up, and washed it out. Knowing this, the Countess grew more and more capricious, intolerably haughty. How could she admit that she was accepting charity? It was out of the question. "Laugh at me, laugh at me now!" she would cry, while her eyes flickered. She could not meet the horrible white stare of the Hangman, Sobriety. "Laugh at me, laugh if you like, but I say I could have bought a dozen Ginos a little while ago!"

To this, Gino always replied: "Dear lady, there is nothing to buy, nothing at all."

The last time I saw her she was trying to cash a cheque. "September the what?" she asked, making blots on the dateline of a crumpled blue slip with a miniature fountain-pen.

A respectable bystander said: "The fourth, madam, September the fourth."

"Of course it's the fourth, I know very well it's the fourth. I didn't need you to tell me that.... Gino, you will cash my cheque for two pounds."

Gino gave her two pounds and, closing her poor smudged cheque-book, slipped it back into her bag. She glared at him and screamed:

"You thief! How dare you go over my bag?"

Gino murmured: "Be nice, put away your cheques. Among friends, one trusts. Away, away—put it away!"

He knew that her cheques were valueless, they always came back; but she, tossing her bewildered head and still trying to write, said: "The *fourth?* ... of what month? Of *September*. September the *fourth* ..."

I heard Gino mutter: "Oh, God, the sea is so wide and the boat is so small!"

But then the Countess, waggling her useless cheque-book, said, with an odious and provocative grin: "I'll tell you something. The Monk Paphnutius looked into my eyes—I was a girl of fourteen—and he said: 'You shall betray and be betrayed, and be loved by one whom you do not love and give your love to one who does not love you. You shall avenge your own victim, and after that you shall order the destiny of an Oriental Empire.' ... You and your dirty two pounds!"

The bar was filling. Gino said: "Dear lady, you are always welcome, but since you are excited, you had better go and rest a little."

On the verge of tears she exclaimed: "And a little while ago I could have employed this creature to brush my shoes, and he would have been honoured!"

But she walked out, pushing the revolving door so violently that it thudded fifteen times. A few seconds later we heard a woman's scream, a screeching of brakes, and a smashing clangor of metal and glass. Everybody looked at everybody else. The door revolved again, very slowly, and the Countess came back trembling, with a pale face.

"It just missed me," she said.

The chasseur, following her, said that she had missed death by inches, having stepped off the pavement in front of a speeding car, which, swerving in order not to hit her, had skidded across the street into some railings. The Countess was ordering a drink. Gino, shaking his head at the barman, said: "No, dear lady, this is all. No more. Just one last drink with me, for your nerves, and then God bless you. You must not come here any more."

She wept.

"The Monk Paphnutius looked into my eyes ... and I, I who rule an Oriental Empire, that *I* should be spoken to like this, oh ... Oh ..."

Gino nodded and said: "Yes, Madame la Comtesse, even you. Good-bye, for God's sake. You have an Empire, and I have a Licence. Enough is enough."

She went away, trailing her old-fashioned handbag, and Gino said: "Monks! Eyes! Empires! Licences! I wish to God Almighty that I was an American sitting on a flagpole."

I never saw the Countess again.

* * * * *

The waiter came back with the cutlets. They were burnt on the outside and raw within. He was unconcerned. While a man at an adjacent table stamped his feet and beat hideous noises out of a cruet with his knife-handle, the waiter talked of Gino and of what a man he had been. "Except somebody sometimes he liked everybody always," he said.

Then the manager came and almost dragged him away.

I knew one of the men whom Gino did not like; a ruffian out of the Balkans, a man with a withered arm, who always had something to sell—a silk handkerchief, for example, with somebody else's monogram; or a fountain-pen—fine to-day, oblique to-morrow—marked with any name but his own. He answered to the name of Stavro, and he was an unscrupulous villain, an unmitigated blackguard, and a swindler by vocation. His right arm and hand were bent into something like the shape of a tired rattlesnake. This deformity appeared to be the result of some recent injury, for the first time I saw him, in the spring of the year of Gino's death, the arm was caught up in a black silk sling, and he had the drawn look of a man suffering persistent pain. Even so, he was handsome in a dark, pantherish way; one sensed the man's power over women and hoped that God would have mercy upon any infatuated creature that fell into his grip, for Stavro would have no mercy at all. I never saw a stonier pair of bright black eyes. Stavro was short but beautifully proportioned, a sort of vest-pocket Hercules, unquestionably a dangerous man in a rough house for all his fastidiousness of dress and manner, and his gentleness of voice. For no definable reason I also detested him. With Gino, it was hate at first sight. Stavro had a disconcerting way of looking at you: he gazed right into your eyes with the hungry, immovable, wide-eyed stare of a pervert or a watching cat. He seemed to be having trouble with a match and a cigarette, so I offered him a light. He thanked me graciously and said:

"This is nothing, this arm. I am almost ambidextrous. I can write with my left hand, even. Look..."

He took out a fat green fountain-pen, unscrewed the cap with the help of his fine white teeth, and scribbled *Stavro* on the marble-topped table. "Do you like my pen?" he asked.

"It is very nice."

"You can have it for two pounds, if you like. It cost me three guineas." He was lying, of course; he was not the man to pay good money for anything. I wondered what he did for a living and concluded that he got a risky livelihood on the fringe of the Underworld, buying things on credit and selling them quickly for cash; walking off with other people's luggage.... Always moving quickly and quietly; elusive; a Disappearing Man in a conjuring trick; here to-day, gone to-morrow; best left alone. Later, Gino said: "I am an old man and you are a young man. Allow me to warn you—keep away from that dark one. He is no good. He is a Pomp." He meant "Pimp" and was not far wrong at that.

Stavro went on talking, purring out self-glorification: "My left hand is as good as my right. I will show you something. There are not many men *you* know can do this ..."

He whisked an elegant pearl-and-silver fruit-knife out of a waistcoat pocket, opened it with two fingers and his teeth, turned his head and pointed to a small wooden sign two yards away, which advertised somebody's Highland Whisky in elegant gold lettering.

"Which do you prefer? The dot over the i in *Highland* or in *Whisky?*"

I did not know what he meant. He explained: "I will dot you the i in *Highland*."

Then, with a casual snap of his powerful fingers he flicked the little knife away. The point buried itself in the centre of the dot he had specified. "Have I earned a drink?" he asked, retrieving his knife and putting it away. I said that he had, indeed, and I bought him one. In the end I bought his fountain-pen.

Stavro frequented Gino's Long Bar for several weeks. His arm, free from the sling, was permanently distorted, fixed in its peculiar, weary, reptilian droop. He told me that all the tendons and muscles had been cut to pieces so that he would never use that arm again. He hooked himself on to me, and to others also. I was not sorry when Gino told him to go and stay away.

"No," he said one morning, as Stavro came in, "you are not coming here any more. Get out and keep out; I don't want you in my bar.... Why? ... Because I don't like your face, in the first place, and in the second place *you* are keeping *nice* people away. Go, please."

Stavro, smiling with his mouth while he murdered Gino with his eyes, bowed and walked out.

It is odd that, thinking of Gino, I should think of the only two customers whom I saw sent away from the genial and kindly atmosphere of his bar. Mourning Gino, I remember his enemies. It is strange....

* * * * *

As I have said, I never saw the Countess again, but I did meet

Stavro once, nearly twelve years later. He had changed, so that I was almost sorry for him. Although he was still elegantly dressed and carried himself, as always, like a gentleman, he had got fat. All his feline litheness, all his supple charm, was dead and buried under an extra hundred pounds of flesh. I recognised him first by his right arm, which was still withered and useless, and then by his eyes, which were still bright and wicked. He, with his swindler's memory, remembered me immediately, and greeted me as if we had parted only a day or two before. He asked me how the fountain-pen was working. I had given it away ten years ago, cursing myself for having been hypnotised into buying it. I told him so and he laughed, and then we went to a nearby wine bar for a glass of sherry.

I looked at Stavro in a mirror, as Perseus looked at the evil face of the Gorgon, and it occurred to me that while some great men may die with their best songs unsung, this fat crook was destined to go to the grave with most of his evil unconsummated. This idea filled me with a strange sense of peace; I knew, then, that while there is certainly a Devil, there is unquestionably a God. I said to Stavro: "Can you do with a couple of pounds?"

He looked at me stunned with astonishment. "Do I understand that you are offering me money?" he asked.

"Without rancour, as man to man," I said.

He was touched. He took the money, bought me a drink with one of the notes, and put the change in his pocket. Then he said: "I accept your money in the spirit in which it is offered. I love frankness, openness, and candour between man and man." He was a born liar. He went on: "And for this two pounds I will give you something worth two thousand. I will tell you the story of my*self*."

Stavro looked at me with expectancy, and made a protective gesture with his good hand, as if he feared that I might be thunderstruck and utterly overwhelmed by his magnanimity. But, observing that I bore up, he plunged straight into the great drainpipe of his past.

He had been a very bad man indeed, worse than I could have guessed. Among other things, he had been a professional killer, an assassin employed by one of the political murder organisations of the Balkans. I knew that the man was a liar, yet what he said rang true; I remembered, for example, the terrifying little trick by means of which he had first aroused my interest, that trick with the knife. He was not, he told me, one of the directors of political assassination; he was an operator, an agent. He might work, for example with a few underlings. He might, perhaps, train and arm a boy like Princip, the crazed student who fired the shot that started the first World War. Stavro had nothing to do with Princip, but he was involved in similar affairs. Several gentlemen (never heard of in Western Europe), big names in the Balkans, met their deaths through Stavro. In important cases he, Stavro in person, with his deadly right eye and terrible right hand, dealt with the killing. He was one of those men who have the knack of pointing a gun at you as I point a finger. He never missed. As for his nerves, he had none. It was not that he was fearless; he lacked the capacity to feel fear, just as he was incapable of understanding the meaning of pity. If it was necessary to torture somebody, Stavro would torture him, quite dispassionately. He was not a sadist; he found no pleasure in inflicting pain—it was all a matter of business, as far as he was concerned.

I believe that in telling me all this he had in mind some rake-off from a fat fee such as the Sunday newspapers were paying for stories like his own. He became explanatory, almost eloquent. With a passionless wink he told me that he knew perfectly well how nothing was any good without a love interest; and if I wanted love interests, good Lord, he could embarrass me with the richness of his love-life: he was Cupid, the indiscriminate gunman.

"There is, though I say so who should not, my dear friend, something in me to which women are—or have been—drawn, I tell you, as iron is drawn to a magnet. I was known as irresistible. Why? I will tell you why. With women, it is pretty much the same as with hunting wild animals; more often than not they run away a little ahead of the noise you make whilst approaching. Irritate them, and—in the case of fierce, proud animals—they will charge you in order to destroy you; and then, if you are a man with a clear eye, a cool head, and perfect confidence in yourself, the animal that charges you delivers itself into

your hands. In other cases, for example shy and bewildered creatures, it is necessary to gain a certain advantage ... to creep up,
having calculated the wind. But that is neither here nor there.
My successes have nearly always been with the wild, fierce ones:
there is infinitely more satisfaction, as your Shakespeare says, in
rousing a lion than in starting a hare. 'The blood more stirs,' I
think he said. I am a big-game hunter. Irritate, stimulate; wound
if necessary; arouse interest; then out of the undergrowth comes
your animal, with slashing claws and foam at the mouth. Poor
wretch! Little does it know that *I* am here with a thunderbolt,
quite unafraid, almost sorry for it. Then ... Bang! A rug for my
study. For example, there was, in a certain city, a woman who
was known as The Golden; gold hair, gold skin, gold eyes, and as
good as gold. I will tell you details ..."

And Stavro told me details. The lady to whom he referred
was a famous beauty who had come out of a good family to
marry into an illustrious one. She was the toast of her country,
and her husband, the well-born and noble gentleman who
adored her, was regarded as a fortunate man, since she remained
unspoiled. The Emperor Franz-Josef had tried to lead her
astray; her virtue was impregnable. Stavro, however, managed to
assail that virtue. In the case of The Golden it must have been
the nostalgia for the mud, such as affects certain women from
time to time. However it happened, Stavro succeeded. There
was a hideous scandal. The lady's husband blew his brains out.
She had committed only social suicide, and lived on. She was
ostracised; she went away, lived a gay life, ran through most of
her money, lost the residue in the War, and went to the dogs. It
was a nasty story. "Good, eh?" said Stavro.

I made no reply. I could feel again in my nostrils the sulphu-
rous bite of smouldering Evil that goes on and on and ends God
knows where. Stavro continued:

"I tell you all these things because I regard you as my personal
friend. You don't know what you have done for me in lending me
this money"—he touched his waistcoat pocket.

"To-morrow is a bad day in my life. To-morrow is my birthday. All my troubles began on my birthday. I was born. If I had
not been born I should never have had any troubles. On my

fourteenth birthday I was punished by my father for something I never did. On my sixteenth I did something and was found out. On my eighteenth, after a certain incident, I had to leave home. On my twentieth I went to prison, and escaped a death sentence by the skin of my teeth. On my twenty-first birthday I did an important job for Zedoff, risking my neck and getting two bullets in the shoulder, and I never got paid, because Zedoff, losing his nerve, ran away to America.

"All my life misfortune has followed me and has caught up with me invariably on my birthday; that is, to-morrow. And if I can, when the calendar tells me that it is here, I spend my birthday in a quiet place, in retirement. Your two pounds will enable me to do this; I shall go to a village near London and spend my birthday in bed. No harm has ever come to *me* in bed. What does your Bible say? 'Cursed be the day ...' etc? Cursed be the day, cursed be the night.... I am not a literary man. This arm, this good right arm, this piece of dead wood which I must carry with me to my grave—I got this on my birthday, too. And here, by the way, my dear friend, is another little incident which might provide food for your satirical humour and material for your penetrating pen.... I am sorry, by the way, about that pen I sold you, and will get you another, even cheaper, and much better....

"I knew it, I knew that if I started important business on my birthday I should come to grief. But there was no way out of it. I was under orders from Marko. It was, I may say, a big job, and I will give you the details of it later if you think you can use them. You have done me a favour and I will do one for you, and we will split fifty-fifty. It is true that you write it down, but without—for example—me, what would there be for you to write about? Do you realise, my dear friend, that *I*, the man you see before you, I, Stavro—*I* was the man delegated to kill a dictator? I will not insult you by asking whether you have heard of Mustapha Kemal Pasha, the Grey Wolf. God only knows what that man has survived. If I were religious I should say that God had chosen him, that God is keeping him for some kind of destiny, since he is the only man who, given to *me* for killing, is not yet dead. There was big money in it too. If I told you that my own share, after everything had been weighed and paid, was to be thirty thousand pounds, perhaps you would call me a liar? Yet this is the case, I give you my word of honour.

"Marko had organised it. Kemal had to be at a certain place at a certain time, and when he got there, a certain gentleman (not a hundred miles from here) was to put a bullet out of a Mannlicher sporting-rifle into him—a semi-hollow, soft-nosed bullet. And there was a crowd, actually and positively a *multitude* of reliable men hired and ready to cover my retreat. I tell you that there are fates, as your Shakespeare has it, destinies that have us in their power whatever we may do. Is it 'Rough-hew our ends?' or 'Shape them as we will?' I am no poet. It was all organised.

"It was organised, *cher ami*, so as to be foolproof, it couldn't possibly fail. I may say that with *me* gripping that rifle—with *my* eye looking along that barrel—Kemal was as good as dead. And I as good as had thirty thousand pounds in the bank. (I mean in the Safe Deposit, because I don't use banks.) All I had to do was catch the boat train from Victoria, and I left half an hour earlier in order to make assurance doubly sure. As I left my hotel I realised that it was my birthday, and fear came upon me. You know what I mean when I say Fear. I told the driver to drive with infinite care. He did, and a tyre blew out. By the time we were ready to start again, a little time had passed and it was necessary to hurry. And then, taking a short cut round Charing Cross and rushing through an absolutely empty street—what happened? Ha!

"Some drunken woman steps off the pavement, my driver spins his wheel, we hit the railings of the church across the road, I put up my hand to save my eyes and the shock of the impact sends it through a window; the glass cuts my arm into a fine fringe, and I am in hospital for two months. I lose my thirty thousand pounds; Mustapha Kemal lives, and I am a cripple. There, for example, is my birthday luck for you."

I said: "If your birthday is to-morrow, that makes it September the fourth, doesn't it?"

Stavro nodded and replied: "*Too* true."

I bought him another drink. "Did you ever hear of the Monk Paphnutius?" I asked.

His eyes narrowed. "What makes you ask?"

I said: "Nothing. And as a matter of curiosity, my dear Stavro, did the lady known as The Golden have a little scar on her face?"

Stavro, tense as a hungry cat and watching me closely, said: "On her left cheek. What then?"

I answered: "Nothing, nothing."

* * * * * *

The waiter, having dealt with his impatient customer, came back with a deplorably soggy portion of pie and lingering, said: "And that other one, that one with the funny arm. Eh? Monsieur Gino, he didn't like that one. And look what happened to him, eh?"

"Stavro?"

"That's it, Stavro."

"What happened to him, then?"

"It was in the papers. The police was after this man with this funny arm, this Stavro. So he goes to Waterloo Station. So he buys a ticket to Walton-on-Thames. So he puts down a pound note. So it is a *bad* pound note. A counterfeit, a forgery. So one thing leads to another, see? So in the end, so he runs away, and— *bomp!* Right into a motor-car. *Smash-bang!* . . . No more Stavro. Last thing he says is: 'So *this* is my birthday?'"

"Ha," I said. "Bad? A *bad* pound?"

"Yes, on his birthday. Coffee, sir?"

"No, no coffee. On his birthday, eh?"

Before I paid the bill I held a pound note up to the light. "Will you look the other way while I steal Gino's spoon?" I asked.

"Take! I give!" said the waiter, looking sideways to be certain that the manager's back was turned. "What is it? You see something?"

"I never passed a bad note before," I said. "Keep the change."

The waiter laughed, and I, having shaken hands with him, went to catch my train.

A Bang on the Head for Dutoit

A queer story is told about an old man who died in 1940.

His name was Dutoit, and he died at the age of eighty-nine. The joy on his face was wonderful to see. He was one of the happiest men in France in the moment of his death. For seventy years, he had been free from all earthly care. His life ended in a blaze of triumph, for he saw the realisation of his one great hope.

He was an old soldier. His military career had lasted about twenty-five minutes, not counting a period of training. He was involved in one of the historic battles of the world—the Battle of Sedan, in 1871. You know what happened then. The French Army, sold, betrayed, and ill-equipped, went out to meet the gathered might of Prussia under Bismarck. Napoleon the Third was Emperor then—a fool blown up with pride.

Sedan was a scene of horror. The Germans were always clever at the use of spies and the purchase of traitors. They had bought Bazaine, the greatest of the French generals. The great mass of French infantry went out singing. It was the old, old story. "To Berlin! To Berlin!" they shouted. But Napoleon III had neglected to buy the fine new cannon that the Krupp factories had offered him. He felt, no doubt, that there were more pleasant ways of spending his country's money. Prussia, you may be sure, had not overlooked the possibilities of the newest kind of heavy artillery. The French infantry marched into a shattering blast of cannon-fire. They went down like skittles. The Prussians were sending over shells of a new and dreadful killing-power. The French artillery replied, out of the mouths of obsolete cannon.

The infantry went to cover.

And behind a bush, safely crouching under a tiny hillock, lay Dutoit and two others.

Dutoit was a mere boy, a student of music who also loved history. He was a frenzied patriot. His imagination had been fired by the old glories of fighting France. He used to dream of the splendours of victory under Napoleon the First. He felt that

56

somehow this other Napoleon would revive the glories of France and the Empire. He thrilled to the imaginary music of a Victory March. He laughed as the shells burst. He was part of France, and riding on the right hand of a shining destiny.

But his companions began to grumble.

One of them said: "What does that pig of a Badinguet think he's playing at?" (Badinguet was one of the third Napoleon's nicknames.)

The other said: "The Prussians are hacking us to bits with their blasted big guns, and we are lying here like animals waiting to be slaughtered."

But Dutoit replied: "Be quiet. This is war. In a war you don't run forward all the time. Sometimes you watch and wait. Do you realise that we are France? Do you realise that we cannot lose?"

"Bah," said the first man.

Shells screamed overhead. The second man said: "They're getting close . . ."

Dutoit went on: "Have courage. What, are you men or mice? Our fathers were in worse holes than this, but they fought through. Where is your spirit? My grandfather fought under the Emperor at Marengo. He said: 'In the end France must always win,' and so it must. Has France ever lost; ever really lost? Think of the Battle of Austerlitz! Eylau! The Moskwa! Sometimes it only seems to go badly. But it is the last trick that wins the game."

"But where is our artillery, comrade?"

"It will come."

"Where are our reinforcements?"

"They will be here."

"Where is Bazaine?"

"Rest assured, Bazaine is on his way with a hundred thousand good little soldiers!"

"Meanwhile these damned shells are coming over like grass-hoppers!"

"Nevertheless we'll win through," said Dutoit.

The first man said: "In my opinion, we've lost Sedan."

Dutoit replied: "Nothing of the sort. We'll win, here as elsewhere. Mark my words, comrade, the Battle of Sedan will be ours; a French victory over the damned Prussians!"

"French Victory my eye!"

"I swear to you that at any moment we shall hear the Advance ... we'll tear into those Prussian guns and silence them, and push on, and win. Sedan is as good as ours."

The other man said: "Bah."

"You wait a minute," said Dutoit.

And perhaps thirty seconds later a shell came whining overhead, and moaning down. It burst twenty yards away. Dutoit rolled over and lay still.

And the French lines broke. There was a hideous retreat under a murderous storm of gunfire. The Prussian cavalry came through. France was betrayed and beaten.

That day, Dutoit was dragged into the temporary headquarters of the Medical Officer. There was a wound in his head. Only the scalp was torn. The bone was intact. Dutoit was unconscious, but breathing quite regularly. They bound up his wound, and left him to recover consciousness. A day passed. A week passed. Dutoit's head healed. Yet he did not come out of his coma. He lay still, like a man asleep.

He was taken to a hospital. A month passed. He still slept. He was sent home. He slept on. As he slept they fed and washed him. He lay motionless except for the rise and fall of his chest. A year passed. The war was over, lost. Governments changed. Dutoit slept. Such cases are not unknown to medical science: there was a Scots sergeant, wounded at Waterloo, who slept for thirty years! The human brain is an unknown quantity. A touch can overthrow or suspend its conscious life.

Dutoit lived on at home. Years went by. He was a recurrent newspaper-story. His case made minor medical history. The family of Dutoit died out. He was taken to a hospital again. The hospital was condemned and pulled down. They moved Dutoit. He never knew. The century turned. The telephone came. So did the motor-car. He was unaware of this. Some crazy men tinkered with little engines and frameworks of cane supporting wings of silk. They thought they could fly! The world laughed. Dutoit slumbered. Man flew! The world marvelled. Dutoit slept. The Dreyfus affair shook France; but not Dutoit. Queen Victoria died in England: he never heard about it. Presidents and

Prime Ministers came and went. Dutoit stayed in bed, blissfully unconscious. There was a mutter of rumour ... a roar of rage. Germany was on the march again, and France and England were in arms against the Kaiser. France spoke of 1870, and revenge. People remembered Sedan: but Dutoit had forgotten it.

1914 ... 1915 ... 1916 ... 1917 ... 1918. A howl of exultation shook the world. Germany had crashed. The Allies were victorious. The thunder of the Kaiser's guns had made Dutoit's bed tremble. But he slept through it all. France went mad with rejoicing. Dutoit remained still, deeply sleeping. His beard had grown more than two feet long. The hair of his head had fallen out. But his face was calm and healthy.

Once in a while he opened his eyes, but saw nothing and slept.

Peace swept France ... a peace more nerve-racking than a war. Germany sank to the depths. Out of the great sadist underworld there came a wild-eyed man with an absurd moustache and a crazy book. He was called Hitler. He became the Führer. France became grave and thoughtful. Dutoit slept on.

Germany rearmed. The rest of Europe went into a frenzy of weapon-making. Everybody knew that war was coming again ... again with Germany. But not Dutoit!

Munich sent Europe on tiptoe. Dutoit lay flat. It was coming! Poland! The world crouched, waiting. Then war broke again. Goose-stepping jack-boots crashed along the roads of France again. The great guns roared. Under a screen of treason the Nazi armies swept down. The Allied armies tried to fight. The French artillery thundered again at Sedan. The Germans rolled over them. The French counter-attacked.

And Dutoit was dying, of sheer old age.

They watched his bedside. His heart was limping slower.

It happened one morning.

A young doctor, standing over the old man, saw him open his eyes. And to everybody's amazement, Dutoit spoke, for the first time in seventy years.

He said: "Where are the Prussians?"

Taken by surprise, the doctor stammered: "We have counter-attacked and driven them back from Sedan."

"I told you so," said Dutoit, with a sweet smile; and he closed his eyes and died.

Macagony's Fist

Having left theological college to become a salesman of corsets, and having left that job on account of an unconquerable habit of practical demonstration, Macagony became a welter-weight boxer. His career in this line is not recorded in the history of the ring. His enemies suggest that he hit the referee with a stout-bottle because he was disqualified for biting. He came to Chicago in 1909, and went into politics in the company of Hinkydink Kenna; was congratulated on having emerged with only a fractured jaw, and jumped the first freight-train to Nevada where he went to work in a copper mine.

Here he found his real vocation—blowing things up. He learned exactly what to do with gelignite. If you wanted to know just where to place your ballistite cartridge so as to remove the front of the foreman's house, or precisely how much damage could be done with an oil-drum packed with black powder, you went to Macagony. He carried with him a high-explosive atmosphere. He had one of those tense Irish faces, with eyes that seemed to burn deeper and deeper into the orbits —you felt that in a few seconds that would touch some blasting charge inside his skull, and then that would be the end of everything. He had the traditional Irish nature, which is compounded of equal parts of poetry and picric acid ... the soul of Dion O'Banion, who sang "The Rose of Tralee" to his aged mother before rushing out to put five bullets into John Dougherty—John Dougherty, who believed in fairies, and murdered Anna Kaniff with an ice-pick.

As soon as the Civil War broke out, Macagony went to Dublin to throw some bombs. He must have been the original Irish Troubles. I lost sight of him at that period, and quite forgot him until I met him in 1936 in Hooligan's Spanish Bar. Macagony had changed; aged; lost flesh and acquired a hunted look. Moreover, there was something wrong with his right hand.

It appeared to be horribly deformed—bulbous, like a turnip, and covered with a woollen thing like a sock.

"Nice to see you again," he said, and added, in the same breath, "loan me five."

I asked: "How was the revolution?"

He replied: "Great. Great! I blew up three armoured cars. Once, I threw seventy-seven Mills bombs in sixty-three seconds, by the clock."

"Is that how you hurt your hand?"

Macagony became furtive. Then, pocketing my five dollars with his left hand, he soared into a good mood. An Irish good mood. When Irish eyes are smiling, watch your step: and when you hear the lilt of Irish laughter, take care to arm yourself either with a quart bottle or a fire-extinguisher. "That ..." he began; then seized my coat, and whispered: "Swear on the head of your mother that you'll keep your lip buttoned."

"You bet I'll keep my lip buttoned."

"I'd get twenty years."

"Do I talk?"

"All right; listen, then. You know I always like a good explosion?"

"Didn't you once put a bicycle-pump filled with gun-powder under my chair?"

"Don't interrupt. Well, you know I was in the troubles, eh?"

"Yes."

"Ssssh! ... Well, it was great. I used to go about with a sawed-down forty-four in my pants pocket, and a Mauser on a lanyard down me leg.... Bombs? Un-limited! I once dropped one down a tuba mirum in a military band. Boy, oh boy, have you ever heard a pineapple explode inside a tuba? You haven't lived, man, till you've heard that. Ahhh ..."

Macagony sighted an acquaintance—one of the waiters—and leapt up to exchange conversation.

"You'd think he was a baby-face," he said, on returning, "but with these two eyes, I've seen him shoot six with his own hand when we burned Dunville's wharf.... What was I saying? Oh yes; me mitt."

"You hurt it in an explosion ..."

"I did not. It was a different thing altogether. Me and some of the boys were making a bit of a raid on the Orpheus Cinema, see?"

"Well?"

"There was Murphy, there was Flash Guinness, there was Guts McGrath, there was——"

"Well, go on."

"Well, first of all, we gets a couple of petrol cans, see? And I fills them nice and tight with sticks of dynamite, see? And I fits a detonator in each cap, runs a wire, presses the button, and up she goes. See?"

"Very nice."

"I wish you could have been there. There wasn't an unbroken window for miles around. It was raining bits of Black-and-Tan for hours afterwards. The dogs in the streets got into the habit of sitting on their haunches with open mouths, making a meal off the falling bits."

"As long as you were kind to the animals."

"Sure. Well, we start to make a get-away, when what should we see but a couple of detachments of the Black-and-Tans coming down from both ends of the street. So we broke into a house, and got on the roof to fight it out. See?"

"Uh-uh."

"I had a couple of tramcar conductors' money-bags full of Mills bombs, and we all had our guns. See? So we held the roof. It was a sight worth seeing. You could hardly see a hand in front of you, for bullets. Murphy got his first. You fire a rifle at a tiled roof, and the bullet will ricochet round and round for weeks. It's not fair. Me, I did my best with the bombs, but we were outnumbered, see? They got on the other roof, and we fought a duel from chimney to chimney. It was great. But they were coming in on us, and I was down to me last bomb. Well, I waited till I should see the best chance to use it. I had me finger in the ring of the pin, and me hand round the bomb, and I waited. Then, at the last moment, I swings the pin out of the bomb, and I throws, ZING!"

"Did you do plenty of damage?"

"I didn't wait to see. I got down on my belly, and make a get-away, across the roof and down a fire-escape, right through the soldiers, hell for leather across town, and down to our hideout."

"Where was that?"

"In a cellar. . . . Well, we get together there, and we lie doggo. The streets are lousy with soldiers, see? We could not dare to move. Then, all of a sudden, Guts McGrath says to me: 'Macagony, what's the matter with your hand?' I looks at my right hand, and what do you think I see?"

"It was bleeding?"

"Bleeding! No. I still had me right hand tight round the bomb. I'd thrown the pin, and kept hold of the bomb. And there we were, not daring to move, down in a little cellar with a live Mills bomb, with me holding down the spring; and if I'd let go, we'd all have been in hell in three seconds."

"Good God! What did you do?"

"Nothing. I kept tight hold. We was down there five days. I didn't get a wink of sleep. I lost me nerve. I didn't dare do anything . . ."

Macagony winced. I said: "But, Mac. You could have wedged the spring down with a nail, or a hairpin, or something."

"I know. But none of us thought of that till later. And me muscles were atrophied, or something: I couldn't open me hand . . ." Macagony tapped his covered right fist.

"And what happened then?"

"Nothing. Nothing, me boy. Nothing. I resigned meself to me fate, and here I am."

"And the bomb?"

"Here it is to this day," said Macagony, pointing to his bulbous hand, "but don't say a word to anybody, I'd get twenty years if you did—hey! wait a minute! Where are you going to, in such a hurry . . ."

Grey Old She-Wolf

Nature is absolutely pitiless. When you can no longer run you lie down. When you lie down, die.

The old she-wolf had run with the pack for many years fulfilling the bitter life-cycle of the species, hunting, killing, eating, starving, fighting, mating and giving birth. Many generations of wolves had come and gone. Only she remained. She had fought time. Time had torn out her hair, stiffened her legs and rotted her teeth.

Now alone she was marked for death. She was starving. It seemed that in the whole breadth of the world no life was stirring. Even the trees might have been dead—frozen to death. Nothing moved, nothing breathed.

She knew that unless she could find food very soon she would be too weak even to walk, then she would lie down in the snow and die.

If an old wolf could think, she might say to herself: "To what purpose should I struggle to outlive this day, since, food or no food, I must die to-morrow?" But above all things comes the will to live. The old she-wolf slunk on smiling, listening, creeping in the strong black shadows between the trees.

The moon rose higher—the big, blinding, white Siberian moon. The wolf moved faster, throwing herself forward with that long, smooth stride with which wolf eats up distance, weaving through the trees. Hunger was gnawing at her stomach.

Suddenly she stopped, crouching. She could smell man—or rather that which appertained to man, fire. It came from miles away to the south. There came into her mind the taste of blood which she associated with that smell, and also a memory of pain. She, with her pack, had once run through the streets of a village and eaten two men. She knew that man had means of biting hard and deep, but she would have fought a bear now, for a scrap of fish.

The miles passed. The smell grew stronger, burning wood. The moon soared higher. The she-wolf ran faster and faster. Saliva hung in a frozen spike from her lower jaw, and her breath hung in little icy diamonds to the hair on her skull.

*   *   *   *   *

Then something bit her. She yelped and tried to leap away. But she was caught by a forefoot in the teeth of a wolf-trap. She tried to pull her foot away. The steel bit to the bone. She stood still, panting.

In the course of her long life, she learned all that a wolf can ever know. She had seen these things before. When they bit they held on, held on for ever, and bites could not hurt them, nor all the tugging in the world tire them, and when the sun rose, a man came with an axe.

The teeth of the trap bit deeper. She opened her throat and expressed her anguish in one utter howl so mournful and protracted that people in the distant village stirred in their sleep.

From the south came always the tantalising smell of life.

She lay down. But neither age nor weakness could change the fact that she was a wolf—more than a wolf: a mother of wolves. She bit at the trap. A tooth broke. She snarled and bit at her leg above the teeth of the trap. Her mouth was sore, and her teeth worn and loose, but she bit hard and fast. It was like an amputation with a dull knife during which even the knife feels pain.

An hour passed. The trapped paw hung by one tendon. She tugged once and was free, but on only three feet. And then she became again aware of hunger.

The she-wolf looked at the paw in the trap, and licked it. It was cold and strange, no longer a part of her. She bit a piece out of it, swallowed it, bit again and again, until nothing was left but a sliver of furry bone between the interlocked spikes. But dawn was coming. She limped on, southward, sometimes whimpering with pain.

From time to time she stopped, sniffed, listened, and changed her path. Her breath came heavily now, and every step was terrible. Needles of frost had begun to bite into the gnawed red stump of her leg. She knew that it would be necessary to use cunning, since men also run in packs and are difficult to kill.

* * * * *

At this hour, very few human beings were awake, and it happened that the only one who had yet ventured out of doors into the awful cold was an old woman called Katka.

She, like the wolf that was coming, had outlived all of her

generation. There was nobody in all the world who could say: "I knew Katka when she was in her prime." She had lived so long that nobody knew how old she was—even she had forgotten, but she claimed to be able to remember the passing of the legions of Napoleon when she was a little girl.

Katka, also, was terribly hungry, and looking for food. If she could have reasoned, she would have thought: "To what purpose should I struggle to outlive this day, since, food or no food, I must certainly die to-morrow or the next day?"

But human beings do not live according to reason any more than wolves—even less, in fact. Katka had begged a little wood for the stove and the village butcher had given her a few scraps of meat such as one might throw to a dog. Another well-disposed person had presented her with a few handfuls of flour and some salt.

There came into her head an idea. If only she had a griddle she could cook herself a griddle-cake of flour, water and salt, to eat with her meat. She looked out of doors and felt the cold and thought: "No, it is too cold to go out. I will simply boil the flour in water with the meat."

But the desire for the hot cake was too strong. She wrapped herself in all her rags, and crept to the cottage of a kind-hearted neighbour to beg for the loan of a griddle. "Before God, I will bring it back to you in an hour. Before God!" she said.

"An hour?"

"Only an hour."

* * * * *

The neighbour handed Katka the griddle, a kind of hot-plate with a long flat handle all of iron. "Take it," she said, "but bring it back. It must be heavy, though, for you to carry."

"No, thank God I am still very strong."

"Listen, Katka, I will give you a cake later on when I make some. Don't bother with the griddle."

"Thank God," said Katka, "I still have my health and strength and can still cook myself a cake, old as I am." She held the griddle on her shoulder as a man carries a rifle. "Good day, and

God be with you. I heard a wolf howling last night, so look after your little ones. They are devils, wolves."

"Nonsense, there are no wolves."

"I heard one. I once saw Napoleon pass. I am old enough to know a wolf when I hear one, I hope? Mark my words."

Katka went out, somewhat offended, carrying the griddle. She had walked, perhaps, twenty yards, when she heard a soft, throaty snarl.

She started and then saw the old she-wolf—bloody and terrible, skeletal in her emaciation, panting so that the breath steamed out of her mouth and nostrils as if her throat were boiling like a kettle, slavering, grimmer, greyer, more gaunt than death itself, crouching for a spring with red ferocity in her desperate eyes, and menace in every bristling hair on her neck.

Their eyes met. They stood still. Then the wolf sprang. Automatically the old woman struck downwards with the griddle, its edge, worn by fire to the sharpness of an axe, struck the she-wolf between the eyes. She fell forward and died in silence.

Katka hobbled back to her neighbour's cottage, crying: "Look! Look! Look! Look!"

The butcher skinned the wolf, and gave Katka the pelt for a bedspread, but for all that she died ten days later of what they called "a cold".

We should have described it as pneumonia, perhaps adding: "The old man's friend".

The Frenchman who Understood Women

The woman with banana-coloured hair seemed to parade in front of herself banging a drum. When the attention of her companions wandered a little she talked louder. When they ran away she dragged them back.

The great room was full of the mutter of a hundred conversations, while, in a hall beyond, fifty couples danced to the music of a fifteen-man band and a negress with a voice like warm honey sang the "Basin Street Blues".

Yet I give you my word of honour; the conversation of that

uproarious woman was clearly audible from where I sat, ten yards away. *Kyak-yak-yak-wak!* It was as penetrating as the voice of a terrified duck in a thunderstorm. She laid about her with punches and coy slaps. Once, with cowish coquetry, she chased a startled youth right round a sofa.

She waddled like a Manatee—one of those shapeless sea-beasts which showmen keep in tanks and describe as "Genuine Mermaids". I wanted to throttle her, tie her up. She embarrassed me, that blaring brass band of a blonde. It was not as if she had even good looks to recommend her. Pig-eyed, buck-toothed, with a face as red and shiny and a voice as shrill as a penny squeaking balloon.

"Bah!" I said to the gentleman who sat on my right.

"Pardon?"

"I said 'Bah'. I was referring to that intolerable woman. Listen to that voice!"

"True," he said. "Her voice is appalling. As Houelle so neatly put it: *There are beautiful flowers which are scentless, and beautiful women that are unlovable*. To my mind, the most beautiful woman in the world is unattractive if her voice is not melodious. Shall we walk into the garden?"

"Why not?"

We went out. He carried himself with a kind of precise grace, that pale and interesting old gentleman. There was something about him that reminded me of Conrad Veidt. The shattering yellow voice pursued us: the blonde was beating a fat man with a carnation. "Women!" I growled.

He replied: "Pigault-Lebrun says: *Those who always speak well of women do not know them enough: those who always speak ill of them do not know them at all*. I am a Frenchman, sir, and have studied women. Having always had reasonable intelligence and a highly-developed critical faculty, as well as a lot of money and (in my youth) a fair share of good looks, I have not lacked opportunities. Are you married?"

"No."

"But you are still young. You are wise not to marry young. I think it is impossible to achieve happy marriage before the age of forty. One must select with infinite care the perfect mate. For, as Petit-Senn says: *Marriage with a good woman is a harbour in a tempest; but with a bad woman it proves a tempest in a harbour.* I was fifty-five when I married, and thank God I have never regretted it."

Over the din of the "Basin Street Blues" came the cackle of the banana-blonde.

"That voice!" he said. "Let us walk a little farther. Yes ... I have had a wild, irresponsible life, my friend, and know women. I was restless. Having an artistic soul, if you will allow me to say so, I sought perfection. I married when I finally discovered the one woman in the world with whom I could happily share my life and fortune. Mark my words, the woman you really love is she who would have been your friend if she had been born a man. She should be your equal, so that you may enjoy life hand-in-hand with her. The perfect marriage should never be founded on passion, for, as Feuchères says: *Every great passion is but a prolonged hope.*

"But a man who has learned all about women in his youth and maturity, he may marry with his eyes open and be happy, as I am. Commerson says: *Marriage is often but ennui for two.* So it is. But I have found my ideal.

"I travelled the whole world in search of her. The variety is infinite. That is why, in seeking a mate, a man cannot be too careful. It is important to discover the one perfect combination. Just as an infinitesimally slight difference in the shape of a key will render it unfit to open a door, so a tiny variation in character may make a wife impossible to live with.

"I know a man who would have forgiven infidelity, but who attempted to assassinate his wife because, in squeezing tooth-paste, she invariably started the tube in the middle and not at the end.

"Pay attention to every detail of the woman you think you love. It is easy to be deceived by a worthless woman. *The destiny of woman is to please, to be amiable, to be loved*, says Rochebrune. But by whom? That is the point.

"Somewhere there is a perfect mate for every man. She may take long to find. As I said, I was fifty-five when I met mine. I had known innumerable women, and found them all wanting.

But one evening at a party such as this I realised that, at last, the great thing had happened. I felt a pang of realisation as soon as I saw her. A blind understanding warned me that she was sublime. She was an American, but had lived for several years in Europe, travelling much, learning much. She had even written a book.

"And while Karr says: *A woman who writes commits two sins: she increases the number of books, and decreases the number of women*, my love was utterly womanly.

"She had intellect, yet was feminine. She had beauty, and intelligence. She was of a happy temperament, yet calm and sweet. Her manners were gracious and perfect. She was wise and kind. And her personality was as vivid as the dawn.

"I begged her to marry me, and after a long time, succeeded in making her my wife. And time, my friend, has improved her sterling qualities. That was five years ago. I had passed five years in Paradise, and love her more and more every day.

"So. Now you, my friend, were speaking bitterly of all womankind on account of the screaming antics of some debased creature inside, there.

"Yet my wife is also a woman. There are women and women. Do not be like Boucicault, who said: *I wish Adam had died with all his ribs in his body*. Seek, and you shall find perfection. Now, let us go in. That unpleasant person has stopped her screeching, and my wife is waiting for me somewhere . . ."

Kyak–yak–yak–yak–yak came the voice of the woman with banana-coloured hair, from whom people were still flying in terror.

"Is that woman never going to shut her mouth?" I said.

"But the singing has stopped."

"Singing? Singing! I refer," I said, "to that canary-headed hag flopping about the sofa like a filleted hippopotamus."

Something struck my chin. It was my companion's fist.

"Sir," he said, his eyes blazing, "that lady is my wife."

Fantasy of a Hunted Man

In Kentucky, in the year 1918, there lived a ferocious old man who was known as the Major. I suppose he was of the kind that carves out empires and breaks open new territories. He was indomitable, wiry, strong as steel in spite of his sixty years, and devoid of fear. An admirable, though far from lovable man, he lived alone, deeply respected and half feared by everybody who knew him. He was something of a madman, terrifying in his fanatical devotion to anything he regarded as his duty. The Major belonged to the hard old days when men, single-handed, fought wildernesses and beat them tame.

Into his battered, lion-like head, there had crept the craziness of race-hate. He loathed foreigners, and abhorred negroes, and was always to be found in the forefront of any demonstration against the unhappy black men of Kentucky—a figure of terror, with his rifle, and his great moustache which curved down like a sharp sickle, and his huge and glaring blue eyes.

That kind of fanaticism seems to bubble dangerously near the surface of the Deep South. A word cracks the skin over it, and lets loose an eruption of murder and cruelty.

One day, a hysterical woman said that she had been accosted by a negro named Prosper. He had, in fact, asked her some question pertaining to firewood; but she had run, screaming for help. (That happens frequently.) She ran, I say, screaming. The drowsy little town seemed to start and blink. The negroes knew what that meant, and they trembled. Somebody passed a word to Prosper. He knew that innocence was no argument: he was a negro black as night, and therefore damned before judgment. He took to the woods, flying from what he knew must come.

A great mutter rose. Men clustered, tense and angry. Mouths twitched up in snarls. Beware of the undercurrent of blood-lust that crawls in the depths of men! Somebody yelled: "Are we going to let that nigger get away with this?" A hundred other voices roared: "No!" The mutter of the mob became a howl, like that of mad dogs. Guns came down from hooks. Night had fallen. Torches flared. Two great bloodhounds, straining at their leashes, snuffled on the trail of Prosper. The men followed the dogs. The mob was out for blood and torture. And the Major led them, with a gun loaded with buckshot under his arm.

But Prosper had a long start, and he knew the woods. The mob hunted all night long, and far into the next day. Then they became exhausted, and paused. But not the Major. He was drunk with hate. When everybody rested, he went on alone. He plunged into the depths of the wood. His long legs had the loping stride of a hunting wolf. The trees covered him. He disappeared.

And two days later he appeared again, and it seemed that he had gone quite mad. He was afraid! He cringed. He staggered towards some people who were watching him, and said: "I didn't do it! I never done nothing! I'm a harmless old nigger! Don't hurt me, white folks! Please don't hurt me!"

Then he fell into a sleep, so deep that it was almost a death. And when he awoke, twelve hours afterwards, he was the Major again … but changed. He was quiet and gentle. He blinked uncertainly—he who had never been uncertain of anything, right or wrong, in sixty years of life—he who had never uttered a kind word in living memory. The Major, the nigger-hater, the lynch-lawyer, the whipper, the killer—the Major was seen gently patting the head of a terrified little black boy who stood paralysed with fear under the unexpected caress.

What had happened to him in that dark forest?

One day he told the story:

* * * * *

When the others had rested he had gone on, and on, until he could walk no longer. His body was exhausted; but not his hate. He determined to rest a little, and then continue his hunt for the vanished negro Prosper. And as he sat resting, sleep came down on him like a deadfall, and he lay among the leaves and snored.

But it was no ordinary sleep. It was a strange kind of sick coma in which the Major found himself. He was caught in the meshes of a dark and nightmarish dream, like a bird in a net. He knew that he was dreaming, and struggled to awake, but could not. And then he found himself floating away . . . and there was a blank, a hiatus, a timeless silence.

He awoke. He found himself crouching in a thicket, in a part of the wood which he did not know. And his heart was thumping in his breast, and he was terrified, disgustingly terrified of something that was following him. The Major was bewildered. He had never known fear, and now he was afraid. He somehow knew that he was going to a hollow beyond the thicket. Something was urging him there. He knew, also, that dawn was at hand, and he dreaded the dawn . . . and yet he also dreaded the dark.

He had lost his rifle. His clothes seemed to have been torn to shreds by thorns. His face was swollen where branches had snapped back at him in his headlong rush through the wood.

He crawled on, footsore and exhausted. Prosper! he had to find Prosper the negro and drag him back to be slaughtered by the mob. But of what was he afraid? He did not know. The Major went on. He got out of the thicket. There, sure enough, dimly outlined in the starlight, lay a hut. He went down towards it. It was a mere ruin. Those who had lived there had either died or gone away. It was empty.

He went in. He shouted: "Anybody here?"—and was surprised to hear the husky rasp of his voice. His throat was dry. He felt ill and weak . . . and still frightened. His mind revolted against the trembling of his limbs. His body was scared, and wanted to hide. As he stood in the hut, shaking like a man in an ague, the first glimmer of day came through holes in his boots. ". . . I must have been walking in black mud . . ." Then he saw his hands. They were black and wrinkled, with whitish nails and pink palms—negro's hands.

Sick with anguish, the Major leapt up. There was a fragment of broken mirror. He looked at his reflection.

The terrified face of Prosper the negro looked back at him.

He does not know how long he stood there, staring. He, the Major, was in the body of Prosper, the black fugitive. Some strange flash of intuition told him that somehow . . . God knew how . . . while he lay in his exhausted trance, and while Prosper also lay in a coma of weariness and misery … somehow their souls in sleep had met and changed places.…

He heard, in the remote distance, a baying of bloodhounds.

The spirit of the Major turned to give battle. But the body of Prosper fainted with horror.

And it must have been exactly at that moment that the body of the Major, gibbering in the voice of Prosper, came staggering through the trees towards the lynch-mob and begged for mercy, so that they took him home while the negro escaped.

And then came the darkness of unconsciousness, out of which the Major struggled to find himself in his bed, surrounded by curious eyes and astonished faces.

That is all. There is only one thing more. The Major went into the wood again, and followed the route he remembered. There was the thicket; and there, in a hollow, lay the hut.

On the floor of the hut, smashed to pieces where it had been violently flung down, lay the remains of a bit of mirror.

The Gentleman all in Black

There is a crazy old fellow who lives—or used to live, in 1937 —in a crazy old skylight room in Paris, and was known as Le Borgne. He squinted horribly, and was well known for his avarice. Although he was reputed to have a large sum of money put by, he shuffled about in the ragged remains of a respectable black suit and tried to earn a few coppers doing odd jobs in cafés. He was not above begging … a very unsightly, disreputable, ill-tempered old man. And this is the story he told me one evening when he was trying to get two francs out of me.

"You needn't look down on me," he said. (He adopted a querulous, bullying tone, even when asking a favour.) "I have been as well-dressed as you. I'm eighty years old, too. Ah yes, I have seen life, I have. Why, I used to be clerk to one of the greatest financiers in the world, no less a man than Mahler. That was before your time. That was fifty years ago. Mahler handled millions. I used to receive the highest of the high, the greatest of the great, in his office. There was no staff but me. Mahler worked alone, with me to write the letters. All his business was finished by three in the afternoon. He was a big man, and I was his right hand. I have met Royalty in the office of Mahler. Why, once, yes, I even met the Devil."

And when I laughed at him, Le Borgne went on, with great vehemence:

* * * * *

Mahler died rich. And yet it is I who can tell you that, a week before his death, things went wrong and Mahler was nearly twenty million francs in debt. In English money, a million pounds, let us say. I was in his confidence. He had lost everything, and, gambling in a mining speculation, had lost twenty million francs which were not his to lose. He said to me—it was on the 19th, or the 20th of April, 1887—"Well, Charles, it looks as if we are finished. I have nothing left except my immortal soul; and I'd sell that if I could get the worth of it." And then he went into his office.

I was copying a letter to the bank, about five minutes later, when a tall thin gentleman dressed all in black came into my room, and asked to see Monsieur Mahler. He was a strange, foreign-looking gentleman, in a frock-coat of the latest cut, and a big black cravat which hid his shirt. All his clothes were brand new, and there was a fine black pearl in his tie. Even his gloves were black. Yet he did not look as if he were in mourning. There was a power about him. I could not tell him that Mahler could not be disturbed. I asked him what name, and he replied, with a sweet smile: "Say—a gentleman." I had no time to announce him: I opened Mahler's door, and this stranger walked straight in and shut the door behind him.

I used to listen to what went on. I put my ear to the door and listened hard, for this man in black intrigued me. And so I heard a very extraordinary conversation. The man in black spoke in a fine deep voice with an educated accent, and he said:

"Mahler. You are finished."

"Nonsense," said Mahler.

"Mahler, there is no use in your trying to deceive me. I can tell you positively that you are in debt to the tune of just over twenty million francs—to be exact, 20,002,907 francs. You have gambled, and have lost. Do you wish me to give you further details of your embezzlements?"

Calm as ice, Mahler said: "No. Obviously, you are in the know. Well, what do you want?"

"To help you."

At this, Mahler laughed and said: "The only thing that can help me is a draft on, say Rothschild's, for at least twenty millions."

"I have more than that in cash," said the gentleman in black and I heard something fall heavily on Mahler's desk, and Mahler's cry of surprise.

"There are twenty-five millions there," said the stranger.

Mahler's voice shook a little as he replied: "Well?"

"Now let us talk. Monsieur Mahler, you are a man of the world, an educated man. Do you believe in the immortality of the soul?"

"Why, no," said Mahler.

"Good. Well, I have a proposition to make to you."

"But who are you?" Mahler asked.

"You'll know that soon enough. I have a proposition. Let us say that I am a buyer of men's time, men's lives. In effect, I buy men's souls. But let us not speak of souls. Let us talk in terms of Time, which we all understand. I will give you 20,000,000 francs for one year of your life—one year in which you must devote yourself utterly to me."

A pause: then Mahler said: "No." (Ah, he was a cunning man of business, poor Mahler!) "No. That is too long. It's too cheap at that price. I've made 50,000,000 in less than a year before now."

I heard another little thud. The stranger said: "All right, my friend. Fifty million francs."

"Not for a year," said Mahler.

The stranger laughed. "Then six months," he said.

And now I could tell, by the tone of his voice, that Mahler had taken control of the situation, for he could see that the strange man in black really wanted to buy his time. And Mahler had a hard, cold head, and was a genius at negotiation. Mahler said: "Not even one month."

Somehow, this affair brought sweat out on my forehead. It was too crazy. Mahler must have thought so, too. The stranger said:

"Come. Do not let us quarrel about this. I buy time—any quantity of time, upon any terms. Time, my friend, is God's one gift to man. Now tell me, how much of your time, all the time that is yours, will you sell to me for fifty millions?"

And the cold, even voice of Mahler replied: "Monsieur. You buy a strange commodity. Time is money. But *my* time is worth more money than most. Consider. Once, when Salomon Gold Mines rose twenty points overnight, I made something like twenty million francs by saying one word, *Soit*, which took half a second. *My* time, at that rate, is worth forty million a second, and two thousand four hundred million francs a minute. Now think of it like that——"

"Very well," said the visitor, quite unmoved. "I'll be even more generous. Fifty million a second. Will you sell me one second of your time?"

"Done," said Mahler.

The gentleman in black said: "Put the money away. Have no fear; it is real. And now I have bought one second of your time."

Silence for a little while. Then they both walked to the window, which was a first-floor one, and I heard the stranger say:

"I have bought one second of your time for fifty million francs. Ah well. Look down at all those hurrying people, my friend. That busy street. I am very old, and have seen much of men. Why, Monsieur Mahler ... once, many years ago, I offered a man all the kingdoms of the earth. He would not take them. Yet in the end he got them. And I stood with him on a peak, and said to him what I say to you now—*Cast thyself down!*"

Silence. Then I seemed to come out of a sleep. The door of Mahler's office was open. Nobody was there. I looked out of the open window. There was a crowd. Mahler was lying in the street, sixteen feet below, with a broken neck. I have heard that a body falls exactly sixteen feet in precisely one second. That gentleman all in black was gone. I never saw him go. They said I had been asleep and dreamt him, and that Mahler had fallen by accident. Yet in Mahler's desk lay fifty million francs in bonds, which I had never seen there before. I am sure he never had them before. I believe, simply, that the gentleman in black was the Devil, and that he bought Mahler's soul. Think I am crazy if you like. On my mother's grave I swear that what I have told you is true.... And now can you give me fifty centimes? I want to buy a meal ...

Strong Greek Wine

"You——" said the innkeeper and then stopped. He had been about to say: "You have had a rough time of it." The newcomer had the air of a man who has been badly beaten. His cheeks were mottled, so that they might have been bruised. Under each eye hung a black pouch, and his lips were swollen. Furthermore, the man had a wild, hunted look and his tired eyelids, struggling against the heavy hand of sleep, blinked rapidly as he glanced from side to side.

"Well?" he said. "What?" There was a hoarse savagery in his voice which the innkeeper did not like. He replied:

"I was going to say, you are welcome."

There was a faint melodious noise. The innkeeper looked away from the stranger's face, and smiled. The man was flipping a large silver coin in the air and catching it as it fell. In the gloom of the tavern you could have seen the flash of the innkeeper's eyes as they followed the flight of the piece of money.

"Wine?" he said.

"Strong wine."

The innkeeper bowed, and lifted a small wine-skin.

"I have something special here," he said. "Extra. Did you say strong wine? This would knock an ox down or resurrect the dead. This is imported stuff. Greek wine."

"Have one yourself," said the stranger. He looked about him. There was only one other customer—a silent, elderly man with a broken nose. "You too."

"I don't mind if I do," said the landlord.

"You're very kind," said the other man.

The stranger nodded and drank. "Greek wine, you liar!" he said.

"My lord," said the innkeeper. "You seem to have some doubts as to the quality of this wine. Let me assure you——"

"Well? Well?"

"Your Honour! Your hand!"

"What about my hand?"

"You have bitten it!"

The stranger blinked at his left fist. From a ring of blue marks, reluctant drops of blood slowly oozed. He said: "What's that?"

"Nothing, your Highness. Only for a moment you startled me, biting your hand like that."

"For God's sake shut up and get some more wine!"

Two more men came in—one fat, the other thin. They saw the stranger and there was something about him that stopped the casual trickle of their conversation. The fat one glanced at the innkeeper, who winked and nodded. "Your Honour, shall I give these gentlemen a drink too?"

"Eh?"

"I said——"

"Drinks!" cried the stranger, in an awful, rattling shout, and smashed his cup to tiny fragments with one blow of his fist.

"Ah . . . there will be a trifle to pay on that," said the innkeeper.

The stranger stopped spinning the coin and hurled it across the counter. Bowing to the ground, the innkeeper murmured: "May you live a thousand years, my lord."

Silence came again. "Your health, honoured sir," said the fat man. "Have you come far?"

"Yes," said the stranger.

"From . . . ?"

"Well?"

"I—I was going to say . . ."

The stranger raised his eyes, and there was such utter desperation in that glance that the fat man gulped his drink and said no more. The thin man tried to make conversation. "Plenty of excitement in town these days," he said. "Hear the latest? Riots. It seems there was——"

"For God's sake!" said the stranger, in a queer, high voice. "Is there no musician here? Does nobody play? Does nobody dance? Does nobody *sing*? Is there nothing in this stinking, dirty, filthy city that.... Are there no women? Then for the love of God bring some wine!"

"Greek wine," said the innkeeper.

"You lie. But bring it." The stranger produced another silver piece, which he flipped and spun with nervous intensity. "Curse you, hurry!" The innkeeper spilt dark puddles of pungent wine in his haste, and set out more cups.

"Long life," said the fat man.

The stranger laughed and drank. The innkeeper whistled. The thin man coughed. Nobody liked the sound of that laughter. "Well?" said the stranger. "Isn't anybody saying anything? Haven't you got tongues? Are you struck deaf and dumb and paralysed? God damn you—talk!"

"It's a hot day," said the innkeeper.

"Coming over dark," said the man with a broken nose.

"Looks like a storm," said the thin man.

The fat man cleared his throat and said: "Yesterday I heard a good joke, but I seem to have forgotten it."

"More drinks," said the stranger.

"Steady on," said the fat man. "I've got work to do. How's business, Joseph?"

The landlord replied: "How's *what?* Business, did you say? What business? Don't make me laugh. Business! I can't pay my way any more. Taxes here, taxes there.... And then, again, I'm at the wrong end of town. It's dead."

"It's slack everywhere," said the fat man. Addressing the stranger, he added: "Don't you find it so?"

"Don't I find what so?"

"Business bad."

"Yes."

Outside, the quiet street lay, salt white in the blinding daylight. A shadow fell over the threshold. Two women were coming in followed by some men. The innkeeper winked and made a gesture, upon which the women smiled and sat at the stranger's table. He looked at them gloomily. One of the women was young and beautiful. The other was older, but fully painted. There were shadows under her eyes, and her ears supported heavy metal rings.

"Drink for the ladies, your Excellency?" asked the innkeeper.

"Yes," said the stranger.

A scarred old man in the armour of a soldier, caressing a chin that was hard and black with calluses from the chin strap of his helmet, said: "Your health, sir. Haven't I seen you somewhere before?"

"No," said the stranger, looking away.

"I'm sure I have! I must have! Let me think——"

"Wine, for God's sake!" said the stranger.

The room was full now. "For everybody?"

"Yes, fill 'em up." The stranger looked at the coin he was spinning, and threw it across the room to the innkeeper, who caught it and pocketed it in one smooth gesture.

"You ought to get some change," said the man who looked like a wrestler.

The innkeeper whispered: "Mind your own business, can't you?"

Somebody began to play a stringed instrument. The elder woman started to sing, some strange forlorn song of slaves; a lugubrious, tortured song in a minor key. Her thick, husky voice seemed to rise and fill the air like smoke.

> "Take me, O Master, to the hills
>   That are to me as the breasts of my mother—
> Lead me to those gentle valleys,
>   In the soft grass and the fresh wind
>   Let me die . . ."

"Drinks!" shouted the stranger. The innkeeper busied himself with the wine-skins. A negro with the body of a god and the humility of a beast carried cups and pots. Noise filled the tavern, drowning the woman's voice. She stopped singing, looked at the stranger, touched his hand, and said: "In trouble, dear?"

"No," said the stranger, and pushed her away.

"Would you like me to sing for you?"

"No."

"Dance?"

"No."

"Will you buy me a drink?"

The stranger was staring out into the street. The morning shadows had crept close to the houses. It was noon. He pushed away his wine cup, which fell to the floor and seemed to explode in a star-shaped splash of glistening purple.

"Did you go up the hill?" somebody asked.

Somebody else replied: "What for? It's all over by now. I've got something better to do."

The stranger pushed his way towards the door. There was a little white fleck in each corner of his mouth, which some unendurable misery had twisted into a narrow, lipless oblong.

"Hey!" cried the innkeeper. "You owe me for one round."

The stranger stopped suddenly as if he had encountered an invisible wall. They saw him thrust a hand into his pouch, fumble, and withdraw a great clenched fist. He swung his hand. Everybody winced and ducked. There was a smash and a jangle of silver. People threw themselves on the falling money in a cursing heap.

"Here," said the stranger. "The other twenty-eight pieces."

The innkeeper, standing in a strange attitude—for he had one foot on a coin and one fist clenched in the air where it had closed upon another—stared after him.

The woman, hiding five pieces in her bosom, said: "He seemed to have something on his mind."

"All the same," said the landlord, "I wish we had a customer like him every day."

The Old Burying Place . . .

The old man said: "Once, when I was no older than you, I went as far away as the Old Burying Place."

"Where is that?" asked the little girl.

"Far away, across the plains and through the forest. Ha, we were *men*, we were *hunters*. But, these young men? Bah. They have good bows and the best of everything, yet they have been away for a day and a night, and where is the meat? All I ask is a bit of meat to suck. I have lived through as many winters as there are fingers on eight men's hands. In my day we had no iron-tipped arrows. We chipped a sharp flint, bound it firm, and —psst! Iron! Bah! Women they are: not men."

"Tell me about the Old Burying Place."

"It's a long, long way away, but I went there when I was a boy. It was one winter, a terrible winter. There was no food. Even the acorns were rotten. All the pigs had gone away into the forests, so we followed them with our bows and our spears—my father, and his father, and myself.

"It was very cold. We walked for five days before we found the tracks of a pig. We followed them all day, our arrows on our bow-strings. Towards nightfall we caught up with him—a very old one, rooting under the snow for food. My father's arrow struck him in the flank. Then, when he ran away again, we followed. There was blood——"

"Tell me about the Old Burying Place."

"Ssh! What am I telling you, then? I was saying: we followed the pig. I was tired, but dared not rest: they would have left me to die in the snow.

"At last we came to a part of the forest full of broken stones. 'We are coming to the Old Burying Place,' said my father's father. 'There are bad things here. Let us go back.' But my father said: 'I fear only hunger,' and drove us forward.

"Soon there were no trees, only stones—the Old Burying Place. This is a place of death and darkness. Nothing grows there—not a weed; nothing. There we found the pig, lying dead.

"We took out his liver and ate it before it got cold. Then we lay down to sleep, having lit a fire to keep away the cats. Only my father's father would not sleep. He said: 'It is not lucky to sleep here. People sometimes do not wake up after sleeping here. There are things walking here that should not be walking.' At dawn I awoke and saw him, still sitting, watching.

"Then my father said: 'Let us open one of these burying places. I knew a man who found good cooking-pots in one of them.' But his father said: 'No. It is not good. There is bad air in these tombs. Why does nothing grow here, not even the grass?' But my father was already striking with his axe at the door of one of the tombs, at a place where the earth had fallen away.

"The door was of iron, but soft. It fell to a red dust. Then there was another door, and a deep pit. We took firesticks, and shouted to frighten away evil spirits, and climbed down, until we reached a great cave. Who could have dug such caves? They go deeper than man can follow, and are lined with smooth white stones, so that the sound of your voice comes back to you again and again, no matter how low you speak.

"We walked for a great distance. The cave was very cold and dark, and our firesticks were burning low. At last we saw bones. They must have been the bones of common people. They had all been buried together; thrown in a pile at one of the doorways— more bones than you could count if you had ten times ten fingers and toes—bones and bones and bones. No cooking-pots; nor iron; nothing except their death-masks."

"Death-masks?" asked the little girl.

"Yes. The buried People who lived here when the world was young used to cover the faces of their dead."

"Why?"

"Who knows why? So; we turned back. The bones of three people lay in a corner; a man, a woman and a child, holding together still, even in death. Nearby there was a doll, such as you yourself might play with."

"You should have brought it for me."

"Fool! When you were not yet even born? My father said: 'I shall not go away with empty hands.' And he tore down a sheet of iron fixed to the wall. My father's father took a death-mask.

"As for me, I picked up a chain of yellow metal that hung on the dead woman's arm. It must have been a powerful talisman, because even as I pulled at it the bones fell apart and tumbled to the ground in a heap like all the rest. Then we went back. The pig——"

"And what was the chain like?"

"Tah! A chain. On the end of it there hung a thing like this——" the old man crossed his forefingers—"with the image of a man hanging on it, fastened by the hands and feet."

"Oh, how pretty. And the mask?"

"I don't know. . . . It looked like the bones of a man's head, but instead of eye-holes there were round plates of something you could see through; and instead of a nose there was a long tube and a bag. As for the iron plate, that is all I have left, and it hangs behind you now."

"Oh, is that it?" asked the little girl. She looked. The plate was long and rectangular; much cracked; eaten up by time. It had been enamelled. Still legible on its surface was one word:

"PICCADILLY"

The girl said: "I wish you had saved the chain."

The old man rose, laughing, as three young men came into the cave, dragging the corpse of a goat.

A Small and Dirty Dog

Yesterday I met a man who had fallen in love with a girl who was playing him up; and I remembered the story....

I used to know a man named Chico. Heaven only knows what has become of him. He was one of those men who are somehow destined to be made fools of by women.

You know the type: drunk with vanity and full of trivialities; boiling over with a sense of stupendous importance—a bore who believed that the whole world waited breathlessly for news of his latest emotional entanglement.

Now one day—it must be about seven years ago—I met him while I was sitting outside the Café des Deux Marronniers.

I was having a drink with a queer little fellow who looked like a jockey and whose name I never knew, when Chico came fluttering about us with all the news of a brand-new infatuation.

"She is wonderful, adorable, and good. She is faithful, devoted, and absolutely divine ..."

So he ran on. And then the man who looked like a jockey turned his head and deliberately spat on the pavement. His leathery little face wore an expression of seething distaste. Then he spoke, and this is what he said:

I have lived about fifty years or so, more or less, and in the last thirty years I have never had anything to do with love as applied to women.

I do not believe that women have any idea of the meaning of devotion. They are like men—too complicated and too tied-up in self-interest.

No!—let me finish! I know what you're going to say ... that the love of a good woman is this, that, and the other! I do not deny that a good woman can love you as much as need be.

After all, what the devil are human beings that they should expect other human beings to be taken in by them to the extent of loving them?

I know all about people in love, because I was very much in love once, a long time ago.

I was in the early twenties. I met a species of blonde who worked for a milliner, and although she was not much to look at (now that I come to think of it) and had a general air of treachery and vicious ill-temper, I took it into my head that she was the most delightful and divine female that ever walked on legs.

So I started to go around with her and buy her presents, spending more than I could afford and making a perfect fool of myself.

We used to quarrel horribly. I was jealous of her, and not without cause, for she was flighty ... and worse.

Then, one day, when I had seen her sitting in a café drinking, when she swore she had to visit a dying aunt, we had a last terrible row and parted.

I was young and a fool. I took to drowning my sorrows in drink. But that, as you know, is no way to drown sorrows.

This went on for weeks. I lost my job. I used up my savings. I went to the bad. I had a little bit of property, and began to sell that, too.

I drank and drank. And then, one wretched rainy night on the edge of winter, I was staggering home to bed, eaten up with loneliness and the horrible depression of the drunkard, when, reaching my doorstep, I trod on something soft that whimpered.

It was a dog. But what a dog! It was the canine equivalent of one of those outcasts of humanity whom you see picking among the dustbins.

It was a mongrel, and a product of five hundred generations of mongrels. It looked like a jackal, it looked like a drowned lamb, it looked like the sweepings of a barber's shop with its hair of twenty different colours.

But the poor beast was very wretched, for it had been injured in a fight with a bigger dog—with a better dog—and was bleeding at the neck.

Now you know the maudlin sentimentality of the drunk: normally I would have ignored the beast, or, if I had wanted to be merciful I would have had him killed.

But now I picked it up and took it into my bedroom; bathed its wounds and bandaged them, and even reeled out to find something to eat for it.

There is nothing that clings to life like your creature of the gutters: the dog recovered, and after that he would never leave me.

You talk about love. I have yet to see a human love equal to the love of that dog.

One night again, being savagely drunk, I beat him; but when he came afterwards to lick my hand—the hand that had injured him—an awful remorse took possession of me and, odd as it may seem, I gave up drinking.

Yes, because of the influence of that small and dirty dog I found myself another job, saved myself from complete wreck and ruin, and began to settle down to the life of an industrious and respectable young bachelor.

And all would have been well. But one day in the spring I saw that accursed woman again. And all the crazy infatuation came back.

We talked. She said that she had never loved anybody but me, and I, only too anxious to believe it, was wild with joy.

Then she looked down and saw the dog, and asked: "What sort of a beast is that?" I replied: "I call him Charles, and he is really quite a wonderful little dog, in spite of his unprepossessing appearance."

And there came into her eyes a look of hate: She was a very bad woman, and she was jealous of that dog.

We decided to get married, and did so as quickly as we could and went to live in my flat. And then the old wickedness crept back.

It had been there all the time, but now she felt that she had me, and words cannot describe the extent of her persecution of me from day to day.

This went on for nearly a year, and again—being a man who has in him a streak of disgusting softness—I began to drink.

She did all she could, for her part, to make my life intolerable. Well, one night I came home drunk.

She was waiting for me with a certain evil smile on her face.

First of all I observed the absence of the dog Charles, who invariably greeted me with frantic caresses.

I said: "Where is he?" And my wife said: "He is where I wish you were."

And then she told me that she had had enough of this little loathsome dog and had got rid of him. I was absolutely stunned. She went on to tell me how she could not bear the idiotic affection I had for the dog. . . . She could not tolerate his appearance, his smell. . . .

And when she said that I knew that I really did love the dog better than her . . . that my affection for her was mere folly and that I really loved the dog for his goodness. And I sat down and stared in front of me.

She said: "I tied a brick round his neck and chucked him into the river. Dirty little beast! The wind blew my hat off. You will have to buy me a new one."

At that I felt myself going mad with rage, and I saw a pink mist before my eyes. I kept a revolver in a drawer. I opened the drawer and took out the revolver.

I swear to you that I was going to kill her. And then, just as my finger was on the trigger, I heard a familiar scratching at the door and paused.

Her face was pale as death. I opened the door. Charles came in.

He was in a pitiful state—almost drowned, shivering with cold, bleeding and dripping with water.

In his teeth he held a black hat with pink flowers—her hat. He limped up to me, laid the hat at my feet, tried to wag his tail, and fell dead. And my rage melted in a great gush of tears.

For that woman I felt, then, only an awful contempt. I picked up the body of the little dog and left the flat.

I looked at that beloved, bedraggled corpse and thought how strange and sad it was that God had sent the mongrel dog to save me from drunkenness, ruin, and murder. I never saw my wife again.

Love! You speak of love! You and your silly little romances! For myself, I have never met in all the world a love to equal that of the small, dirty dog Charles.

Doctor Ox Will Die at Midnight

"Inspector, please pay attention. This is terribly serious. I am Doctor Pelikan, psychiatrist, of the Magog Asylum."

"I am honoured to meet the celebrated Doctor Pelikan. What can I do for you?"

"Order four or five of your strongest officers to guard the apartment of my colleague, Doctor Ox!"

"But why?"

"Because to-night, at midnight, Papke the Ripper plans to murder him."

"But, Doctor Pelikan, Papke the Ripper is in a padded cell in your own asylum."

"I know, I know! But all the same, I warn you, I warn you!"

"Very well, doctor: but let us discuss it calmly. Have a cigar. Please step into my office. You do not mind if the sergeant also listens?"

"Not at all."

"You have no objection to my locking the door?"

"No, no, no! But please be quick. There is no time to lose."

The big door closed. The heavy lock clicked. The tiny doctor, his haggard face macerated by insomnia, sat opposite the gigantic inspector, whose cigar, gripped hard between his iron jaws, stuck out under his stone-grey moustache.

"Tell me, doctor, is not Papke sufficiently guarded?"

"Inspector, he is locked in a cell from which a fly could not escape, in a corridor through which a mouse could not pass without attracting attention. Nevertheless, send four strong men to guard the apartment of Doctor Ox: otherwise, Papke the Ripper will murder him at midnight."

"But how can you possibly say that?"

"I see that you do not take me seriously. If I explain, will you do as I say?"

"Certainly, doctor."

"Very well. Listen. It sounds fantastic, but it is the most serious thing in the world. You have heard of me. I know the minds of madmen better than anybody else on earth. I have devoted my entire life to the study of the insane———"

"I have read your *Studies in the Psychopathology of the Murderer*, doctor."

"Good. Then I can be very brief. Two years ago, I had a certain argument with Doctor Ox. In short, we discussed the physical basis of thought. I argued that it was possible for the intellect to operate independently, apart from the physical brain. Ox laughed. 'A theory,' he said. 'A fact,' I replied, 'and I will prove it.' 'I wager five hundred kronen that you cannot,' said Doctor Ox. I said: 'Very well. To-night, when you go to your room, stay awake until three o'clock. Take a book to bed with you. Read it; make a marginal note. In the morning I will quote to you the exact words you have read and written.' 'That is a bet,' said Doctor Ox."

"But could you?" asked the inspector.

"Yes. The higher faculties, the intellect and the will, are separable from the body. I could show you how. This, in a nutshell, is the technique. Wait until the small hours of the morning, when everything is quiet, and physical energy is at its lowest ebb. Lie down comfortably in the dark. Concentrate every shred of your will upon yourself: see yourself as a body, lying on your bed. Endeavour to project your sight and your powers of reasoning to a point two or three feet above the centre of your body. Then look down upon yourself with a detached mind. Practise this. Try and try. Fifty times, a hundred times, you will fail: then you may succeed. Make your mind travel across your room. Observe every object, but ignore obstacles: will yourself through walls and doors. Cover only familiar ground, going from object to object, observing every foot of the way. In this manner, you may project your mind into another room, another house—even another city."

"That would be a useful accomplishment for people involved in espionage, Doctor Pelikan!"

"Please do not interrupt. I was telling you of my wager with Doctor Ox. Doctor Ox lives in the flat immediately above mine. I had been there a hundred times. It was easy. I won my wager. When we met, at eleven o'clock, I said to him: 'You were sitting up in bed, in new red pyjamas, reading *Dead Souls*, by Gogol. On page 308, where Murazoff says to Tchitchikoff: "Yes, it seems to me that you could prove a *bogatuir*," you wrote in the margin: "Here, the conscious weakness of Gogol takes its revenge on the iron will of Tchitchikoff." Then you put out the light.'

"Doctor Ox was amazed. I tell you this in order that you may not disbelieve the amazing facts that follow. This happened two years ago. Even then I was highly skilled in the technique of the experiment. But since then, I have acquired an infinitely higher efficiency, and if you doubt me, I am prepared to prove every word I say!"

"No, no," said the inspector, "please proceed."

"I began to project my mind into the cells of the asylum, at night. I am familiar with every stone in the building: it was not difficult. I took the opportunity of making observations of the inmates. True, I achieved nothing of very great practical value; but it was interesting.

"Then, a year ago, they brought in Papke the Ripper."

"A dangerous man, that, Doctor Pelikan!"

"A horrible man, inspector! A devil, a perfect devil. Investigating that man's mind was like diving down and down into a bottomless pit full of horrors, as in one of those frightful Oriental legends—an abyss without end—a hell, I tell you, a hell! A——"

"You have broken your cigar, Doctor Pelikan. Permit me to offer you another."

"Thank you. Excuse my emotion. Papke was terrible—a beast, possessed of a tremendous elemental force—less than a man, but far more terrible than any animal. He used, in fact, to wrestle with bears in a circus. Oh, why didn't they hang him when he murdered that poor little girl, instead of sending him to me? He gloated, secretly, over the memories of fifteen horrible murders——"

"Fifteen!"

"Fifteen. And he had all the intuitions of the wild animal. He could tell when an eye was looking at him. I tried many times to watch him through a secret spyhole in his cell. He would sit like a statue, and say nothing. Later, he would say to me: 'And did you enjoy watching me earlier this afternoon?' We could do nothing with him. Doctors and attendants were afraid of him. But one night, I projected my mind into his cell, and, watching him as he lay asleep, I thought that I might actually get *inside his brain*, and wrestle with him, intellect against intellect, will against will, out of the reach of his awful hands."

"Good God, doctor! And did you?"

"I tried, night after night, for eight weeks. Finally, I succeeded. The intellect of Doctor Pelikan found itself side by side with the mind of Papke the Ripper. And what I saw horrified me. I watched plan after plan rise to the surface of that amazingly cunning and tortuous mind, like bubbles in a cesspool. And at the basis of each plan was a weapon, a razor. He had a genius for concealment. Stripped, bathed, and thoroughly searched, he had nevertheless managed to bring with him the blade of a French razor, which he had hidden in the padding of his cell. I forced my will then to fight against him. I ordered him to surrender this weapon. My order must have come upon him as an impulse. 'Here, take this away from me,' he said—while his real self shrieked *Kill! Kill!*

"Inspector, I have fought many battles of will, but never a battle like that. The savagery of Papke the Ripper beat at me like a high wind. And it won! At the last instant, when I thought that the victory was mine, the proximity of the attendant and the feel of steel combined with the thought of blood to let loose an absolute typhoon of ferocity. He leapt away from my control. A child might as well have tried to hold back a mad bull. With one slash, he almost severed the hand of the attendant. Blood-lust boiled up like a volcano. I was scorched, flung away, and beaten out. I saw him, waving the red razor above his head. My nerve broke. I fled. Morning found me, sick and terrified, worn out by the struggle, and obsessed by the fearful memory of that hour in the soul of Papke the Ripper.

"But that very next night, I went back. I went back into the mind of Papke, and fought against it. I fought powerful memories of ancient evil pleasures. I fought strong resolutions, even as they formed. I struggled between memory and resolution, but it was like trying to hold back the North Sea.

"I withdrew. Then I thought: 'Although I cannot overcome the beast, why should I not forestall him?' I became even more ambitious. If I could send my will through space, then why not through the other dimension, Time? And you must believe me, inspector, when I assure you that I succeeded, in a small way. Yes. After the most terrific efforts, my disembodied mind was projected through short distances of time. First, one hour. Then three, then eight. And finally twenty-four hours. I am too weak to do more than that: but that much I can do."

"A useful accomplishment if one happens to be a gambler on horses."

"Ask Goldberg, commission agent, exactly how much I have won from him in the last six weeks! He will tell you: Five hundred and seventy thousand kronen. This is by the way. I can move twenty-four hours ahead in time. That is why I am here, warning you—warning you, I say, to guard, with four of your strongest men, with their revolvers loose in the holsters, the flat of Doctor Ox, who, as surely as I sit here, is going to be torn to pieces—dismembered—horribly murdered, by Papke the Ripper, to-night at midnight."

"Well, well, doctor, if you insist . . ."

"I do. And I will tell you why. Last night a curious thing happened. I was worn out. I lay down on my bed, intending to project my will into the cell of Papke. But I was too tired. I fell asleep. My vitality was low, very low. I believe that my mind slipped away from my body of its own accord. Less vividly than during consciousness—as in a bad dream—I found myself in the mind of Papke the Ripper, not fighting it, but *involved* in it. It was like a well, in which I was drowning. I saw the completion of a resolution to kill Doctor Ox to-night, together with a plan."

"But what plan?"

"I do not know. It was vague. It was simple. It was brutal, bloody, horrible! I awoke trembling. I tried, then, to cast my will forward a few hours. Again, my mind slipped over hours of time of its own accord. This time I saw everything vividly. I saw myself in Doctor Ox's room, looking down upon something which I had discovered—all that was left of my dear colleague, my old friend Doctor Ox.... Then I saw myself running ... running.... And somewhere in the shadows, the face of Papke the Ripper—laughing, laughing.... This will happen tonight, inspector, at midnight. And that is why I am here—to beg you, quickly, quickly, to send four, six of your strongest men, to save Doctor Ox from Papke the Ripper, who will be at large with a knife in the streets of this city at midnight! I beg you, call me insane, if you will, but act upon my intuition before midnight. I am a little incoherent: that is because I am worn out with overwork, and insomnia, and too much anxiety. Doctor Ox will die at midnight!"

"At midnight?"

"Yes."

"To-night?"

"Yes, yes."

"Very well, Doctor Pelikan."

"You will do as I say?"

"Certainly."

"Thank you, inspector, a thousand times!"

"Please do not mention it, doctor. On the contrary, it is I who have to thank you. Sergeant—call in Officers Paschkes, Schoff, Vasatko, and Schmidt," said the inspector.

Four huge police officers came in.

"But, Doctor Pelikan, may I ask you one little question?"

"Of course, inspector!"

"First of all—another cigar."

"Thank you, inspector." Two "Virginia" cigars began to smoulder. "Now, proceed."

"In your vision of last night, where did Papke the Ripper hide the head?"

"The head of Doctor Ox?"

"Yes."

"In the cistern."

"Thank you, Doctor Pelikan. You did not mind my asking?"

"Not at all."

"That, you see, was the only portion of Doctor Ox which we were unable to find."

"Huh?"

"It will not be to-night at midnight," said the inspector. "Papke is still in his cell. It was to-day at midday. Since then we have been looking everywhere for you. Sergeant . . ."

The Earwig

Mr. Scripture had been caught in the grip of a bad dream. Something was clinging to his feet, dragging him down. That, alone, seems little enough, but it was attended by all the horror of the dark. Even as he slept, he told himself that it was only a dream, and struggled to wake up; then, with an awful start found himself awake in a tangle of bedclothes, and sighed with relief to see the dim daylight and the familiar objects in his bedroom.

He sat up, glad to be alive. But when he looked at the clock, the terror of the nightmare was swamped by a bigger, blacker fear. For it was nearly a quarter to eight. There remained seven minutes in which he had to wash, shave, dress, and reach the station in time to catch the seven-fifty-two.

For a moment, Mr. Scripture looked from side to side with the futile desperation of a trapped bird; then fled headlong to the bathroom, shaved in about fifteen wild strokes and cut the corner of his mouth, plunged into his shirt, buttoned his waist-coat all awry, and then, putting on his boots, almost wept as a lace broke.

He was afraid to look at the clock. There was still something of the atmosphere of the nightmare clinging to this abominable October morning. It was not properly light. It seemed to Mr. Scripture that the day would really never break. High up, there hung a dirty yellow suspicion of fog. His heart jumped to meet a ridiculous hope: *Perhaps there is fog down the line! Perhaps the train will be late!* But he knew there was no fog; that the train would not be late; and that there would be no excuse.... No, no, he was lost, lost!

He snatched his overcoat, banged on his hat, and ran like a rabbit into the melancholy wet wind that was blowing along the street. As he passed the newsagent's on the corner, he caught a glimpse of a newsbill:

FRANCE

TO

ACT

(Special)

Then he looked in front of him and ran along the High Street as he had never run before. He did not look at his watch: he could not spare the time to look. The street was almost empty. A pigeon, pecking at something in the gutter, flapped away in terror. Mr. Scripture heard the beating of its wings; and, in the same instant, the noise of the train entering the station. But there remained at least four hundred yards to cover, and his breath was almost gone ... and the road was like a road in a fairy-tale—it seemed to get longer and longer.

Mr. Scripture had lost count of time. He only knew that his chest hurt, and that sweat was running behind his ears. And so he reached the station, with his heart banging and rattling like horses galloping over a wooden bridge. He was just in time to see the back of the train swinging past the far end of the platform.

All hope departed from the heart of Mr. Scripture. He threw himself on to a bench, and sat there, panting, too miserable to think, exhausted, absolutely used up. But after ten or fifteen minutes he calmed himself, and began to brood upon the enormity of the situation.

The station-master who was passing said: "Missed your train, I see, Mr. Scripture."

"Yes."

"Never mind, sir, there's another one due at 8.20, and that'll get you in around 9.20."

"God!" said Mr. Scripture; and suddenly felt sick.

The station-master went on: "Nasty morning. Sort of weather that gets you down. I can feel it, I don't mind telling you, with my rheumatism. When I got up this morning, I fair hollered out with pain."

Then he went away, and Mr. Scripture thought: 9.20! *Oh, Lord, this is the end of everything....*

He was quite sure of this. It was true that, in the eleven years during which he had worked for Sir John Hardesty, he had never once been late. But in Hardesty's offices, no one ever was late. Unpunctuality was a crime, a black crime which Hardesty could never forgive.

"Time is money," he said; and believed it. So many minutes, so many shillings; if you were late, you were robbing him; you were a thief. You felt fortunate only to have been sacked; you were grateful that he had not called the police. Hardesty was a cold man, cold as ice. And a brute. Little Mr. Yorke had worked for him for fifteen years, only to be ordered out of the office like a dog, on account of a miserable fifteen-minute lapse.

With Hardesty, you knew what to expect. He was the big, bad business-man of fiction. By incredible toil and superhuman toughness, he had made his way out of the back-alleys of a Liverpool slum.

He was hard and mean. You felt that he begrudged even the words he spoke to you: he flung them into your face in stony monosyllables, which he snapped off with implacable, slitted, steely lips. He was inhuman; a believer in the maxim: *No friendship in business*. Friendship? With Sir John Hardesty there was nothing but enmity.

Everybody hated the man. God help the wretch who owed anything to Hardesty! Sooner ask for three days of grace from the Angel of Death than ask Hardesty for a little more time to pay. And woe to the man who came to Hardesty for charity! There was more kindness in the paving-stones; more gentleness in the winter rain. Starvation was easier to bear than his brutal contempt. In a way, he was just; but even his justice was bitter, mathematical, and lifeless....

And this is what I must face this morning! thought Mr. Scripture, with a qualm of terror. And there came into his soul a desire for flight. Dismissal was inevitable. Then why face the ordeal of it?

Blown by the wind, a crumpled piece of tin-foil from a cigarette packet slid along the platform and touched his foot. He started, and looked at his watch; stared, with dumb fright. Time had stopped!

No, only his watch had stopped. The station clock said 8.10. Then why was his heart beating so fast? He adjusted his waistcoat, stamped his feet to warm them; and remembered, with peculiar vividness, the nightmare of the thing that clung to his feet . . . the unseen thing that had dragged him down and down. . . .

Pure fear took hold of him, on that long, windswept platform. He lit a cigarette, though he never smoked before midday; inhaled smoke, and felt better. He wanted a cup of tea, a very strong cup of tea . . . he wanted a cup of tea more than he had ever wanted anything in his life. Approaching the ticket-collector, he said:

"What wouldn't I give for a cup of tea!"

The man replied: "Ah! Or cocoa with milk."

Then the train came. Mr. Scripture chose the compartment which, he calculated, would stop nearest to the exit at Liverpool Street. From there, with luck, he could run to the office in five minutes. Hardesty always arrived at 9.15. There was a chance—a feeble ghost of a chance—that on this unholy morning, the great man himself might be a few minutes late.

It would be a miracle, but miracles sometimes did happen. Poor men won £30,000 in sweepstakes, or football pools; coincidences occurred, mad coincidences. . . .

Somebody had left a newspaper on the other seat, a vulgar picture paper, such as Mr. Scripture scorned to read. He saw the black headline: FAMILY DROWNED AS YACHT CAPSIZES, but had not the heart to read. The train rumbled on. He felt that he had been riding in that train since the beginning of time.

Exhausted, he dozed; felt a horrifying sensation of dizzy flight; opened his eyes again . . . closed them; and with shocking inevitability there recurred the dream of the clinging thing, and the downward sinking. He cried out, and awoke. A voice cried: "Liverpool Street!" and Mr. Scripture ran out, still half asleep.

It was only when he reached the street that he remembered his hat, which he had left in the train. But he did not pause. He ran until he reached the office, and crept into his own little room. The unopened mail lay on his desk. He glanced at it. The uppermost letter was from Thompson's—nobody could fail to recognise the long, pretentious blue envelope.

Now ... thought Mr. Scripture; and his mouth became dry. He smoothed down his hair, and knocked at the door marked *Sir J. Hardesty. Private.* There was no answer. Crazy hope sent his heart into his throat. *He's not here! Not here!* Then he opened the door, and hope died.

Hardesty was sitting there, waiting for him; grimmer than death; with eyes like agate marbles, and a face like a granite death-mask.

"Come in, Mr. Scripture," said Hardesty.

Scripture closed the door, stood before his master in a humble attitude, and said:

"I ..."

"I know. You're late."

"Sir ... Sir John, I ..."

It was at this moment that Mr. Scripture, looking down, saw the earwig.

It was crawling across Hardesty's formidable glass-topped desk, towards the blotting-pad. Mr. Scripture stared at it, fascinated. An earwig! On Hardesty's desk!

It approached Sir John's hand—that heavy, uncompromising hand. In another few seconds, it would touch him. . . .

"You know my rules, Scripture," said Sir John.

"I ... I ..." Scripture forgot what he had been about to say. The explosion of a bomb could not have dragged his attention away from the earwig. The earwig! The earwig! How close to death that earwig was!

"You'll tell me that you've never been late in eleven years. I know. You'll say it'll never happen again. It won't. I pay you five hundred a year. I expect my rules to be obeyed ..."

Scripture was dumb. He was still watching the earwig. It crawled to within an inch of Hardesty's hand; then turned and crossed the desk again. . . .

"So take a month's notice, Scripture. No, on second thoughts, draw a month's salary, and get out. You're sacked. Good day." The earwig reached the edge of the desk; hung there for a moment, then fell on to the carpet; wriggled; disappeared.

As when the unseen thing had clung to his feet, Mr. Scripture shouted, within himself: *I'm dreaming! This can't be true!*

And that, indeed, was the end of the dream; for he awoke with a loud cry, and found himself in his bedroom, almost weeping with relief.

Yes, he was awake, really awake; unmistakably wide awake.

He sat up, looking towards the window. It was a dreary morning. Then he looked at the clock, and his heart stopped beating.

It was a quarter to eight.

He had seven minutes.

He was stunned. Life had overlapped with nightmare. For a second he sat, looking about him; then leapt up and into the bathroom; shaved with lunatic haste, and dressed.

Snatching a hasty glimpse of himself, he felt in his chest a sensation as of something contracting. He had cut the left-hand corner of his mouth; and his waistcoat was buttoned awry. *Steady!* he told himself, *you're letting yourself be influenced by a dream!* He tied his bootlaces with extraordinary care.

One of them broke.

Then he was out of the house, running desperately; desperately and hopelessly, like a man running away from his destiny. *I will not look at the newsagent's shop*, he decided. Indeed, he had almost passed the corner, when an impulse too strong to be denied, made him turn his head. . . .

FRANCE TO ACT (Special)

shrieked the placard. It was after him! It was on his heels! The nightmare, the nightmare was upon him! The flapping of the wings of the pigeon shook him like the shock of gunfire. *Why am I running?* he wondered, *I am finished. Why run? In another instant I shall hear——*

Khsssh! shouted the train in the station; and Mr. Scripture still ran, under the bitter yellow sky; and arrived, as he knew he would, in time to see the train steam out.

He sat.

A voice said: "Missed your train, I see, Mr. Scripture."

"Yes."

"Never mind, sir, there's another one due at 8.20, and that'll get you in around 9.20.... Nasty morning. Sort of weather that gets you down. I can feel it, I don't mind telling you, with my rheumatism. When I got up this morning, I fair hollered out with pain."

I am caught, thought Mr. Scripture; and bowed his head.

Was this also a dream, a dream of a dream? He sat. He waited. He felt like a character in one of those old, macabre German films ... a clock ticks; a shadow approaches; you know what is about to happen, and it happens—and because you expect it, it is all the more shocking.

The tinfoil slid up to his boot, with a tiny metallic rustle. Yes! Time ... no, the watch had stopped....

Tea.... "Ah! Or cocoa with milk." The train! The compartment. There will be a newspaper. Yes, there *is* a newspaper....

I must not forget my hat. I shall not be able to afford another.

"And I mustn't go to sleep," said Mr. Scripture, aloud. He was afraid of the nightmare of the clinging thing ... the horrible sinking....

But he slept; and he dreamt; and he awoke with a cry as the train reached Liverpool Street ... ran in panic, half asleep, and, when he reached the street, groaned when he remembered his hat.

Yes. There was the mail. There was the blue Thompson envelope. There was the door. There would be no answer to his knock. There was no answer. No, there was no hope. There sat Sir John Hardesty, grimmer than death, saying:

"Come in, Mr. Scripture."

"I ..."

"I know. You're late."

"Sir ... Sir John, I ..."

Inevitable, also, as a figure in a familiar horror-tale, there crawled the earwig. Across the desk it crawled ... towards the blotting-pad ... up to Sir John's left hand. Mr. Scripture was hypnotised. He could not move. He could not speak.

"You know my rules, Scripture?"

The earwig held him, even as it had held him in the dream. He struggled to tear his eyes away; writhed, and forced himself to look up and meet Hardesty's gaze.

Then he was able to speak. He heard his own voice saying:

"You will say to me: '*You'll tell me that you've never been late in eleven years. I know. You'll say it'll never happen again. It won't. I pay you five hundred a year. I expect my rules to be obeyed. So take a month's notice, Scripture. No, on second thoughts, draw a month's salary and get out. You're sacked. Good day.*'"

He saw Sir John's expression change. The knotty forehead wrinkled in astonishment. Then Mr. Scripture looked down again, in time to see the earwig reach the edge of the desk, pause, and fall.

As it wriggled, he put out his foot and crushed it.

Sir John Hardesty said: "How the devil ..." then paused. "What makes you think ..." He bit the end off a cigar, cleared his throat, and shouted:

"Who are you to put words into my mouth? Get back to work, and don't let it occur again!"

Once again Mr. Scripture told himself: *I'm dreaming! This can't be true!* But it was true; and he leapt zealously to the door as Hardesty snapped:

"Quick. The Thompson correspondence, Scripture. Wake up!"

Who Wants a Liver-Coloured Cat?

There is a *café* near Cambridge Circus which is open all night, and into which strange men creep in the small hours of the morning. Let us call the café Rocco's Coffee Bar.

If you wait long enough in Rocco's you will see about forty per cent of all that is queerest in London.

There, between chocolate-coloured walls, under the fly-blown alabaster lamps that hang from the smoky ceiling, mysterious men sit, making small cups of coffee last, sip by sip, for hours after midnight.

I used to frequent Rocco's. It was there that I met the man with the liver-coloured cat.

He was an exhausted-looking man, dark and pale, with a blue jaw. There was something wrong with one of his legs, he dragged it after him like a dead weight. He had none of the air of the habitual night-bird. Yet he was always in Rocco's Coffee Bar, night after night, doing nothing, saying nothing; simply sitting, killing time ... or rather, staying still while time killed itself.

He spoke to me for the first time late one night in November, 1938.

He said: "Like cats?"

"I don't mind them," I replied.

"Ah," he muttered, sipping his coffee. "I do." Then he said something strange. "Ever seen a liver-coloured cat?"

"Liver-coloured?"

"Sort of liver-coloured. Dark gingerish colour, but with a kind of purplish look about it. Liver-coloured. A tom-cat, very well grown."

"I've never seen a cat like that," I said.

"I have," the strange man said, and shivered. "I've got one. I don't like it."

"Can't you get rid of it?" I asked.

He laughed. You can tell just how tired a man really is when you hear him laugh. This man was weary to death, used up.

"You might think I'm crazy," he said. "Perhaps I am crazy, but I don't think so. Now, listen. What would you make of this? I swear to you—as God is my judge—that this is just what happened.

"Last month, I got home from work at about 6.30, and saw this cat sitting on the rug in front of the fire. There was a saucer of milk in front of it. It hadn't touched the milk. The poor beast looked wet and bedraggled.

"I said to my wife: 'Since when have we had a cat?' 'Since this afternoon,' she said. 'When I came back from shopping it was sitting on the rug. I don't know how on earth it got in, but I didn't have the heart to turn it out. Perhaps it's ill. It won't eat or drink.'

"I said: 'Oh, well, let it stay, anyway.' I had a meal and then drew my chair up to the fire. I couldn't get comfortable.

"It was that cat. It was a nasty colour . . . sort of liver-coloured . . . and there was something queer about it. It didn't wash itself, or close its eyes as other cats do in front of a fire. It kept staring.

"I went to bed early. Before I went to bed I opened the front door and bent down to pick the cat up. I was going to put it out. But I didn't touch it—it snarled at me like a leopard, and ran out of its own accord.

"I saw it on the stairs. Then I shut the door quickly and went to bed. My wife asked me: 'Did you put that cat out?' 'Yes,' I said, and she sighed with relief and said: 'Thank goodness.'

"Next morning I was up at seven. I went into the kitchen. I had to pass through the living-room. I nearly jumped out of my skin. There, sitting on the rug, was the cat.

"I swear I saw it run downstairs. Yet there it was. I had a very unpleasant feeling when I saw it there. But I was prepared to admit that it might—just possibly—have slipped back past me.

"I brought my wife a cup of tea. She said: 'What's the matter?'

" 'Matter?' I said.

" 'Yes, you look pale.'

"I said: 'Oh, nothing. Bit of a turn. I'd swear I put that cat out last night. But it's still here. But I'll tell you what. You don't like that cat. No more do I. I'll ring the cats' home and have it taken away.'

" 'For heaven's sake, do that now,' she said.

"So I went out as soon as I was dressed and telephoned. Then I went to work.

"That evening my wife told me that the man had come and taken the cat away in a basket. We both felt better, because there was something about that cat that somehow scared us.

"We turned in early. In the middle of the night I woke up suddenly. I had a . . . not exactly a dream, but something like a *thought* . . . an unpleasant *feeling*.

"I sat up, wide awake. I listened. Nothing. I got out of bed and went into the living-room. The doors were shut. The windows were shut.

"But down on the rug there were two green things. Eyes. It was the cat.

"Yes. The same cat; there aren't two cats of that colour. I'm no hero, but I hope not more of a coward than most men. But I was scared—and angry.

"You may know that I'm on the road for P—— and Co., and use a car. That same morning I borrowed a sack. I caught the cat and got it into the sack, and tied up the mouth of the sack with more string than was necessary, really. Then I dumped both cat and sack into the car—it struggled like the devil—and drove, hell-for-leather, out as far as Thornton Heath.

"I dropped the cat, still in the sack, on the steps of a house, and drove back. It was a Saturday. I didn't go out to work on Saturdays. When I got back my wife was in a flutter.

"'Where have you been?' she asked.

"'Well,' I said, 'that's disposed of that confounded liver-coloured cat, anyway.' And I told her what had happened.

"She said: 'You've been dreaming.' And she pointed. On the mat in front of the fireplace . . . yes. *The cat!*

"Can you explain that? I looked at my wife. She looked at me. 'Don't think I'm mad. I'm not—only fed up,' I said. 'But I give you my word of honour that I dumped that cat ten miles away half an hour ago.'

"She said: 'I don't think you're mad. There's something uncanny about this . . . cat. I'm afraid of it. It's not natural. It doesn't eat or sleep. And it keeps *staring*. And—John—I *know* the man from the cats' home took that cat away. I *saw* him take it. And then . . . I came out of the bedroom, and there it was, sitting, just looking at me. John—*what is it?*'

"I said: 'I don't know. But, my dear little girl, all the cats on earth aren't worth your little finger . . . and so you and I are going to take this cat to a vet., and we're going to have it put to sleep once and for all.'

"My wife put on her coat. The cat let me pick it up and carry it. It felt damp and cold. We took it to a vet. four streets away. We stood by when he put it in a gas-chamber. We waited. Then the vet. opened the box, and said:

"'Now, that's strange!'

"I didn't ask him what was strange. I guessed. The cat wasn't there. 'Where can it have gone?' he asked. I could have told him where.

"My wife and I were afraid to go home. But we went. And there sat the cat.

"It's been there ever since. My wife has gone to stay with her sister in Beckenham. I go there week-ends. But I don't go home. To be frank, I'm afraid to.

"Would you like to take my key? You can go and see for yourself—a liver-coloured cat, sitting by the fireplace. I'll wait outside for you. Do you want to go and see?"

It was very late. I said I could not go. But then, later still, I had an unpleasant sensation of having missed something strange and true. I went back to Rocco's. The man with the limp had gone. I never saw him again.

The House of Relish

In the year of Our Lord 1796, Absalom Relish founded the House of Relish in a potting-shed, in Clodpuddle, in the County of Kent. The foundation of this business represented the consummation of a lifetime of honest endeavour. The son of humble parents, he left the land on account of an inherent weakness of the knees, and entered the service of Baron Soyle of Clodpuddle in the capacity of knife-and-boots boy. His integrity, willingness and sagacity did not escape his master's eye, so that before twenty years had passed Absalom was elevated to the dignity of second footman, from which he worked his way, in the course of ten or twelve years, to the position of butler to the Baron, and the secrets of the recipe-book and the pantry. Punches, sauces, and metal-polish, soap-boiling, jam-making, and elderberry wine were as an open book to Absalom Relish; nor were the secrets of game-hanging and the putrefaction of Stilton cheese unknown to him. But above all, he became possessed of the recipe for the famous Soyle Pickles, which for centuries had been the envy of the nobility of the county. This was the corner stone of his house. Unjustly dismissed on a wrongful suspicion of delinquency as to Port wine, he left the Baron's service in righteous indignation and determined to devote his remaining years to the dissemination of pickles. His stock-in-trade consisted of one large tub, one large wife, some wooden spoons, fruits and vegetables, and a few stone jars. The story of his meteoric rise, which should be an inspiration to the young of all times—and was, indeed, adopted as the official prize book of all Supralapsarian Boarding schools in the year 1869—was committed to print by Horatio Relish in his Memoir, published privately in 1867. The manuscript is still preserved in the Relish Museum. It tells of Absalom Relish in the beginning. He started small. Yet, by dint of thrift, enterprise, humility, energy, and devotion, he extended his circle of patrons until, when he died in 1828, his son Matthew inherited a business of which the turnover was no less than three hundred jars of pickles a week, supplied by a factory housed in a spacious new shed, and manufactured by a staff of five—Matthew Relish himself, his wife, and his son; Jonathan Stuffings, an orphan nephew afflicted with scrofula; and Elizabeth Tippett, a woman of ninety, who had wet-nursed old Absalom Relish sixty-eight years previously.

Matthew Relish was a true son of the old stock. He stood like a rock in a fluctuating world. With a will of iron he resisted any form of change. When his wife once said to him: "Matthew, my love, do you not think that we might have cut a cheap wooden block to print the labels for our jars, since my handwriting is not so legible as it once was on account of the rheumatism, and our son Horatio has warts on his fingers from the vinegar in the mixing-tub, and can but with difficulty ply his pen?" Matthew cut her short with a stern: "Silence, woman! Your prattle is enough to make my father turn in his grave. No more of this. What was good enough for him is good enough for me! And as for the child's warts, send him to Winifred Stooge, the Clod-puddle witch—she will charm them away for sixpence."

On another occasion, when a commercial poet who was famous for his couplets popularising a well-known brand of boot-blacking, forced his way into Matthew's office, and held before the astonished gaze of that sound man of business, a series of verses beginning:

> How did Bold Dick Turpin ride to York?
> On Relish's Pickles and Cold Roast Pork!

The outraged Matthew drove him from the pickle-shed to

Clodpuddle Green beating him about the head with a heavy wooden mixing spoon.

Time proved Relish right. Without vaunting self-praise or vulgar display, the output of Relish's pickles literally soared; until, by the year 1850, the transport of the country combined, in barge, coach and sometimes even railroad, to rush over the home counties no less than one thousand two hundred jars every week.

But at this point the anarchy of war came to shatter the calm atmosphere of the thriving factory. England declared war on the Russian Bear. Hosts of troops poured into the Crimea. Scorched by the blazing suns, bitten by the Russian frosts, choked by the fogs of the Black Sea, the scurvy-tainted blood of the British Bulldogs cried aloud for pickles.

Horatio Relish, whom military history does not record, had become friendly with a gentleman on the Government: he announced to the aged Matthew that Opportunity had knocked at their door, and that he had contracted to supply the Army with pickles.

"Nonsense, Sirrah!" cried old Matthew, "stuff and nonsense! Not to be thought of. Why, we could scarcely produce, in a week, enough pickles to add relish to the meals of a few companies; let alone an army. Are you mad, sir? Have you been drinking, sir? Has success turned your head, sir? That you dare to think in terms of thousands of jars of pickles? Have you been at the ale, sir? What, where will we get the jars? Where will we get the vegetables? How will Simpers write out so many labels?"

"Dear Papa," said Horatio, "we must buy more jars, and arrange to purchase fruit and vegetables from the farmers of the county. Indeed, if necessary, we must have them brought to us in carts. And as for labels, we must have a wooden block made, and print them——"

"You have your mother's tainted blood!" roared old Matthew. "But indeed, what more could I expect from one of the Surrey Futtercakes? Leave the room, sir! Leave——"

But at this moment, his face swelled and darkened to the colour and texture of an aubergine, his eyes became red, and bulged, so that they assumed the appearance of two young onions in the pickling-vat, he uttered a choking cry, and fell prone at his son's feet.

He was laid to rest in the Clodpuddle Supralapsarian Cemetery. His undutiful son, Horatio, unmindful of his father's dying wish, employed several more men and boys; extended his sheds, bought more bottles, vinegar, spices and vegetables, and within a few months—such was the vigour and determination of young Horatio, inspired by an evil impulse—hundreds and hundreds of jars of Relish's Pickles, grossly embellished by printed labels, so that each jar resembled its fellow, were conveyed in packing-cases in the hold of the *Rule Britannia* to soothe the stomachs of the furious frost-bitten Britons and goad them to more savage bloodshed.

Mindful of the moral welfare of a wild soldiery deprived of feminine company, Horatio omitted certain costly spices such as had been considered essential to the original recipe, and which, according to eminent medical experts, might be calculated to heat the blood. Virtue is its own reward. His conscience, as well as his purse, was thereby inflated. He contributed a new stained-glass window to the Clodpuddle Supralapsarian Church, depicting Saint George, in the likeness of Absalom Relish, standing triumphant on the carcase of a prostrate dragon.

But after the war was over, Horatio Relish was stricken by the pangs of conscience. It is necessary for the reader to understand that the man was not wholly evil. He had been carried away by the exuberance of youth. He sold, now, thousands of jars of Relish's Pickles every week. He was a wealthy man. So he repented. He dismissed, without warning, an artisan named Adonijah Wiggins, who had been with the company, man and boy, for forty years, for venturing the suggestion "That if it so pleased the master, the Suckling Preserve Factory had taken to boiling the jam by steam". He hardened his heart to the foibles and fantasies of his young sons, who, with all the ardour of thoughtless youth, might have permitted their heads to be turned by new and unsound ideas as to advertising. "The name of Relish," said Horatio, "is not to be painted on posters or exhibited in shop windows like the name of a clown or an opera-singer. My father, sir, would have disinherited me for such ideas—yes, sir, cut me off with a shilling. Let me hear no more of this flim-flammery, sir, or it may be the worse for you."

"But, father," protested young Absalom, "might one not, in a chaste announcement, enlivened by tasteful woodcuts, draw attention to the fact that such celebrities as Mr. Joseph Grimaldi, Doz, etcetera, have enjoyed Relish's pick——"

"Leave the room, sir!" roared Horatio. "Or by G——, I'll put you to the door!"

"One thing more," begged Absalom, "only one little thing. I have heard, from a representative of the Beedlebotham Glass Blowing Company, that Sucklings are considering glass jars to pack their preserves in——"

"What, sir? What? Pack Relish's Pickles in glass jars, like a two-headed abortion preserved in spirits of wine at a fair? Have you been at the brandy, sir?"

"Our customers often complain, father, that large numbers of jars are broken in transit. We are the losers on account of this. Do you not think, therefore—nay, strike me if you will, father, but hear me out; only hear me out!—do you not think that we might stuff the interstices between the jars in the wooden boxes with shavings or sawdust, instead of old newspapers? Would——"

"D—n me!" shrieked Horatio, "d—n me, I'll be the death of you, by G—— I will. Go! Leave the room!"

Absalom left the room, and shortly afterwards, receiving an offer from the firm of Slapdash, Skelter and Blast, left his father's company for India, where he died unrepentant of the yellow fever, fifty-three years later, an awful example to undutiful sons.

His younger brother, Matthew, however, more than recompensed his father for his erring brother's downfall. He followed in his father's footsteps. When Horatio died, of the stone exacerbated by port wine, in 1875, young Matthew took his chair.

A portrait of Horatio Relish, done in oils by Lickspittle, hangs to this very day in the Board room of Relish's. It depicts a blonde, portly man, remarkable for his whiskers, which, it was said, surpassed in luxuriance and quality those of the Emperor Francis Joseph of Austria-Hungary. His solid frame, substantially encased in a black frock-coat, of superlative cut, seems to bulge out of the canvas and into the room. Across the grey

waistcoat, tastefully embroidered with red spots, like the back
of a fine Scots plaice, hangs a solid gold curb Albert watchguard
of undeniable value. But the face, above all, arrests the attention.
Low down on the forehead, which is neither excessively high nor
unduly broad, grow his short wiry curls. His eyebrows are im-
mensely thick and virile. The eyes beneath them are extremely
small and of a very pale blue colour, like the eyes of all far-seeing
men. Under each eye hangs a dark, rugose pouch, exactly similar
in appearance to half a pickled walnut. It was well known that his
heart was in his business; you might think, to look at him, that
his body, also, had been. His nose is somewhat large and has so
many excrescences that it resembles one of those delicate sprigs
of cauliflower which are a feature of Relish's pickles; his cheeks
have the hue of red cabbage; each lip might be one of Relish's
gherkins, pallid with over-pickling, and attached to his face with
gum; and between the masculine bushes of his whiskers, his little
round chin peeps coyly out like a ripe shallot. Over all, there
hangs a pickled atmosphere; an air of vinegary permanence and
starchy adulteration.

* * * * *

When Matthew Relish became head of the House of Relish
in the 1870's, the greatest civilisation the world has ever seen
was progressing to its unassailable peak. God and Bismarck
had smitten Paris, the Modern Sodom. Wagner was still hissed.
The Supralapsarian Mission was penetrating the Kasai River;
Matthew's subscriptions alone, it was calculated, had concealed
the benighted loins and barbarian bosoms of no less than seven
hundred cannibals of both sexes beneath corduroy and black
Manchester cotton. The machine-gun was coming into its own.
The ardent blood of an Empire-building generation craved an
intenser stimulus. Pickles! Pickles! was the universal cry.

The demand became imperative. Wild-eyed ladies in that
delicate condition which gives rise to sudden fancies, insisted
on saucers full of Relish's Pickles, threatening that if they were
denied this delicacy the desire might work inwardly and result
in onion-faced gherkin-headed monsters. The Roast Beef of
Old England became meaningless without Relish's Pickles as

its complement. The Clodpuddle factory reeled in a wild whirl of the mixers churned in the tubs; boys and girls of tender age fell asleep with their faces in the vinegar, and mixed pickles in their dreams. Pickle-Mixers' Palsy and Label Stickers' Tongue smote the population of Clodpuddle, and it was a proud day for Matthew when the name of Relish found its way into the Medical Dictionary in connection with Relish's Scurvy, an affection of the skin due to the irritation of pickle-vapour, which, Matthew hoped, might in the course of time, rival Phossy Jaw in prevalence.

Matthew remained in tolerable good health, except for periodic attacks of the hæmorrhoids—a consequence of the sedentary life which his activities forced him to lead. The Seat of his Intellect, however, remained uncongested, and the business prospered phenomenally until the year 1879. In this year, the House of Suckling, a company of jam-boilers notorious for their degrading lust for new ideas, insinuated themselves into pickles. In fantastic glass bottles, the contents of which were disgustingly naked to the glance of every Tom, Dick or Harry, they forced their product on the counters of weak-minded and undiscriminating shopkeepers. Suckling stopped at nothing. Theirs was not the honest tactics of healthy competition. They devised posters which depicted a revoltingly vulgar little boy, his face plastered with a sickening yellow mass, standing on a stool to pilfer handfuls of Suckling's Pickles from a jar on a high shelf, and exclaiming: "Oh my, they *are* good!"

Their unwarranted intrusion did not escape the eagle eye of the Relishes.

"It seems to me," said Horatio Relish, Matthew's only son, "that these people constitute a genuine menace to Relish's Pickles. The hydra-headed multitude is notoriously fickle, and incapable of discrimination. They take what they see clearest. I suggest, therefore, that we, also, purchase a machine for mixing pickles; have designed some tasteful and attractive pictures of a high moral tone, to attract the public eye; and even put our pickles in glass jars."

"In other words, cry our pickles from the house-tops," said Matthew in a tone of menace.

"Yes, sir; as the great Bodger cried the Gospel."

"Hm.... In other words, make a popular spectacle of ourselves."

"Yes, sir," said the ardent young man.

"Boy, you are taking leave of your senses."

"No, sir. People are purchasing Suckling's Pickles. We are selling less."

"Ho! And so you propose that we spend the remaining part of our waning profits on gimcracks and fancy bottles, hey? Bah, sir, bah!"

"Father, I have been thinking of this matter, and it seemed to me that the vegetables and fruit which we use are too fresh. If we added to our mixtures a moiety of *not*-too-fresh vegetables and *very* slightly spoiled fruit ..."

"Well?" said Matthew, in a more reasonable tone.

"Listen, Father. I have been talking to Doctor Willies, and he has assured me that the rare spices which we use in our pickles irritate the bladder and are bad for the nerves. He also expressed the opinion that it might be arguable that vegetables fresh from the earth might be injurious to the stomach. The Reverend Colick-Jones, also, suggested to me that highly-spiced foodstuffs might well inculcate a taste for the Fleshpots of Egypt and render discontented the cold-meat-and-pickle-eating classes of this country. Such discontent might result in bloody revolution. It is therefore our bounden duty to use less expensive spices, and slightly spoiled fruit."

"Hum ..."

"By this means we may starve out Suckling and Satan. Satan thrives on spice. A salacious story is called *spicy*. We must rise above that."

"Neatly put, son, neatly put."

"Improve the soul as well as the body of the pickle eater. And do no harm to our own interests. By judicious alteration of our mixtures, and installing steam-driven machinery, and so forth, we can produce two-and-one-half bottles for the price of one. And since we sell our bottles at the same price as before, we double our profits."

"My lad, your arguments are not without some show of reason. Adulterate——"

"O Father, I beg you: not that word!"

"Adapt our pickles. . . . Hum. . . . Yes, indeed, there is a certain modicum of something resembling logic in what you say . . ." said Matthew. "And I can see in this some similarity to the tactics of the great Martin Luther. He drove away the Devil by throwing an inkpot at him. We will pelt him with very slightly spoiled fruit. Ha, ha!"

"I would further suggest, dear father, the addition of the word 'Pure' to our labels. 'Relish's Pure Pickles'," said Horatio.

"A fine word. But . . ."

"True, Father, true. A *true* word."

"Ye-es, of course. Our intention *is* pure."

"Then, Father, shall we say 'Pure'?"

"Why not 'Warranted Unadulterated and *Absolutely* Pure'?"

"Yes, Papa," replied Horatio, that dutiful son.

The House of Relish suited the action to the word, and, within two or three months, long cylindrical jars of Relish's Pickles, glassily transparent and stuck with a pink oval label, overshadowed the squat, green-labelled Suckling pickle-jars on the counters of the tradesmen. Cheek by jowl with every Suckling poster there appeared a larger and brighter poster calling attention to the pure and unadulterated product of the House of Relish. Horatio spared neither effort nor expense. He became a patron of the Arts, sometimes paying no less than half a guinea for a design for a poster. "Show us something with some *work* in it," he would say. It is true that he paid Hungerford Ribb eleven shillings for the famous Purity Poster, which has no more than one human figure in it; but he ordered the artist to "make up the deficiency by putting in a lot of flowers, trees, pickle-jars, clouds, birds, cows in the distance, a church, and a couple of dogs and sheep". The poster has gone down in history. It depicts a rosy, fresh-faced English maiden, dressed in the Union Jack, and holding up a jar of Relish's Pickles. Below, appear the words: "Pure and Undefiled."

Content to behold his son's development, Matthew withdrew from the business and busied himself with Supralapsarian affairs. He presented to the Clodpuddle Church a new font, made of old Absalom Relish's original pickle-tub, embellished with a silver rim and mounted on an elegant and complicated brass stand; and when he died in 1889, he was laid to rest in the Relish Mausoleum. The discomfited and envious Suckling, on seeing this superb edifice, which is nearly as large as the Marble Arch, and has almost as many knobs as the Albert Memorial, was heard to mutter: "Old Relish never told the truth in his lifetime. They did right to carve above his name the words: 'Here Lies...'"

But in spite of his unflagging efforts, Suckling was never able to equal the success of the House of Relish. If he lowered his prices, Horatio sternly undercut him. If he introduced a new cork, Horatio surpassed it. Above all, Suckling could never quite achieve the public appeal of the word 'Pure'—that inspiration of a noble mind. By virtue of that word, Horatio seemed to have seized the public in an unbreakable lock-hold. People said: "Try a little Relish's—they're pure, you know"; and "Oh, come, Relish's won't hurt you. They're the purest going." In a certain slander case at the Courts of Justice, a certain Mr. Trollip passionately exclaimed: "My Lord, Relish's Pickles themselves are not purer than my daughter."

Horatio, long before this, had married the daughter of Admiral Effingham Fawcett, who had presented him with twin sons, Absalom Effingham and Matthew Fawcett, in 1882. The two boys went into the business in 1903, and there Matthew soon displayed the business acumen and sound selective brain of his father. Indeed, since he and Absalom had proceeded, so to speak, from two halves of the same cell, it was to be assumed that all the good points had fallen on Matthew's side, leaving Absalom entirely devoid of brains, character, and virtue. Matthew's brain was as heavy, hard, and solid as a brick: Absalom's was like so much wax, ready to receive the flimsiest new impression and retain it. The father, Horatio, stood like a rock; Absalom drifted from idea to idea, like a rudderless boat on a sea. Horatio was the rock against which Absalom broke.

The time came when Absalom, seduced by some feather-brained theoretician from America, dared to set himself up as a critic of his father's methods.

"What you've done," he had the temerity to say, "is all very well. It was good enough for the eighteen-eighties; it may even be good enough for to-day. But the time is coming, Dad"—he had been only too ready to acquire the gross slang of the gutters: he called his male parent "Dad!"—"The time is coming when you will suddenly find yourself too far behind the times to catch up."

"Silence!" shouted old Horatio, "you have gone too far! You take too much upon yourself. I have been manufacturing these pickles since eighteen——"

"Yes, yes, you've been manufacturing these pickles since eighteen hundred and one, if you like. But that doesn't mean to say you know anything about selling them in the twentieth century. If the Zenz Corporation came to England——"

"Silence!"

"England is England, and America is America," said young Matthew; for even in those years he did not falter at the most profound philosophical propositions.

"You mark my words," said the hysterical Absalom, "one of these days Zenz will shove you off the market."

"Insolent young puppy!" roared Horatio. "Leave the office!"

"Why don't you go to your Zenz Corporation, then?" suggested Matthew with fine irony.

"All right," said Absalom, grinding his teeth in a murderous fury, "I will go to Zenz. But before I go let me tell you that your whole business is run like a cockle-stall; the packing is ridiculous; the advertising is childish; the——"

"Get out!" bellowed Horatio. "Get *out!*"

"That's right, get out," said Matthew.

Absalom left the office, slamming the door with such vicious force that one of the brass Cupids which decorated the panels fell off on to the carpet. He never came back. Rumour hinted that he had gone to the devil. One thing is certain, and that is, that he joined the Zenz Corporation, an American company of ill repute, addicted to such slogans as "Get the Zenz Bill Pickle Habit—It Pays!"

Nobody mentioned his name. Matthew, however, was a man of his father's kidney. He realised that the business was so firmly established that nothing on earth could shake it, and knew that nothing more needed to be done. This righteous young man, like his father, was a pillar of the Supralapsarian Church, and had engraved upon his watch the noble motto: "Everything is for the best in this best of all possible worlds." He consoled his father for Absalom's worthlessness, and when Horatio breathed his last in the treacherous autumn of 1912, he said, with his dying breath: "It is with an easy mind and a joyous heart that I leave the control of the House of Relish in the hands of my beloved son Matthew."

Absalom, meanwhile, was consorting with birds of his own feather in the Zenz Corporation.

* * * * *

Matthew was a man of strong character, unaffected by the changing of the times. He adopted as the trade mark of the Company an extraordinarily realistic picture of a gigantic pickle-jar immovably imbedded in a pedestal of solid rock, and this symbol figured prominently on the letter headings of the firm, between the picture of the factory and the intricate scroll-work which bore the name of Relish. Matthew's speech imprinted itself unforgettably on the minds of all who heard it.

"The rock is our sign; we shall not budge!" he cried; "we shall resist, with all our might, the new American influences which, like a destructive volcanic eruption, are creeping insidiously into our everyday life—we shall endeavour to nip them in the bud before they can take root and inundate us."

In an interview which he granted to a writer for *Sputters*, a popular weekly paper, Matthew uttered more immortal words:

"America attempts to conquer the world. But we shall not be conquered. The motor-car is something that must pass away: this is plain logic. Otherwise, for what purpose did the Creator devise the horse? ...

"The safety-razor twines itself about our feet like a scourge. Soon, every beardless boy will shave. It is for England to stop this ...

"Man will never fly. Does it not occur to these crazy dreamers that if we were meant to fly we would have been born with wings? ...

"The kinematograph will die out. The public must have Reality...

"Modern advertising? Stuff and nonsense! The public know that Relish's Pickles are the best. Otherwise they wouldn't buy them. And since the public continue to buy Relish's Pickles, what good can be done by advertising? We shall, therefore, spend less on advertising in the coming year..."

The firm of Suckling, however, was inspired by no such lofty ideals. They scrambled for orders. They clamoured from every hoarding. They presented a copy of *Alice in Wonderland* in exchange for twenty labels from their two-pound jars of pickles; a set of boot-brushes for fifty labels; and a silver-gilt-type combination shoe-horn and pickle-fork for a hundred and fifty labels. Other firms were not slow in following suit. Sickerbeit Marmalade offered a buttonhook for fifteen labels. Rodent Tooth Powder provided a wash-leather eyeglass-wiper for every seventy-three empty tins; Dual-Purpose Soap gave a scrubbing-brush and a tastefully embroidered floorcloth for four hundred wrappers; Bifurcal Barbed Hairpin stunned the world with a sensational offer of a jug, basin-soap-dish, and night-pot of willow-pattern crockery in exchange for two thousand empty packets. A wild philanthropy seemed to be animating the larger commercial houses, and there is no saying where it all might have ended, had it not been for the outbreak of the War to End Wars.

Matthew Relish had scorned to involve himself in the gift-schemes of his competitors. "If," said that far-seeing man, "these people have to bribe the public with gifts before they can sell their products—if they find it necessary to adopt the trickery of slogans and catchwords—it says little for the state of their business. We do not have to do such things. It is true that, as a result of Suckling's gift-books and pickle-forks, we have sold a few jars less. But the public will realise, gentlemen; the public will realise." And, as a final gesture of contempt, Matthew closed down his Advertising Department, and relegated all his publicity to the hands of a very reliable old gentleman named Arnold Sucklethumbkin-Dithers—a churchwarden of the Supralapsarian Church, distantly related to a Mrs. Drool, who had a nephew on *The Times*. Mr. Sucklethumbkin-Dithers, we feel bound to say, was a sufferer from asthma, corns, and halitosis, and his method of organising a publicity-campaign was to whistle the words: "Same as before." His secretary was a lady named Miasma, who, in spite of the fact that her gums had withered so that whenever she spoke she was compelled to hold up her front teeth with her right hand and keep down her lower teeth with her left, afforded him much assistance. "Miasma," said Dithers, "is invaluable."

Notwithstanding this, when the First World War came, the House of Relish, incredible to state, was doing relatively poor business. But Matthew was right. Relish's needed no publicity. England rose to defend the right, and hordes of sturdy Britons marched across the plains of Flanders to defeat the insatiable Hun. There, their souls yearned for the old, familiar Relish Jar. A gentleman from the War Office called on Matthew, and suggested that Relish's should supply the forces with pickles. Matthew was a patriot to the core. He readily agreed to this, and quite soon the Clodpuddle factory was packing as many pickles in one week as it had previously packed in six months. But with all this increased prosperity, Matthew did not change. When somebody said to him: "Would it not be advisable, Mr. Relish, since you are winning us the war so rapidly, to have labels printed in the German language for use in Berlin?" Matthew replied: "On no account. They must learn to speak English." He learned, with deep regret, of the English losses at Passchendaele, and was heard to say: "The flower of our manhood! Who will be left to eat my Pickles?" His prosperity still increased; his bank-balance assumed fantastic proportions, but this did not spoil the man. He still served his country. He threatened with instant and ignominious dismissal any of his male employees who did not volunteer for active service, and had erected on Clodpuddle Green a Roll of Honour in marble, upon which he engraved their names as they fell. A happy inspiration struck him, and he surmounted the memorial with a very elegant scroll, bearing the inscription: "Greater Love Hath No Man Than This." It soon became evident that Matthew Relish could not possibly receive less than a Peerage.

Nothing could stem the flow of his humanitarianism. When he heard stories of German atrocities, his soul revolted. *German Officer Eats Belgian Baby*, said the *Daily Squirt*. "Oh, barbarous, barbarous!" cried Matthew. "Had the child been baptized?" No. "Oh, disgusting, disgusting! And did the German officer eat pickles with it?" No. "Oh, unspeakable, unspeakable! We must destroy these people as the Lord destroyed Amalek." When the Armistice was declared, Matthew became pensive. "Have we punished them enough?" he said. "Ought we not to continue the war for another nine or ten years? It would teach them such a lesson..."

Nevertheless, peace came, and a grateful country endowed Matthew with the title *First Baron Clodpuddle*.

But what, in the meantime, had happened to Matthew's wicked brother, Absalom? Absalom had gone to America, to join the Zenz Corporation; a firm devoid of dignity and decency, which had assumed considerable proportions in that unpleasant continent where actors and actresses shamelessly court publicity by getting divorced before committing adultery; where one half of the population lives by giving the other half something which it calls "The woiks"; and where the attention of the consumer is attracted to goods by the most revolting physical details. Absalom was in his element. As might be expected, he went from bad to worse. He rose to eminence in the firm of Zenz by his advertising campaign—the notorious "*Owch!*" series which depicted men and women screwing up their faces, with their mouths full of half-masticated pickles, and saying: "Owch! That pickle bites! Why don't you get a *blended* pickle?" Under the pictures, huge black capitals scream:

ZENZ BLENDS NEVER BITE BACK!

He left Zenz, and went to Blitz Novelties, where he slid a little farther down towards the limbo of the Utterly Lost. He took two sticks of wood, tied them together with a bit of coloured string, and called the absurd result "Snickit". Then, through a nation-wide campaign, he so popularised "Snicket" that the entire population of the United States paid ten, fifteen, and twenty-five cents for those pieces of wood and string, and wherever one went, one could see nothing but Snicket-addicts endeavouring, with tense faces, to balance one stick on top of the other. Policemen played it in the streets; judges adjourned court to play "Snicket" with the District Attorneys; and an old lady in Kalamazoo died of excitement on seeing Trixie Pyetpaskud-niakov, Snicket Queen of Peoria, achieve the almost impossible "Snick".

Thence, Absalom, now known as "Ab. Relish", proceeded to Samovar Soap Inc., and caused the entire American population to sniff anxiously at one another by his "Smell Clean" campaign. Under pictures of men and women locked in an erotic embrace, appeared the words:

HARVEST MOON ... BLUE? ROMANTIC NIGHT ...
HEARTS THRILL AS LIP MEETS LIP IN
LINGERING ECSTASY ...

> *But are you sure that when your arms encircle her, she does not hold her breath?*
> Can you be sure you smell clean? Perspiration damps romance. Wash with Samovar, and feel sure!
> 10 *cents a tablet.*

From this, Absalom returned to the Pickle industry; for there was nothing sacred to this fellow. Not content with soiling soap with his touch, he must needs return to the trade of his fathers. Pickles ran in the veins of the Relishes; he could not keep away. The Zenz Corporation offered him a salary which was assessed at about nine times the salary of the President of the United States, and Absalom returned to take charge of their vast Publicity Department.

He began by undermining the morale of certain celebrities. Film stars, politicians, aristocrats, gangsters—any man in the public eye was demonstrated as being addicted to Zenz products. Mrs. Ten Billion was portrayed, in riding-dress, conveying a Zenz Pickle to her scornful lips on a golden fork; the glamorous Etta Gobrag was shown eating pickles out of the jar on the "set", and saying: "Leave me; I want to be alone with my Zinz Pickles"; Machine-Gun Toots Boloni was shown in gaol, devouring his favourite sandwich, which consisted of a joker and a nine of hearts and Zenz Pickles; a visiting Duke was posed with a monocle and a jar, saying: "What bally ho, dear old thing, Zenz Pickles are most frightfully nice."

A radio programme was organised, devoted to the merits of Zenz Pickles—the first of its kind in the United States.

"By the courtesy of Zenz Pickles," and "Zenz Pickles now send you ..." resounded in every home. The most popular artistes were hired at fabulous fees. But this was only the beginning. Magazines, newspapers, hoardings, all blazed with new, fantastic slogans, arresting photographs, and disturbing statements. Rugged-looking models, dressed as pioneers, engine-drivers, telegraph-wire stringers, newspaper reporters, all-in wrestlers, weight-lifters, and public speakers declared: "Yuh kin go further on Zenz Pickles." "Funny thing, I can't go half as far without Zenz Pickles." "Gee, I get breathless when I miss my Zenz Pickles." Little boys looked up at healthy American mothers, and said: "Aw gee, mom, Zenz Pickles make me strong," or tossed mighty mouthfuls of meat into their systems while their admiring parents whispered: "We don't have to coax him to eat now we have Zenz Pickles." The healthiness of Zenz Pickles was harped upon until it burned its way into the soul of the people. A boxer could almost vanquish his opponent before the fight, simply by ostentatiously eating Zenz Pickles. Anybody who ate any other brand of pickles felt hopelessly handicapped in the battle of life.

"And now again," said Ab Relish, "we got to consider the elderly element of the population. What burns up the old folks? The fact that they ain't so lively as they used to be. Lively. Get what I mean? All right. Now you get some doctors, see? And get the scientific angle on just how onions and vinegar tickle up the glands. Get me? Then we can work some sort of angle like: *Zenz Glandular Pickles*, or *Rejuvenate While you Eat*. A picture of some old fellow looking regretfully at the legs of some Follies girl: *Not so young as he used to be. Why?* Why, because his glands want stimulating. Therefore eat Zenz Pickles. And again, the same old feller with the wrinkles ironed out, making whoopee on a dance floor, with a paper hat and a blonde, or something: *Young again!* Why? You know why. Get it? Health, health, always health. Since the war, people feel they know what's good for 'em. All right. Appeal to their intelligence. Sure, I know they ain't got any intelligence, but make 'em feel scientific. You can take it from me, there's no hooey to beat scientific hooey. Pictures of nerves and guts; diagrams of glands. Get the angle? Well ..."

Zenz Pickles swept America. Meanwhile Matthew Relish, carried along on the crest of the book of the nineteen-twenties, was sweeping England. When he heard of Zenz, he laughed. And when he received news of the Coming of Zenz to England, he still laughed, with the deep, whole-hearted laughter of an impregnable man.

Large, gloomy, well-groomed New Yorkers looked over factory sites. Absalom booked a passage on the *Megalomania*. Relish was about to meet Relish. A waiting world held its breath, confronted at the end of the centuries with an impending answer to the ancient conundrum of the irresistible cannon-ball and the immovable post.

In the spring of the year 1928, Absalom Relish landed in England.

*   *   *   *   *

Shortly after he landed, Ab Relish visited his brother Matthew at Clodpuddle. It was a momentous thing, this meeting of the two strong men, who had gone down their diverging roads to their different destinies. Light came face to face with darkness; Order met Anarchy. Matthew could scarcely recognise his twin brother in the person that now confronted him. Absalom had become lean. He had none of that Relish embonpoint—that neatly rounded abdomen and that soft duplication of the chin which lends dignity to the gentleman of middle age. Feverish activity had planed Absalom down. His eyes—unlike Matthew's, which time had rendered more prominent and delicately tinged about the balls with yellow and red—were of a distinct blue. In receding modestly to display the fine shining pink of his scalp, Matthew's hair had run to a profusion of adorable little curls at the nape of the neck; Absalom's, unlike that of his biblical namesake, was cut short. A habit of non-committal lip-pursing had formed Matthew's lips into a rosebud; Absalom's mouth slammed like a closing door as he bit off flying splinters of brutally direct speech. Absalom was dressed like an ordinary man, in grey; Matthew would have felt stark naked without his cutaway coat, white slip, stiff cuffs, high collars, cravat, pearl pin, watchchain, white spats, long woollen pants to absorb the perspiration, gold studs, and pince-nez on a black ribbon.

They looked dissimilar enough; but as soon as they began to converse, you would have said to yourself: "Not only are they not brothers; they are strangers and enemies from two different worlds."

"Do you expect, like the Prodigal, to be welcomed back to the Fold?" asked Matthew.

"Listen, Matt: to hell with your fatted calf—the only fold I've come back to is the bill-fold."

"I understand that you propose to establish the firm of Zenz in this country."

"That's right."

"To poison the stream of British commerce with your American methods of publicity."

"Uh-huh."

"It is you—you, a son of the House of Relish!—of whom I have heard in connection with advertisements which the vilest coal-heaver might blush to hear mentioned."

"'Smell Clean'? Feminine hygiene, armpits, and all that stuff? Sure, that's mine."

"And you come *here?*"

"Why not?"

"Leave my office."

"Just a minute. I've got a suggestion. I'm coming back to England to sell Zenz Pickles. And I will sell 'em. I'll stuff 'em down the public throat in double handfuls. Get me? That means war. You'll go under. Now listen, Matt; you're a hundred and fifty years behind the times. Zenz is prepared to make you an offer. Sell out!"

"*What?*"

"You've got money. Sell out; retire. You're finished."

"How dare you?"

"Look at the way this business is run. Haphazard, slack. It's all very nice, playing at merchant princes; but you're living on the past. Your pickles have got a reputation. All right. I can explode it. You can't fight me. You're too much of a mug to use the right weapons to fight with. Look at your publicity! It makes me sweat blood. 'Eat and Enjoy Relish's Pickles, Warranted Absolutely Pure and Unadulterated.' Where are your eyes? How did you come to miss the Vitamin angle, for instance? 'The Five-Vitamin Pickle'—hell's bells!—Vitamins A, B, C, D, E, conclusively demonstrated by graphs! Buy a couple of Viennese doctors: —'Professor Splots, the Eminent Health Authority, says...' See? Health! 'Sunlight on the Breakfast Table'—'Restores the Tissues like a Ten-Hour sleep!'—'You May Not Be Able to Afford A Six Months' Holiday—But You Can Afford To Eat Relish's Pickles.' Vitamins, see? Or Slimming! 'Eat less Starch: Eat More Relish's'—give away a free diet-sheet: 'How to Keep That Girlish Figure.' Illustrations: 'Before': picture of somebody with a bust down to here"—Absalom placed his hands in the region of his umbilicus—"'After': picture of somebody with a similar face, with a figure like Evelyn Brent. You can get models to look alike. Hell, when I worked that slimming angle, I worked it with two pictures of a woman who had got dropsy. Smack it into 'em! You don't sell pickles by saying 'Eat and Enjoy Pickles'. That's a thing of the past. Tell 'em they can't *live* without Relish's Pickles! They can't have *babies* unless they eat Relish's Pickles! Organise baby shows, with free cabaret and tea; chorus of fat, healthy kids: 'The Relishy-Wellishies'. Sponsor boxers! 'On my Right Knockout Floorboards!'—and up jumps Knockout with RELISH'S PICKLES FOR HEALTH AND STRENGTH in letters a yard high on his dressing-gown. But don't sit there picking your nose! Why——"

"This is disgusting! Get——"

"—there's a pickle-angle in everything. Get pickle-minded! Pickles make you sleep; pickles make you wake up. Look at your pack! What the hell is it supposed to be—a model of the Leaning Tower of Pizzer, or what? Didn't you have the sense to stick the muck in a jar that could be used as a flower-vase, or a highball-glass, or a milk-jug, or something? Look at your label!

It looks like nothing on earth. And no carton. Why no carton? Why not a carton that the kids can play with? Hell, I was doing a Felix the Cat pack years ago. Why not a book of recipes? A lot of paper. What does it cost you in the long run? Damn all; but look what it gives you to talk about! Oh, hell, you've got no idea. And I tell you, once we get going, you'll stand as much chance as a bug in a gearbox——"

"Sir! Before I ring the bell and ask my secretary to show you out, let me tell you one thing: England is not America. We shall fight you, and drive you back. You shall not take the bread and butter out of our wives' bosoms. We have the market, and what we have, we hold. You think that the British public are fools——"

"Just like any other public. They're bigger mugs than they used to be, because they think they know more. Once a sucker has read a few newspaper articles about vitamins and ductless glands, he's easier to play than before—he'll take the shirt off his back to pay four and sixpence for a bottle of formaldehyde and water, or something. You got to keep on giving 'em new angles. One day it'll get down to pickles being good for dressing wounds, making mud-packs, getting grit out of the eye, and bleaching collars.—'A Jar of Pickles Accidentally fell into the Washtub.... Judge my Surprise when Archibald's diapers emerged as White as Driven Snow ...' Hell, why not? One tea-spoonful of ... No."

"Get out!"

"Okay," said Absalom. "You'll see."

"Tiddlebotham, show this person out."

"Remember—we're all smart Alecks until our time comes. All right, I'm going."

It was dog eat dog—war, war to the knife!

Absalom flung himself into the organisation of the English branch of the firm of Zenz. He worked eighteen hours a day. His office became a kind of dump, ankle-deep in a chaos of showcards, posters, displays and pickle-jars; a wild confusion, of which he alone knew the secret. A map of the British Isles covered one wall, bristling with little red flags that were to mark the spread of the Zenz anarchy. Another wall bore an immense sheet of graph-paper, which, Absalom had determined, should soon be scored diagonally by a red line running up at an angle of about forty-five degrees. Absalom sat at a large desk by the window. Papers and sheets of cardboard encroached upon him, like virgin jungle over-running a clearing. Stripped of his coat, and belching smoke as he gnawed his way savagely down cigar after cigar, he seemed never to stir from his seat. Perhaps he derived some nourishment from the tobacco-leaf that he swallowed: he seemed to take no other food, except slippery elm tablets, cedarwood (he ate two pencils a day, sucking the lead before throwing it away, with the zest of an old lady sucking a fish-bone), and warm milk. He worked in a kind of delirium, and rarely stopped talking:

"Where's your imagination, you sissies? Public interest —gimme interest—oh, for the love of God gimme something that'll hit 'em in the front teeth! Show me one more 'Eat and Enjoy' crack, and I'll stuff it down your throat . . .

"Oh, Pete? Is that Pete? Listen, Pete, I've got a honey of an idea. Curious Oaths. Yes, Oaths; you heard. O for Obsolete, A for Ass, T for Tonsils, H for Hell, and S for Stupid. Got it? Get me a list of peculiar old English oaths still in use about the country —you know, things like 'Shiver my Timbers', and 'Well I'll be Gormed', and 'Gord Stuff me Gently', do some research, and work up some sketches, and snap into it, and have half a dozen at least ready by to-morrow midday. Yes. Shut up. Good-bye . . .

"Hey, what in the hell is this? A jar? Get out of my sight. The place for a thing like that is under the bed, not in the shop window . . .

"Now listen, Professor Schweinerei-Ochsenschwanz; not a cent more than five hundred do I pay. You gimme dope about vitamins in my pickles, and sign it, and I pay you five hundred. Professor Yix would do it for three-fifty and he's a bigger celebrity than you. Only I want a long name. So don't get ideas or it's no deal . . .

"Hey, Mick! Get photos of that footballer, Hugginham, kicking a vegetable marrow over Saint Paul's Cathedral after a feed of pickles, will you? And ask the Duchess of Blick how much she wants to be photographed at her dinner-table surrounded by the Blick Plate, with a jar of Zenz Pickles on the table: she ought to take a thousand; Salsabianca is going to put the brokers in at the Castle for the hairdressing bill ... Get going! Oh, and, Mick—get me a ballet-dancer. Approach Turnova. 'Sylph-like Suppleness on Zenz Pickles.' 'If it were not for Zenz Pickles, I would never have lived to dance in Ballet ...' You know. 'Bye ...

"Whaddaya call that? A poster? Gimme colour! Gimme life! Hand me any more about little boys raiding the pantry, and I'll tell you what you can do with it ...

"Hey, Pete, here's a line: 'Our Onions Are Odourless'. Something about the strengthening quality of the onion—in South America, any peon can carry a grand piano up to the top of Mount Popocatepetl without stopping for breath, because he lives on a straight onion diet. We have a secret process of preserving the virtues of the onion and abolishing its smell. You know: 'The Onion Builds You Up Physically—Don't Let It Tear You Down Socially' ...

"Hallo, Yankelovitch's Theatrical Agency? Yankelovitch? This is Ab Relish. I want thirty-five fat little girls.... No, you mutt; for an act. What do you take me for? I'm going to call them the Zenzy-Wenzies. They better look healthy ...

"Hallo, is that Blue Peters? Listen, Blue, I want you to compose me a theme-song for the Zenzy-Wenzies. Something sprightly. Yes, I got a lyric:

"Zenzy-Wenzies bright and gay,
        Bright at work, and bright at play,
        Eat Zenz Pickles every day——
        Happy Zenzy-Wenzies!

"*You're* telling *me* it's good? Hah! All right; get on the job, Blue —some sort of hot variation on 'Pop Goes the Weasel'. And you might work out another one, more suitable for adults:

"Hold that Zenzy!—Hold that Zenzy!
        Hold that Zenzy!—Hold that Zenzy!

"You know: 'Tiger Rag'. Never mind about that, though. Gimme kids! Let me have the child until he's seven, and you can keep him for the rest of his life. I'll make them kick their mothers on the shins and scream their tonsils through the ceiling for Zenz Pickles . . .

"Great big jars! Give 'em a lot of jar!

"More Pickles for the money! . . .

"Blended Pickles! . . .

"Zenz Blends! . . .

"Zenz!"

In less time than it takes to tell, the public was stunned, bewildered, swamped, flooded, and swept off its feet in a pickly cataclysm.

The House of Relish wheeled itself into the combat with a hoarse bellow; but it was as if the Fat Girl of Peckham had gone into the ring with Jimmy Wilde. Relish's arose from their long sleep with the creaking incertitude of Rip Van Winkle. Fifty thousand pounds were placed at the disposal of a reputable advertising agency, with strict injunctions concerning the dignity of the firm. A letter was unearthed, from Lord Nelson to Lady Hamilton, which said: Most Divine Lady, my arm gives me much pain; I long to see your sweet face once more. My Lady Dumdora called on Saturday night, with a jar of most excellent pickles. Relish's, which did much to alleviate the Fever. . . . GOOD ENOUGH TO NELSON! cried Relish's; but quick as lightning came the Zenz riposte:

EVERY GREAT MAN SINCE CÆSAR KNEW THE ZENZ BLEND

Such a claim might have seemed fantastic; but Absalom, with minute historical data, indicated that the Zenz recipe had been in existence for fifty-eight generations. Now in fifty-eight generations, one has had the astronomical number of 288,230,376,152,121,344 ancestors—actual fact, disgusting to consider—so that it may not unreasonably be assumed . . .

ZENZ ADDED FIRE TO CLEOPATRA'S KISSES!
WILL ADD FIRE TO YOURS!
288,230,376,152,121,344 ANCESTORS CAN'T BE WRONG
THEY MADE YOU WHAT YOU ARE TO-DAY!

At this, Zenz sales soared until the graph looked like the red trail of a skyrocket, while the Relish graph descended in sickening jerks, like steps leading down to the river.

Matthew became green and white in the face. By 1932, he had wasted away until he weighed scarcely more than fourteen stone. His eye had lost its calm; his hand shook so that his port tossed like an angry sea; his appetite, also, had so woefully declined that it was with difficulty that he managed to eat his four square meals a day, and it was observed with profound regret that he who once had wielded a trenchant knife and fork now turned with distaste from the eleventh course at dinner, after he had eaten scarcely more than a couple of soles and a roast chicken at luncheon. It was obvious to all the world that his heart was breaking. Suppressed grief was causing his neck to swell; unshed tears were causing his blood-pressure to rise. It came to be whispered: "Poor Matthew has met his master; it is breaking him up.... Yet what a great business man he used to be, before his brother came back! How gentlemanly was his deportment! With what dignity could he cough!" He was already spoken of as a figure pertaining to a glorious but obsolescent past....

Meanwhile, Matthew's son, Horace, flying from the screaming Sabbatical sopranos and Sunday morning ballad-singers of London Regional, could not turn the dial of his radio without being knifed in the ear-drums by the penetrating voices of the Zenzy-Wenzies, boosting Zenz pickles over the air from Radio San Marino. Zenz propaganda masked by hot jazz, low comedy, and juvenilia, burned itself into his brain until he succumbed to it. Horace was a true son of his father, and could wear a black coat with the best; yet he was young, and therefore impressionable. He finally found courage to speak to his father about the matter:

"Father, don't be offended, but I've been thinking——"
"You been what?"

"It seems to me that since Zenz is cutting our throats, and nothing that we can do can touch Uncle Absalom . . ."

"Well?"

"Don't you think you might make friends with him again?"

"Never. Don't suggest such a thing again."

"But, Father . . ."

"Not another word!

"Silence!" roared Matthew at the top of his voice, "your uncle is my enemy!"

"But all the same, it seems ridiculous to be enemies when you might be so much better off by being his friend. And after all, he is your brother."

"I would starve rather than be friends with that man. He comes here and steals our market, takes the bread out of our mouths, and you—you—you——"

"Father, don't excite yourself!"

"You suggest—you *dare* to suggest that we, *we*, should—gggh . . . gggh . . ." Matthew inserted a finger under his collar, became black in the face, spun round like a top, and fell down dead.

He was buried in the Relish vault: the last of the old order.

Absalom looked gloomily at his nephew.

"What did you say your name was?"

"Horace."

"Pah. What are you going to do about the business?"

"Continue with it. Perhaps, Uncle, we might be friends?"

"Yes, I suppose so. Bah! You better combine with us. It's a pity, but there it is. . . . Ah!" Ab Relish sighed very deeply.

"What is a pity?" asked Horace.

"This is—all this combining. Hell, if I had been you, I would have spat in my eye: I would have said: 'Uncle Absalom, you are the son of a bitch, and I'll fight you tooth and nail, biting, gouging, and concealed weapons not barred! Friends! Bah! Friendship! Combine? What does that mean? It means to say there's nobody left to fight. It simply means to say we sit down on our fannies and grow fat bellies. What's the good of that? And you say 'Combine'. I'm ashamed of you. To-morrow morning, you take off that black coat, and get the village blacksmith to unrivet that collar, and you start in the cleaning rooms. Any arguments? Hey?"

"No, Uncle."

"No, Uncle. Of course not, you sissy, you! Why not? Why didn't you smack me in the mouth and say: 'Who in the hell do you think you're ordering around?' Mouse! Pah! *I* got to combine with *you*. You ain't big enough to fight. Oh hell, hell, hell, I'm fed up. Friends! Friends! Gimme enemies! Gimme enemies: then I can enjoy life."

"Pickles ..."

"Pickles ... I'm fed up with pickles. There ain't a soul left to stand up to me. It's time I quit."

"Retired, Uncle?" asked Horace.

"Retired, Uncle! I mean, quit pickles and start a fresh line; something really competitive; something with a little excitement ..."

Dustin—the Broken Man

They brought Dustin back after forty days and forty nights. He had an air of awful dejection, of emptiness and utter weariness.

All deserters have that look when they are caught, or when misery or conscience makes them give themselves up.

Dustin looked sick as he stood in the grim, dim light of the guardroom. The police-sergeant, with a glare in his eyes like candlelight on ice and a rat-trap snapping of his wiry, breakback jaws, said:

"A deserter, a gutless yellow deserter; and a fool to think you could get away with it. Shove him inside!" And his mouth clicked shut; and the cell door clicked shut, and darkness and silence swallowed Dustin until the next day when I saw him scrubbing the guardroom floor.

I do not like deserters, and cannot pity them. But the unmistakable haggard drag of heartache in Dustin's face moved me to say:

"You poor mug. What made you do it?"

"Fell for a girl," said Dustin, and laughed again. "Me. Just fancy that."

"Why not you? It happens to everybody some time or other."

"Me!" Dustin fished a dirty floorcloth out of the pail and wrung it out.

"Me! I was married once. I had seven years of it. I had all the misery in the world with that woman.

"She ran about with other fellows. She stole everything she could lay her hands on, ran me into debt. I was fond of her. She played me up, led me a dance, and then left me for somebody else. I was a fool.

"She died just before the war, I heard. I don't know how: I didn't care any more.

"Last leave, I went to see a man I used to know up North. He had a sister. The sister had a lady-friend that she introduced me to.

"Her name was Dora. She was about twenty-eight. Her picture is among my papers. She's the prettiest woman I ever saw in my life. I fell for her. I fell bad, hard, terrible hard. She's dark. You ought to see her eyes. If there was such a thing as black stars . . ."

He scrubbed at a grease-spot.

"The craziest thing is that she fell for me, too," said Dustin. "She's a widow, with a bit of money of her own, just enough to live on. That had nothing to do with it. We used to go for walks together.

"She showed me her house over by the edge of the town; a pretty house right in the middle of a sort of park. We got engaged. I gave her a gold ring my father gave me.

"We couldn't bear to be away from each other ... that's the funny part of it; she couldn't bear to be away from me. She told me so a thousand times.

"Afterwards, she wrote to me about it ... couldn't eat, couldn't sleep for thinking about me. Was eating herself up, crying her heart out, *had* to see me, had *got* to see me.... But that was a wonderful week. It was!

"We just walked and talked and stayed together, and we couldn't bear to say good night, but stood and talked and talked, even in the rain.

"We arranged to get married as soon as I could get leave.

"But when I got back to camp, good Lord in heaven, how rotten and empty everything was.

"I couldn't sleep or eat or find any interest in life, couldn't do anything but think about her.

"But I stuck it out as long as I could, and sweated on my next leave. And my leave was just about due, when I got into trouble. It was through thinking about her, looking forward to seeing her again. Madness. But there it is.

"I was out on field training. I was dozy and dreamy. I lost a pick and a spade; just left them somewhere—— I forgot where, forgot all about them.

"I got called in on orders, forgot myself, was off-hand in answering, made a rotten bad impression, got fourteen days' C. B.

"Well, fourteen days is a terrible time to wait. That meant twenty-eight days' loss of privileges on top of the fourteen and then my leave put back fourteen more.

"I went crazy. The first *Defaulters* on the revally of the day after, I just went sullen; didn't show up; got put in the report. The company officer was all right. He could smell something wrong. He talked to me like a gentleman.

"If he hadn't done so, I was in the mood to answer back. I didn't care. I didn't care if I died. The first three days crawled. They crawled so that they drove me mad. It's like waiting to get somewhere in a hurry on a matter of life or death.... And you get in a dead-slow train that stops every station for—it seems a year....

"So one day I was coming off a Defaulters' drill in the afternoon, dressed up in my best to get by the inspection dressed as it might be for leave.

"Buses come through the camp. All of a sudden I jumped on one, got to the station, got to London and then found that I didn't have more than a pound in my pocket. I had to get right up far North.

"I got a train as far as Rugby, and started to footslog it from there. I walked like on a forced march. I must have been mad, I dare say.

"I slogged up those roads, and couldn't think of anything but her, and couldn't find patience to stop and eat and couldn't do anything but slog on though I was dead on my feet."

Dustin wiped sweat from his forehead with a lean forearm, and as he looked up at me he seemed to have aged ten years.

"In the end I got there. Nobody stopped me. It was sheer luck.

"I got to this little town. It was night. I went straight to her place up there by the park. She was still up. I knocked. She opened the door, and nearly fainted for joy when she saw me.

"Then she took me in and showed me why she'd been staying up. She'd been writing me a letter saying that if I didn't come soon she'd die.

"And after a bit I said: 'Dora, don't let on I'm here.'

"She asked me what I meant. I remember she was looking at me. I told her what I'd done.

"And then all of a sudden her whole face got different. It kind of iced up, skinned over with ice like a pond overnight in a frost.

"I said: 'Dora, what is it?' And she said: 'So, just because you couldn't have patience for a little, just because of that, you go and throw everything down the drain. What kind of man are you?'

"She said: 'Did I go running away to you? But I'm fond of you the same as you are of me. What kind of a man *are* you to drag everything back because of me, because of not waiting for a few days? What sort of a mind have you got, that you want to load us up with a rotten name for the sake of a few days?'

"And she called me Marrdie—spoiled baby kind of thing—and said: 'I don't like you. You're marr'd and soft: go away from me.'

"So I went away. And I hung about, sort of dead, but alive. And in the end I gave myself up at Bedford."

A Corporal of Military Police appeared, and said: "Shullup, Dustin, and get on with that swabbing job." To me he said: "Let him get on with it."

I went. I caught a last glimpse of Dustin. He was scrubbing the floor, on his knees, crouching.

It occurred to me that his fate had beaten him down into that position, and there he would remain—unhappy man!—until death lifted him up and away.

Let Lying Dogs Sleep

Things were grim enough that night without murder.

Groombridge Junction sprawled, soaking, under a steady,

heavy rain; stone-blind with an ebony black-out. Miserable queues of water-logged people fought like cats and dogs for seats in the trams which clanked up and down the High road.

They just wanted to get away from things and sleep. There was nothing we could do. Wild horses could not have dragged one laugh out of the population of a suburb sodden with rain and wretchedness.

I was watching the audience as I laboured with my jokes.

A couple of pounds' worth of riff-raff gloomily crunched monkey-nuts in the gallery. A disgruntled handful of the local aristocracy hung on to their gas-masks in the best (two-shilling) seats and snarled at all the funny bits. There were naked wildernesses of greasy green plush. Nothing could save us from a dead loss in Groombridge Junction that week.

I was exchanging patter with Charlie Wood, the comedian, but nobody even smiled. Then I caught a despairing sidelong glance from Charlie, and saw Ruby Tinto gathering herself for her spectacular entrance in the wings behind him.

Even in that moment I was struck by the extraordinary hardness of that woman. She was still beautiful. (But why do I say "still"? She was only twenty-six.) But cold, hard—Arctic ice.

Her eyes were blue and clear, but passionless, like as the glass marbles they used to use as stoppers for soda-water bottles. And her face was inhuman—bitter, sneering, lifeless. She reminded me of Ruth Schneider, the Icicle Blonde.

And then I withdrew with a sigh of relief, and Ruby Tinto danced on. She drew a crackle of applause even from the scattered citizens in the auditorium. There was sex-appeal in every line of her, and from that distance her face was radiant, her hair was a Niagara of live gold.

"That Ruby," said Charlie Wood, as soon as we were within talking distance.

As Johnnie Jackson, proprietor as well as compère of Johnnie Jackson's Follies, it was my duty to maintain a diplomatic balance. I said: "What about her?"

"She's making trouble again," said Charlie Wood. "Between me and Helena. One of these days she's going to get what's coming to her."

I said: "If you'd stop behaving like an overgrown school-boy . . ." and left him standing. I walked away with dignity.

Big Marco was standing in the shadows. As I passed him I heard a burst of clapping. "Ruby's done it again," I said.

"Ruby!" said Big Marco.

He is a Swede—or perhaps a Norwegian; a Scandinavian, anyway—of unbelievable strength. He has, also, the stupidity that often goes with such strength.

But while most silly giants are easy-going, Marco broods. He sulks, lashes himself to acts of violence, and then breaks things. A fool and a bully, with the thews of Hercules and the conceit of Narcissus; such is Big Marco, a dangerous man to fool with, quite unlike his brother, Little Marco, who is as decent a fellow as breathes.

I said: "And now, what have *you* got against Ruby?"

"One dese days maybe somebody cut her troat," said Marco. "She make me for a fool."

"She's too late," I said. "You were born one of those thirty years ago."

"One dese days maybe somebody break her neck," said Marco.

"Gah," I replied, and walked on.

Bitter draughts swept the leprous, whitewashed passage. A patter of worn-out feet announced Johnnie Jackson's Glamour Girls. They trotted downstairs, a strangely assorted collection of misguided women.

Helena Fay was the last. She paused for a moment to say: "Hey, Johnnie, for goodness' sake speak to Ruby."

"What now?"

"Making trouble," she said, and darted away with the other girls.

I sighed. The blistered bar-hatch flew up, and the aged bar-maid poked out her battered head. "Mr. Jackson," she said, "I'm not here to be insulted, and I won't have it."

"What have they been doing to you?" I asked.

"It's that Miss Tinto."

"Oh, and what have *you* got against Miss Tinto?"

"She called me an old hag," said the barmaid.

"I'll speak to her about it," I said; and the hatch slammed down like a guillotine.

Just then Joy seized me by the lapels. "Johnnie," she said, "you've got to do something."

"Mind my carnation," I said. "Do what?"

"That Ruby."

"Ruby, Ruby, Ruby," I cried. "All I hear from morning to night is Ruby. What——"

"Well," said Joy, who is a good singer and a handsome woman of excellent heart, "you know that photo of King Francis-Joseph that poor old violinist Wladimir loves so much?"

"Emperor Francis-Joseph?"

"I said Emperor. Well, somebody smeared it with lipstick. Deliberately scribbled all over it with a lipstick."

"And how d'you know it was Ruby?"

"Only Ruby uses cyclamen-coloured lipstick."

Wladimir came running down. He calls himself the Great Wladimir, and is a violinist. His name is not Wladimir; nor is he great. Yet he looks great, and is very amiable. He was weeping.

"Mit his own hands ze Kaiser Franz-Josef gif me dis picture!" he said. "Ant now somebody paint him mit lip-paint! If I know who it is that does zis, bei Gott, I kill. You hear me? I say I kill!"

"After this," I said, "Ruby leaves my show."

She passed at this point, and told me to go and take a running jump at myself, sneered abominably and ran upstairs.

The night grew thicker. The black-out grew blacker. The rain fell more heavily. I was never more glad in my life than I was when that evening came to an end.

As I was putting my overcoat on, Angelico, the saxophone-player, said to me: "I don't know if you've heard, but Ruby Tinto is making herself very unpopular round here."

"Go to the devil and take Ruby with you," I said.

I was the last to leave the theatre. The last tram was full. I had to stumble three blind miles to the nearest bus stop. It was very late before I got home.

It was ten in the morning when I awoke. The telephone was ringing.

"What now?" I muttered, yawning.

It was Angelico's voice. "What now?" he said. "What now? You'd better come quick. Ruby Tinto's dead. She's been killed. Somebody's stuck a knife in her. It's murder."

"Trouble, trouble, trouble," I said. "All I get is trouble."

I dressed and hurried to the theatre. It had been a perfect night for a murder, anyway. And now it was an ideal day for hanging. Groombridge Junction still wallowed in mire and rain. The death of Ruby Tinto had attracted far more people to the theatre than my show had ever drawn. A large, satisfied crowd nuzzled the steps and hung about the stage door. They felt a personal interest in the matter. It was *their* murder. Mothers reprimanded stage-struck girls: this was what came of being a singer. Cadgers mulcted strangers in free drinks because they had seen her from the gallery. . . .

The detective-inspector was inside. All of my people were lined up. Poor Ruby, she had built up a dreadful atmosphere of hate. They were slightly shocked, but could not conceal the fact that they weren't particularly sorry.

Big Marco was actually grinning; it took a murder to make that ape smile. Wladimir, with black circles under his eyes, was protesting to Charlie Wood: "I did not do it. She put lip-paint on my Emperor, but still . . ."

Everybody said: "Here he is." The detective-inspector addressed me with easy courtesy:

"Ah! Mr. Jackson?" (It is amazing what Philo Vance has done for criminal investigation.) "No doubt you've heard . . . ?"

"Why, otherwise, should I be in this stinking hole at this ungodly hour of the morning?" I replied. "Who did it?"

"That's what I'm here to find out. Do you know this weapon?" He held out a long hunting-knife.

"Why, yes," I said. "That's a prop. We use it in a burlesque. I had to chase Charlie Wood round the stage with it last night. I bought it in the Caledonian Market. . . . I forget when."

"And who has charge of it?"

"Well, it's usually knocking around on my dressing-table."

"In your dressing-room, Mr. Jackson?"

"That's where dressing-tables most usually are."

He frowned and said: "Please remember that this is a

very serious matter. Who would be likely to have seen it there?"

"Almost anybody. This is a devil of a show. Everybody is in and out of my room. I never was a disciplinarian. Everybody except women, I mean. I don't allow the girls to go in men's dressing-rooms. And vice versa."

"Does anybody share your room?"

"Charlie Wood."

Charlie Wood came forward. By daylight that funny man does not look in the least funny. He has a pallid, heavy face, a troubled look, and a habit of clutching himself by the lapels as he talks, in the manner of a politician.

"I lent the knife to Joe Angelico at about eight o'clock last night," he said.

Angelico is a peculiar, lachrymose saxophonist who deserves something better than his position of leader of my five hot musicians. His face alone is worth money. It is profoundly gloomy, but otherwise expressionless. When he plays his cheeks fall in and his eyes close.

"I wanted the knife to cut up some newspaper with," he said. "Sometimes just for a gag, I pull a sheet of paper out of my pocket and tear it up."

"And did you bring it back?"

"Now that I come to think of it," said Angelico, "I left it lying on my trunk."

"That's right, Johnnie," said the trumpeter, "I saw it there."

"When?" asked the detective-inspector.

"Oh, round about eight-thirty."

I questioned the others. . . .

"Me, I didn't notice," said the drummer, a tiny man with ferocious eyebrows, who is known as Rabbits.

The other musicians shook their heads. They hadn't seen the knife either.

Wladimir shook his head too. He had taken out his fiddle, a handsome old instrument of the colour of a well-smoked kipper, and was gently stroking it. I noticed, then, that he was staring at Helena Fay, one of the chorus-girls.

There was silence for a moment. Then Helena Fay spoke. She

said: "I borrowed it. I saw the knife on the trunk, and I borrowed it."

"What for?" asked the detective-inspector.

"I . . . there was a bit of loose leather on one of my shoes, and I wanted to cut it off."

"And what did you do with the knife then?"

"I forget. I put it down. I don't remember."

"Helena!" cried Charlie Wood, grasping her by the hand. "What are you talking about? You didn't borrow that knife. I cut that bit of leather off for you with scissors earlier on in the afternoon. Don't take any notice of her, inspector. I had that knife. I went into the musicians' room and took that knife back off Joe Angelico's trunk. Don't listen to her, inspector. She's trying to shield me. I did it. I killed Ruby. She'd been making my life a misery. I'm in love with Helena. Ruby was trying to ruin everything. I'd often wanted to kill her. She'd been making mischief. I said so to Johnnie Jackson last night, didn't I, Johnnie?"

"Well, yes, you did," I said; and my heart bled for that lovesick funny man. . . .

There was silence after Charlie Wood's confession to the killing. A silence that left us all a little embarrassed. The girls got ready for the weeping act they'd seen on the films. I cursed, inaudibly but with bitterness.

Playing a theatre in a one-eyed wilderness like Groombridge Junction with a seventh-rate concert party was bad enough: to be dragged to the theatre on an empty stomach to attend an inquiry into the murder of one's leading lady was plumbing the depths.

There is a limit to everything.

One of us was guilty.

Charlie wanted the honours.

We all goggled a bit as we waited for him to justify his outburst.

He did it well . . . emotion flooded out like Groombridge rain.

The women didn't know whether to weep or faint—I pictured the whole scene re-enacted at the Old Bailey.

"Go on, Charlie," I said. "Go on, Charlie . . ."

"So," said Charlie Wood, "I was passing the boys' room, and

the door was open, so I looked in. I saw the knife on Joe's trunk and put it in my pocket. I left among the first last night, and waited for Ruby to come out."

"And then?" said the detective-inspector. "You simply stabbed her in the back?"

"Yes."

Everybody gasped. I remember saying: "What a mug you turned out to be!" Then the detective-inspector took a pencil out of his pocket. I thought he was going to take notes. Instead, he handed the pencil to Charlie Wood.

"Show me how you did it."

Wood seized the pencil in his red right fist, and inflicted a terrible backhanded stab on the empty air. Two or three people standing near him leapt out of the way.

At this point, Vernon, the man who guards the stage door, raised a piping voice.

"Yer couldn't of taken that knife orf that trunk. I took it orf the trunk and put it on the table. I went up to the musicians' dressing-room, because I 'ad to take Mister Wollymire's——"

"Wladimir!" snapped the old violinist.

"—I 'ad to take '*im* up a pot o' tea for one. I put the tray on the trunk, an' I took the knife off the trunk, see? I put that knife on the table."

"Anyway, I picked it up," said Charlie Wood.

"Why didn't you mention that before?" asked the detective-inspector, turning to Vernon.

Vernon looked sullen; like so many people vaguely connected with the theatrical business, he is a bit mad. He was a juggler until he took to drink; then he missed things, scattered glass balls in the auditorium, and so went to the dogs. He never could have been any good, anyway. He is an absolute fool.

"I forgot," he said.

I told him that he was an imbecile. Vernon shrugged. The detective-inspector spoke to Charlie Wood again: "And then you walked up behind the lady and stabbed her in the back?"

"Yes." Charlie Wood lit a cigarette.

"All right," said the detective-inspector. "But she wasn't stabbed in the manner you demonstrated."

"Oh, hell!" said Wood. "How should I remember just how I held the knife? I stabbed Ruby Tinto in the back, and leave it at that."

"Right," said the detective-inspector, and beckoned to a man with heavy shoes.

Helena Fay screamed. "Wait! Don't! He's only saying that to shield me. Can't you see that? It was me. I killed her. I was jealous. I thought she was trying to take Charlie away from me. I saw the knife on Joe's table and put it in my bag——"

"For God's sake take me away," said Charlie Wood. "Isn't it obvious she's lying to cover me up?"

"I'm not!"

"If you two are so much in love with each other," said the detective-inspector, "does either of you see the other home?" He tapped Vernon on the arm. "Did these two go out together?"

"No," said Vernon, "'e went last. She went first. I stayed be'ind for a bit."

"I said I had to have a drink with a fellow," said Wood. "I finished Ruby first. Then nipped along to the 'Red Lion' just before closing time."

"I waited on the corner of the theatre until Ruby came out," said Helena. "Then I came up behind her and stabbed her. And I'd do it again! I'd do it again!"

The detective-inspector sighed. "Neither of you know where you found the knife. Neither of you know how you held the knife. And you both stabbed Ruby Tinto in the back, from behind. Well, as a matter of fact, she *wasn't stabbed from behind*. Nor was she stabbed in the back."

And then something incredible happened.

Big Marco stepped forward holding out his hands. I shall never forget the amazement with which I looked at those mighty, hairy fists, held close together. "Take me," he said. "It was me who done dis. I tell Yonnie Yerkson last night I am goink to cut her troat ..." He swore a tremendous Scandinavian oath which sounds like thunder but, I think, merely means: *By the big Japanese trumpeter who blows ballads.* "An' I kill her. I was yoost a little mad. She make me for a fool. She lead me up dem garden.

Dan she laugh. She make me fall in lof vit her. Dan she tell me
she lof my brodda."

Little Marco's face was wet with tears. He threw an arm about
his brother's ox-like back and said: "No, Ib! Ib, you fool! Hey,
you! You copper! Look!" He thrust a hand under his coat. Big
Marco wheeled, throwing out a fist like a bung-starter. It would
have knocked a buffalo off its feet. Little Marco went down with
a crash, in a cloud of dust.

"I am sorry, Olaf," said Big Marco. But the little one was
already rising from the floor. His hand came out from under his
waistcoat, with a bundle of cards and papers. "Look," he said,
and threw the bundle to the detective-inspector.

I looked over his shoulder as he tore away the elastic band.
The bundle consisted of Press cuttings and photographs.
"Gaucho, the Hatchet King," said the caption, and above it
stood Little Marco, in South American costume, with a shining
chopper poised in each hand. Beyond him, strapped to a board,
leaned a handsome blonde, outlined in a murderous-looking
bristle of axes, knives, and swords.

"That is me," said Little Marco. "I used to be a knife-thrower.
I am still good. But once there was a scandal; in Australia. I
nearly killed a partner. So I joined Ib in his act. I quarrelled with
Ruby. She should have been my girl. But she loved Ib better. I
am only a little runt. I said to her: 'If I don't have you, nobody
will.' She drove me mad. I picked up Johnnie's knife, the prop
knife. I can throw anything with a point on it. I am still good. I
went out and waited, just a few seconds, because I knew she was
coming. There was nobody else in the street just then. I could
just see her in the dark; she carried a little torch. I threw the knife
and saw her fall. Then I walked on and caught up with Ib. And
then he says he did it—to save me!"

"Idiot!" said Big Marco. "I wish I smack you stone blasted
cold before you say dat, little fool!"

"My God," I said. "I'm sorry about this. Little Marco, you
stupid——"

"You dunt call him no names," said Big Marco, "dat little
lousy mug."

"Let's go," said Little Marco.

"Then," said the detective-inspector, "I suppose your real name is Hugo Brenner?"

"My real name is Olaf Ibsen," said Little Marco.

"Yet you were Ruby's boy-friend?"

"She made me think so."

"Hm," said the detective-inspector. "Well, I suppose we'd better take you along, Mr. Ibsen."

We all followed them. In the passage the detective-inspector paused to glance at the notice-board. "Hard luck on these people," he said, pointing to a quarto sheet. It said: ... I forget the exact words: it said that all the boys and girls in Johnnie Jackson's Follies would have to consider themselves sacked as from such-and-such a date.

"Yes, tough," I replied.

The detective-inspector took out a wallet, and produced a sheet of blue paper. He looked at it, and then at me.

"You are Hugo Brenner," he said.

"I am Johnnie Jackson," I replied.

"That makes no difference," he said. "There's just one or two points ..." He spoke, as it were, to himself: in a half-audible monotone.

"Now that I come to think of it, the girl couldn't have been killed by a knife thrown as this fellow describes. The stab was almost vertical. It went into the neck where it joins the shoulder, and right down into the lungs. It cut the big artery. It went in up to the hilt. You'd have to throw a knife almost straight up into the air for it to land like that, and then it would be impossible to hit a moving target in a black-out, even if it was carrying a torch. That was an overhand stab, by somebody standing directly facing her. And again, she was found in a shop front. Whoever killed her went over her bag. Not for money, because her purse was untouched."

"The poor girl only made a fiver a week," I said.

"Yes. There you are. Yet somebody wanted something in her bag. What? Papers, letters? Now in her bag there was a kind of extra pocket in the lining, with a packet of letters, all signed 'Hugo Brenner', or 'Hugo', and quite obviously written by her husband."

"What!"

"Her husband. She appears to have married Hugo Brenner. Now, Mr. Jackson, I happened to see that notice there, and I recognised the writing." He stood in front of me, blocking the passage. "You are Hugo Brenner."

"I am John Jackson," I said, "and you are haywire. Let me see that letter."

He held it before my eyes. "What, me write like that?" I said: "I am no illiterate, my friend, even though I may run a small-time pierrot show. I . . ."

I read the letter. Something inside me turned over. I felt—how shall I put it?—as water must feel when it is congealing into ice. Something behind my eyes seemed to swell and strain to bursting point. I felt that I had suddenly dropped a mile in empty space, leaving my heart and stomach above me.

I shrieked: "These letters are dated 1933!"

"Yes."

The thing behind my eyes burst. I was suddenly drenched in perspiration. I heard Helena say: "He's laughing," and so I was.

"Then she was a bigamist," I said. "I didn't marry her until 1935. I needn't have paid her money all these years. I could have married Joy. I needn't have killed her at all." I roared with laughter. "I could even have blackmailed *her*."

If I could have bitten my tongue out before I said all that, I should be in my own comfortable bed by this time, looking forward to another dawn.

But it will all be the same a hundred years hence.

Did I say years? Days. Did I say a hundred? One. I hang to-morrow.

Red Gentleman of Staffordshire

I saw Gavin Eld twelve weeks after he got back. He used to have the kind of head a five-year-old child could portray in ten seconds—a jug-handled lop-sided oval enclosing a couple of arches over a pair of dots, representing eyes and brows; an *O* for a nose and an almost straight line intended to be a mouth. But in the eleven months of his absence something had been at work on his chalky sketch of a face: in one or two great strokes it had been marked with a power, a calm, and a certain dignity. It takes anguish to do that. Pain strengthens the face as weightlifting strengthens the body . . . provided you do not compel yourself to carry more than you were made to bear. Yes, some master hand had shaded him, giving him weight and depth. And something else had tried to deface him. His forehead and left cheek were scribbled over with scars. Eld still grinned his rabbit-tooth grin, but in a lop-sided way, and behind his eyes, which had been expressionless as the grey glass marbles that used to cork lemonade bottles when the world was young, there was a strange shadow. Suffering had thinned him. His skin looked burnt, and hung loose: he walked with a sort of wolfish lope.

Mine was the only face he knew when he came into camp. He had little enough to say . . . that he had been captured at Louvain but got away. For forty weeks Gavin Eld had been on the run in dangerous territory, eating and sleeping like a hunted beast in gulps and snatches under hedges and in shadowy doorways. About Eld's headlong assault against a thousand miles of fantastic distance, there was something crazy and wonderful: It had the madness and the grandeur of the charge of Bohemund's God-intoxicated men at Antioch. Hopelessly lost, quite alone on the gloomy plains of France, he had walked home. He was convinced that the war was lost. He wanted to get back to die. France and Belgium had slid into the depths like shale off a cliff. Eld found himself stumbling in the débris of a great grey ruin. He knew that he had travelled eastwards, so he walked westwards.

I asked him: "What did you eat?"

He said: "What I could get."

"Where did you sleep?"

"Where I lay down."

They gave him a Military Medal. He drew twenty-five pounds of back pay. One week, or fifteen pounds later, I saw him in a cocktail-bar in Woking. He was sitting on a red leather stool sipping mild ale. Next to him sat a sulphur-headed woman in slacks holding a lead attached to a bull-terrier. Eld was staring at this dog with gloomy eyes. When he saw me he said, in an audible whisper, jerking a careless thumb: "Great fat cowardly bitch."

The woman said: "I *beg* your pardon?"

Eld said: "I mean yon dog, lady, not thee. She'll weigh forty-eight pounds, give or take a pound?"

"I don't know, I'm sure."

Eld said: "I lay five pounds she's fast."

"Fast?"

"Ay … fast to come, fast to go. If she was mine I'd put her in sack wi' a stone, and chuck her in t' Cut."

"Oh you would, would you?"

"Lady," said Eld, "I know dogs. It was me as owned Skylarks. That's foreign for Tearer."

"*Scylax*," I said.

"Ay, Tearer by name, tearer by nature. Bitches' choice, and the greatest dog ever pupped."

"Greyhound?" asked the sulphur-headed blonde.

"No, lady, a pit-dog."

"A pit-dog? I've heard of pit-ponies——"

"Lady," said Gavin Eld, "a Staffordshire bull-terrier, lady, a fighting dog, lady, a killer. The greatest battler that ever breathed, a red dog, a real Staffordshire bull, a pit-dog, a proper gentleman of Staffordshire."

"I'm afraid I don't quite understand."

"A fighting dog, lady, a thirty-pound fighter. He could kill anything God stood on four legs, or know the reason why. He saved me twice."

I believe that Gavin Eld must have drunk a lot of mild ale. He was never a talker. But he talked now. We edged away from the bar and sat at a table. I remember that the woman in slacks came with us, followed by her great square-chested bull-terrier. Eld felt its neck and sneered. "Skylarks would have taken her guts out in seven minutes," he said. "That was a dog. That was a dog of the old fighting breed. You or I, Gerald, couldn't wish to have a better father and mother. And he saved me twice."

Then he told us. I shall not try to reproduce his strange, ugly nasal-throaty accent. Once in a while he dropped into slang.

The blonde stared at him, fascinated. I did too. He began to talk about fighting dogs; and as he talked I swear to you that there crept into my nostrils a strange, acrid smell of dogs and beer and tobacco-smoke and the small hours ... I seemed to see a public-house parlour in the Midlands.... Men were waiting: leather-faced men with clamped mouths, eleven or twelve of them; and about six dogs ... little dogs, with a certain viperish triangularity of head, a doggedness of jaw, a peculiar width between the eyes. I tell you that I saw it and I smelt it. Perhaps you associate the dog-fight with ancient history. But dogs still fight: the ancient breed of the fighting dog is still maintained; the descendants of the crop-eared bear-baiters are still bred—terrible dogs, good for nothing but mortal combat, but shockingly good for that. They mate them, still, in the north of England and the Midlands: Staffordshire terriers that would rather fight than eat. I had often wondered what Gavin Eld had done for his living. In that absurd cocktail-bar as he sat with the sulphur-blonde on his left hand and me on his right, he seemed to peel himself off. He stripped off his present life like a plaster.

He talked:

*   *   *   *   *   *

Skylarks was a great dog. His father was great, and his mother was a great bitch. You don't know the Staffordshire bull. He is a wonderful dog. It's an instinct of women, and other she-animals, to protect the weakest of a litter. (Haven't you seen how a woman will stand by a humpy-backed child?) But a Staffordshire bitch will choose, always, the finest fighting dog of the litter. You called him *Scylax*. I meant to call him that, but I never had your education. I called him Skylarks. He was a great dog—ginger as a chorus-girl, cobby, balanced like scales and—so to speak— almost hanging in mid-air. He was a great fighter, and he saved me twice.

I dare say you know that I get my living, when I get my living, out of dogs. I keep 'em and I breed 'em. I breed only fighters and killers. I have had one dog that got me £350 a year for two years. He was killed. He was a Staffordshire bull and it was a Staffordshire bull that killed him: his throat was torn out after a fight that lasted one hour and forty-eight minutes. I had Skylarks' mother for a long time. Skylarks was out of her by Ripper. They were red and he was red—a very red dog indeed, ginger as they come. You know, I dare say, how you train one of them bulls ... you wear heavy boots and kick them, toe up. No need to go into details. I will tell you all you want to know: only two things are needed to train a Staffordshire bull—heavy nailed boots and a steel bar. They don't feel nothing else.

I trained Skylarks for fighting. When he was a mere puppy I chucked him in a fighting mongrel, and watched Skylarks kill him and take out his liver and eat it. Soon, I lived on that dog. I can't tell you what he looked like: I can only tell you some points. Give or take a pound, he weighed thirty pounds and was red. He had a head like a coal-scuttle, a little tiny tail and a stocky body. As it so happened, he was born with cropped ears. I have not known this to happen before. His ears needed no crop. Everything that you can imagine in the way of fight, all that you ever thought of in the way of guts and courage was in that dog. At three months he would have fought a lion. I trained him, I trained him as I never trained a dog in my life before or since. Ah! Nothing in the world, lady, nothing in the world, Gerald, can come up to a good Staffordshire bull—a good pit-dog of breed. There's blood there! Give me blood! Against all the world, give me breed and blood; because if you produce a little naked rat that's got blood and breed, he'll fight, although his soul is bigger than his body.

But Skylarks. This was a dog. For over a year and a half I lived on him, and I'll swear to you by the soul of my father and my mother that I loved him like a brother. You may not believe it, but in those eighteen months he won thirty fights. Not a dog that stood against him lived to brag about it, except one—a lemon-coloured dog—whose master threw in the towel. Tearer by name, tearer by nature. He would run in, stop in, hold, kill, come out wagging his little tail and sleep. I used to take him to the pit in a pram with my kid. That dog that would have fought a leopard—ay, by God, and kill him or died—he would lie down next to the kid, holding his little hand between his teeth and never dreaming of hurting him. That is your fighting dog, your Staffordshire bull. A swine with anything on legs, but a lamb with a child.

Well ... I ran into some trouble and worse than any in my life I wanted some money. Now Skylarks was a great dog, and everybody in the world knew him as such. I would have backed Skylarks with everything I ever possessed against any beast that ever had a leg in every corner of itself. But I couldn't get a match; and there was a certain party called Joe Blue that wanted to buy Skylarks off me for twenty pounds. I dare say you know one can get to like a dog. I wouldn't sell. And then the brokers came in and I went to Joe Blue and said I'd sell; but he wouldn't buy. He offered me ten; and I spat on it.

He said: "Look. I'll tell you what. How much have you got?"

"A fiver," I said.

He said, lady ... Gerald, he said: "Will you match him against two Alsatians?"

I said: "Yes."

And so I took Skylarks along to meet Blue's Alsatians. You know that Alsatian. He runs in and slashes. Blue had a dog and a bitch. Skylarks killed the dog in a minute and a half, and the bitch had slashed him to ribbons and they were locked jaw to jaw. Skylarks had the sense of a man. You know, when two dogs are fighting, how you take them apart—the dog that has the hold, you push him forward and then pull him back. Skylarks manœuvred himself loose like a Christian and got a hold on a pinch of skin in the Alsatian's throat, and shifted, and got a proper grip, and killed her. By God, my God, that dear little dog ... he was a warrior and he was a gentleman and God send us all a heart like the heart there was in that dog! It was all over in five and three quarter minutes, and Skylarks was standing by me, and I was dabbing peroxide of hydrogen on his cuts. Because he was cut, that lovely dog—he was cut up like macaroni. I collected my stakes. Then Blue said:

"Do you want to make yourself, or lose yourself some money?"

"What way?" I said.

Blue said: "He holds."

I said: "In life or death."

Then Blue said something horrible. He said: "He was holding with his jaw nearly broke. Do you think he'd hold with a leg cut off?"

I said: "How do you mean?"

He said: "I'll lay you thirty pounds to ten he'd drop his hold of an iron bar if I took off a paw with an axe."

I thought. I was disgusted, because, as I said, I had a liking for that dog. But then again, the brokers were in: The lass was sick and a kid was coming. I said to Skylarks: "Skylarks, brother, brother dog, brother Skylarks, I like you and I don't want to do it to you ... but, Skylarks, I've got to do it. Skylarks," I said, "I'd sooner cut off my own paw. But nobody will lay a bet on that because I'm a man, and you're a dog. But, Skylarks, forgive me, I got to do it because t' old lass wants t' brass and there's a kid coming. So make ready, and lay hold."

He understood. They held up a bar and he laid hold like I told him. And then Blue took off his off fore-paw with an axe, and that dog, that red dog, that lovely gentleman, he still kept hold; and I collected my money, and I cried like a child.

I fought him again on three legs, and another red dog, a fine red dog, killed him. And on another bet—although it broke my heart to see him lying there—we opened him, and let God be my judge, three minutes after he was dead ... in-out, in-out, in-out, his heart was still beating.

My lovely Skylarks, my beautiful little Staffordshire gentleman! I wish he had been my father or my son. A man has a duty, but I loved him, I tell you that I loved him better than the old lass and better than the kid that came. I'd change anything. I'd give anything for him back.

And when I broke away and I was lying there, dying ... dying of hunger, hunger and cold and misery out in those plains, lying in a ditch ...

... Do you know what it's like to dream of hunger? When your belly is eating itself up because there is nothing else left for it to eat? You dream of waves, of a sort of fog in waves like a misty day; only it moves like a sea and carries you with it ... and then when you wake up you're sick, and cold, and you want to give up. I'm telling you something. I would have given up a dozen times in them months, lady. Yes, Gerald, I would have given up time and time again ... only I kept on thinking about that Skylarks. That lovely red Staffordshire gentleman. And I ask you—could I be less than a dog? He was better than most things: but he was a dog, only a dog. And I'm a man. Could I be less? So I broke through in the end.

Gavin Eld made rings on the table with his glass. He was speaking in an undertone, now, like a man alone and talking to himself. Had the beer overtaken him?

He muttered:

"Thalt fight na more, my red beauty; thalt ne'er fly in agen at t'enemy's throat with tha grand heart of iron banging lak a drum and a glow in tha black een lak cals. I'll not feel tha bull's neck in my hands, nay never agen, never. Eh, tha wicked swine, nobbut death'd separate t'enemy and thee, and tha shamed me back to life. Ay, tha didst, tha knows tha didst ... and but for remembering thee I'd 'a gone back lak a coward. Thoroughbred to t' bone as thart, could I let thee think tha master was nobbut a cur?"

Then he rose, not very steadily. "He was only a dog," he said. "But I'm only a man."

Reflection in a Brown Eye

A vivacious young literary man, recently discharged from the Army because he was "temperamentally unsuitable", had been telling us a funny story about his Company Sergeant-Major who liked to play with plasticine. In the blacked-out privacy of his bare room, the Company Sergeant-Major modelled fantastic figures—gnomes, devils, faces, and impossible birds. At bedtime he would heave a big sigh, beat the things he had shaped into a neat flat oblong, and lock the modelling-clay in a little-drawer. The story was well told, and there was a burst of laughter; but between two *ha-ha's* I became aware of a little zone of cold silence. Looking sideways, I saw a Lieutenant of Commandos pursing his lips in an expression of intense distaste.

He, I could see, was an old regular soldier: every muscle in his body betrayed the fact. The arteries in his neck were big with shouting; the tendons of his throat were stiff with old, swallowed anger. He reminded me of Quarter-Master Sergeant Spontoon. Spontoon, who had a hand like an over-baked loaf and ears like scrambled eggs, made silly little pictures of ladies in crinolines by sticking coloured tinfoil on bits of glass: he framed them and gave them away to his friends. And he was reminiscent of the man we used to call Corporal Punishment, who wrote poetry like this:

> *The heat is awful as on parade I moil and toil.*
> *My perspiration pours from me like boiling oil.*
> *Oh, if I only could feel just now*
> *Your lovely ice-cold lips upon my fevered brow . . .*

The Lieutenant, I guessed, had—like the literary man's Sergeant-Major—his private creative impulses. Men under discipline, who sit out the leisure-hours of their youth in barracks, need some way of using up the chopped-off odds-and-ends of yearning that litter the lockers of their minds. One makes a little picture; another makes a little rhyme; a third tries to invent a little machine; a fourth cuts off the tail of his shirt and patiently shapes a collar, or hacks a regimental badge out of a bit of brass. They want to make something durable, these good, quiet fighting-men. For example, Mr. Cosstoe, with a box of coloured chalks and a sheet of brown wrapping-paper, wanted to make an immortal masterpiece. Poor old man!

* * * * * *

He was eighty-seven years old, and I was nine: he was in my way, when I met him first. I wondered what right he had to litter the lawn with his bent body when Bill Baldwin and I wanted to play soldiers.

"That's my great-grandpa," said Bill Baldwin. "He's my mother's grandfather."

It had never occurred to me that mothers could have grandfathers. I glanced enviously at Bill Baldwin, and then gazed at

Mr. Cosstoe who sat sunning himself twenty feet away, making marks on a piece of paper while a very old spaniel sat at his feet, panting in the sunlight and looking up into his face. In spite of his years, and the white whiskers on his cheeks, there was a youthfulness about old Mr. Cosstoe; an indefinable something, like the optimism at which middle-aged men smile, saying: "Ah, boyhood!"

I remember that I was impressed by the pearly cleanliness of his hair and the clearness of his eyes, which were pale blue. His dog's name was Jack, and Jack, also, was almost too old to be alive—fifteen years old, unsteady, asthmatic, sore-mouthed, too heavy for his legs, malodorous. He would not leave the old man, but sat at his feet in the sunlight, wheezing, while Bill Baldwin and I played on the lawn.

"He was in the Crimean War," said Baldwin. Then he added, in a nasty voice that was not his own: "He's a nuisance to himself."

An intuition informed me that Bill Baldwin had heard his mother say this. She was a little, boneless, white-blonde woman who—soft and sour as she was—made me think of fungus in a vinegar bottle. Her husband was in the Civil Service. Her father had been a school-teacher: he was dead. But Mr. Cosstoe went on living—battered, disreputable, carrying with him the tobacco-laden atmosphere of the barracks. It was irreligious: the old man was eighty-seven. A man's allotted span was threescore-years-and-ten; pension or no pension, he was seventeen years overdue.

I did not like Bill Baldwin's mother, but I found myself overcome by something like affection for his great-grandfather. One day I asked him what he was doing with his chalks and his brown paper.

Mr. Cosstoe said:

"Why, I'm drawing Jack's eyes, don't you see?" He showed me something like a smear of chocolate, full of high-lights, and shaped like a wheel.

"Yes, sir," I said.

"*Do* ye though?"

I hesitated. Mr. Cosstoe shook his head and said: "No, ye

don't. No use talking, son, ye *don't*." He crumpled the paper in his big, knuckly, shiny red hands, and threw it down.

I asked: "Why the dog's eyes?"

He said: "Ah .... D'ye know what dog that is, son?"

"A spaniel, sir?"

"A Cocker Spaniel: you're not far wrong. For forty years, now, I've been trying to draw that dog's eyes."

I could not understand the meaning of forty years, and so I shook my head.

"Thisyer dog is Jack," said Mr. Cosstoe. "The one before him was John. Before John there was Jim, and before Jim there was Joe. They're all related, d'ye see. Now, you look at Jack's eyes, sonny—look straight at 'em, and tell me straight what you see."

The old, gasping dog still looked up. I put my nose close to his and looked into his eyes. There was nothing to see but a re-flection of my own face, distorted as in a pair of convex mirrors.

"I see *me*," I said, "like in a spoon."

Mr. Cosstoe nodded. "Quite right," he said, "quite right too. That's what I'm after."

"I beg pardon, sir?"

"*Me*," he said. "I always liked to draw a bit. I was at Inkerman when we went for the Rooshians with stones in our bare fists: I was in the Army thirty-six years. Right, we'll hedge that. You'll find out, sonny, *you'll* learn. Dear little boy! God bless you and love you . . . I was telling you . . . what was I telling you?"

"About the dog's eyes, sir."

"Ah, we're both getting on, Jack," said Mr. Cosstoe, caressing the spaniel's ears, "good old dog, good old boy! You got no sense, then, have you, Jack? Oh dear, oh dear, poor old Jack!" He toyed with his chalks. "You see yourself, God bless you, in that dog's eyes," he said.

"Yes, sir."

"Me too. Before you was born, before your father was born, I see myself in a spaniel's eyes; and *that's* what I'm after, and that's what I'll get, too! . . . There, there, Jack old boy; poor old boy! . . . One day I come home, and—never mind what, sonny, God spare you! I finds myself all alone with the dog . . ."

He paused, shaking his head, and then went on: "It struck me that my dog, Joe, hadn't guarded the house properly, don't ye see? Somebody—I mean to say, something—was missing. And there was nothing but the dog. I go to hit the dog. Then I see myself in his eyes, d'ye see? And I go cold. Oh dear me, dear me!—I see myself as the dog sees me, in a brown looking-glass with all my face pushed forward and a fist raised up to strike; while the dog sits, wondering what *he* done to me; and him with a paw bent. . . . My goodness me! I see myself in the dog's eyes, and I think: 'Let me draw this eye, and me in it—the dog's eye full of love, and me full of rage! Let me draw this, and if I can make others see it the same way as I see it, why . . .' Well, what I'm after is *me* in that dog's eye, little boy. But I can't hit it, I can't hit it."

"Yes, sir," I said. "I mean, no, sir."

He patted my hand. "You see what I mean?" he asked.

"I don't think so, sir."

"Good for you," said Mr. Cosstoe. "Tell the truth and shame the devil!"

Then Bill Baldwin came out of the house, into which it had been necessary for him to withdraw for a few minutes. The old man picked up a stick of chalk, started to smooth a fresh sheet of brown paper, then threw the chalk away. It broke on the sunbaked lawn. He pushed the paper aside and let himself relax in his arm-chair. "Oh dear, dear, dear, dear me!" I heard him say. "Dear me, dear me!"

I was taken away to the seaside next day. When I came back a month later, Bill Baldwin told me that his great-grandfather was dead and buried.

"About time, too," he said, in his mother's voice. "He was a nuisance to himself."

"What about the dog?" I asked.

"Mother had him put to sleep," he answered. "He was too old."

Maria's Christ

To this very day the old woman called Maria believes that while she slept, angels—or, at least, kindly spirits—moved invisible by her side and carried for her the burden which her aged hands were too tired to lift.

By the greatest good fortune she lives, now, in Switzerland. She is more than seventy years old, but strong and vigorous still. How shall I describe her? Her face is brown and dry, like earth. And like sun-baked earth, it is reticulated with tiny intersecting cracks. There is something of the quality of good earth about old Maria: the sun may dry her, the rain may flood her, and the wind may blow her from place to place ... and yet she always survives, in one place or another. Anxiety and the years have corrugated her forehead and plucked out her eyebrows. What remains of her hair is white. In the middle of it there is a parting —or rather, a path—more than an inch wide. The rest is drawn back and fastened in a knot no bigger than a walnut at the nape of her neck. Since time immemorial she has worn nothing but severe black, and nobody in living memory has seen her without beads and crucifix. Nothing on this earth—nor in the heavens above, nor in the waters under the earth—can shake her faith in a personal, benevolent Providence.

She came off a wine farm where they lived on bread: bread boiled, bread fried and just bread. At the age of twelve she became a servant, and for about fifty-five years remained, profoundly devoted to a good family in Barcelona. She was one of those servants who become involved in the life of the family. With her own knotted hands she brought up the little boy, whom she called Juanito. She called him Juanito still, when he was a harassed man of forty-five, somewhat involved in the Spanish equivalent of the Liberal Party. When Franco came, through blood, to what passes as power, Juanito, who was the last survivor of the family, saved himself and went to France. He assumed, perhaps rightly, that nobody would bother to touch old Maria. But he did not count upon the fanatical loyalty of the old woman; who would look after Juanito! Besides, if he were in France, quite obviously, her place was in France too. The Fascists were approaching Barcelona. She wrapped her most treasured possessions in an old shawl, and set out for the border.

It is not quite clear what Maria valued most among the few things she had managed to accumulate in her long, hard life.

One thing is certain: there was a heavy ebony crucifix with a white ivory Christ; some kind of silver-gilt drinking cup, and a few clothes—particularly two hats of a more or less ornate nature, which she had never worn, preferring, quite rightly, the graceful and time-honoured shawl. The bundle contained, also, two books which she could not read, and three ornaments for the mantelpiece such as one wins at hoopla in a fun-fair. Heaven only knows what people preserve as treasures, and why! The whole bundle must have weighed about fifteen pounds, and there was hardly an object in it which anybody would have bothered to pick up if he had seen it lying in the street. But she tied it very firmly together and set out from Barcelona over the long, bitter, dusty road away from something she recognised as a menace but could not understand.

Her old feet rose and fell with a mechanical regularity. She reached Gerona. She had, of course, food and water with her; she, of all people, would not have forgotten that. But perhaps it was the shock of her uprooting from the place in which she had lived so long. Such a shock may weaken a person like the shock of a wound. At Gerona she felt herself growing strangely weak, and sat, always clasping her bundle, by the roadside. A family, also in flight, passed in a large car; then stopped, and offered her a lift. They were going, they said, to Figueras, where one of their relations was to join them; as far as that they could take her. She thanked them, climbed in, and drove on.

They said good-bye to her at Figueras and, all alone, she walked on. She realised then that, for the first time in her life, she was sick. It was not a sickness of the body: it was a sickness of the soul. Remember, she was being torn away from where she belonged; and she was not accustomed to being alone.

She reached Peralada. The roads were choked with people who wanted to get away, anywhere, away from the Fascists. She says that her feet felt like dead feet, and that each of her legs seemed to weigh as much as a paving-stone. More and more frequently she had to sit down and rest. Then her shoulders began to ache. It was the weight of the bundle. She began to be aware of it. She shifted it from left hand to right, and from right to left, every hundred yards. Then she had to sit down and rest again.

Time is long to the weary. She had lived seventy years, but the sum of all those years seemed less than the time that passed on her infinitely slow and painful journey between Peralada and Llansa.

Llansa had the air of an encampment on the edge of the wilderness during the Exodus from Egypt. There was a kind of hideous cavalcade of the homeless on the run. She, who had always been proud of her strength, found herself raising hopeful hands towards passing cars and lorries. But every vehicle was full. Between Llansa and San Miguel Maria felt that her strength had quite gone out of her. She sat away from the road upon her bundle and closed her eyes and waited for death. Understand that this was a peasant woman who had relied upon herself and grown accustomed to being relied on for half a century. And now, when her own force was failing her, she felt that she was as good as dead.

There was an atmosphere of death hanging over that hideous road. People, running away, had taken with them all they valued. Then, as the way became hard, they had bit by bit abandoned the possessions that encumbered them. Oncoming refugees had pushed things aside. The road was hideously lined with the pathetic droppings of families in flight. Near where Maria sat there lay a vast brass tray which had once held a Moorish coffee set. Near this, lying on its side, a child's cradle, seven copper saucepans, and a lamp. Dust was already drifting over the surface of a mahogany table, which loving hands had polished for eighty years. A large black marble clock disgorged a quivering spring: it had burst where it had fallen. Four cushions lay piled upon a dusty stone. An immense feather-bed let out a thick white stream of down, which the wind of passing cars stirred in small swirls. The refugees were throwing down the things they had wanted to save. They were even leaving their means of conveyance by the roadside. Here, a juiceless car stood, hot and dusty, but silent; there, a bicycle lay very flat with a broken fork. There was also a little patient donkey, quite dead, perhaps from exhaustion.

Maria saw the significance of all this. It is hard to save both yourself and the things you possess. She sat for a long time thinking. Could she save, at least, the ebony crucifix with its patient white Christ? No. She would leave it all behind her and go on. Somewhere, on the other side of the frontier, she would find Juanito. Then she would resume her career, her service. She stood up, and without looking behind her, trudged on, reached San Miguel. She had a little money, with which she bought more food to take with her; then left San Miguel, threading her way along that nightmarish white road which rose in powder as her feet struck it, and seemed to cling to the roof of her mouth in dry astringent dust. The way was more and more encumbered with dropped treasures. Maria was numb with fatigue and with the misery of change. Was it the will of God, she wondered, that in her old age she must lose all she ever acquired and die alone and poor among strangers whose language she could not speak? She drove the thought away. Her will lashed her failing body forward.

At last she reached Port Bou. The people who were passing seemed, now, to move faster. They, also, were exhausted. But Port Bou represented the beginning of the last lap, and so they hurried as people do, when they are reaching the end of a long and wretched journey.

She remembers that there was a railway tunnel ... a sort of black cave into which people were throwing themselves. It looked to her like an open mouth, but she drew herself together and walked into that thick and dreadful darkness thinking of the Valley of the Shadow of Death and how one should fear no evil. That tunnel is not very long, but to Maria it seemed to have no end; and when she felt that, like a woman in a nightmare, she was condemned to walk for ever and ever in thick darkness.... When she began to wonder whether she had become blind ... she saw a little semi-circle of light which was the end of the tunnel and so came out and reached Cerebere.

And there she lay down by the road and closed her eyes and slept. She was on safe territory. Before she slept, quite un-reasoningly, she prayed "Dear Lord ... my ivory Christ ..." she wanted it back. And so sleep came upon her and when she awoke the day was fading. She sat up. It had been her habit, before she had abandoned her bundle, to reach out her hand after resting and ascertain that it was still there. She reached out her hand and touched a familiar rough surface. It was her bundle.

Now there is no doubt at all that somebody, finding the bundle she had left, had picked it up and carried it with him; and in due course abandoned it: and that somebody else had picked it up, with a view to opening it later on, and in turn thrown it down ... and that this bundle had gone from hand to hand all along that road, to be finally abandoned near where Maria lay by the roadside at Cerebere. There is a perfectly logical explanation that fits it.

But Maria swears that it was a saint, or a spirit, or just the power of her prayer that somehow brought her ivory Christ back to her, as it were, out of a deep sleep. She knew then, she says, that all would be well. It is certainly a fact that she found Juanito, and they live in comparative peace in Switzerland to this very day.

Destiny and the Bullet

It was at the beginning of the war. There was a smell of stuffiness and of doom. Rumour, that lying slut, had reared her bedraggled head. Nobody knew where everything was going to lead. I was in a corner with three other men. I remember that one of them, a lank-faced pale man, said: "Where is all this going to end?"

And then another man spoke. I liked the look of him the moment I set eyes on him. He was a small, dried-up man, with that air of sun-matured toughness, that appearance of teak-like hardness which you find in men who have lived rough and healthy lives in the tropics. He was wearing a well-preserved suit of old tweeds and an open-necked shirt. But these clothes hung upon him as if they did not belong to him. They say that clothes make the man. This, to a certain extent, is true: a military tunic is never really shaped to fit a soldier—a soldier is made to fit his tunic. And it was quite obvious that this little man had worn a uniform and conformed to an established way of carrying himself for many years. His hair was of a neutral tint somewhere between yellow and sandy white. He had a moustache which might have been a sprinkling of silver sand on his upper lip. He smoked a pipe, and had a certain bird-like way of cocking his head as he talked; and his tone was half-amiable and half-authoritative—the tone of a man who has grown accustomed to combining threats with promises in ordering a platoon. He said this: "And who knows where anything in the world begins or ends? What do you mean by looking as if you'd lost a shilling and picked up a farthing just because you don't know where everything is going to end?"

About ten minutes later, easing himself into conversation like a foot into a shoe, he told us this story:

When I was a nipper I knew everything. Yes, when I was about fifteen years old nobody could tell me anything at all. People didn't tell me, I told them. That is ignorance. It's like that that you stay ignorant. Well, I lived and learned. I lived a hell of a lot, and never learned very much. I'm sixty now, and I've only just begun to realise that the sum total of all I know is sweet Fanny Adams. This gentleman here was giving us a patter about not knowing where things end. Now look, I'll tell you something.

Years and years ago I was in China. I was a soldier there. I got most of my military experience there. I liked the Chinese, because I always found them a decent sort of people; honest and hard-working, and in general clean in their personal habits. Never mind that for the moment. I was a private soldier then. One night I was on sentry duty, on a certain bridge over the Soochow Creek. There had been a lot of stealing going on. It had to be guarded against. There are good and bad of all sorts. There is no place in the world where you won't get thieving. In this case, rifles and ammunition were sometimes getting stolen. Well, in every community there is a class that is willing to pay for fire-arms. I was on sentry-go. It was in the middle of the night and there was a damned great moon. I was pretty young, and it was all a bit new and ghostly. I had not been there more than an hour when I saw something move, and caught the glint of the moon on a bit of steel. I gave the challenge, and nobody answered. I gave it again, and the shadow started to run away. I ordered it to stop or I'd fire. It was a man. He panicked, and ran

like the wind in the moonlight. I had my orders, and I ups with
the old bundhook and fires, intending to hit him in the leg. But I
was excited, and in a hurry. The man went down, and I went over
to him. Instead of hitting him in the leg I'd hit him in the back
and shot him straight through the heart. He must have died in
a split second. I felt queer. This was the first man I ever killed.
It didn't feel nice. When I looked down, to see what he'd been
stealing, I saw that all he had was a few pounds of old iron and a
few bits of brass and copper, in a big tin can.

I got a bit drunk, next, but I felt a bit conscience-stricken.
The man had been some kind of a poor starving workman, and
I dare say he had only tried to pinch a few farthings' worth of
scrap metal to buy a bit of rice for his kids. I didn't feel much
of a hero. But time passed, and I got married. I left the Army
and left China. I went to Singapore. This was years and years
later. I settled down in Singapore, and was very devoted to my
wife. She was a nice girl. I got a job on a plantation, and did
well. I got myself a servant; or I should say, that I got my wife a
servant—a Chinese girl who, I don't mind telling you, was the
best servant anybody in the world could wish to have. In the first
place, she was as loyal and faithful as somebody out of a fairy-
story. She waited on my wife—who wasn't very strong—hand
and foot, and seemed to like doing so, because my wife was
always kind to her and I don't believe that she, poor girl, had had
much kindness in her life. We did not have any kids at first, but
after we had been married about five years my wife told me the
glad news. She was going to have a kid, and I was in the seventh
heaven. We were a long way from anywhere and I had made ar-
rangements that, a reasonable time before the business was due
to start, my wife should be taken to another place where there
were women and doctors and everything.

Well, when there was about another two months to go, I had
to go, on very urgent business, a long way away. I left my wife
in the care of the Chinese girl; but I did not feel very easy in
my mind about it all. I had to be gone just over a week. When
I got back the child was already born. It was a boy and he is
thirty years old now, and more than six feet high, and strong as a
buffalo. But he was born before his time, and he was one of those

kids who, you would think, hasn't got enough life in him to open his eyes. He was too weak to cry. My wife had had a terrible time. She would have died, I tell you that she would have died as sure as God made Heaven, if it had not been for the servant. Yes, this Chinese girl pulled off the whole affair. She handled my wife like silk or porcelain, and she fed the kid with a fountain-pen filler which I used for an old-fashioned pen I had. She played doctor, wet-nurse, midwife, and everything. And it is to her that I owe my wife's life and that of my son, who is now a doctor.

I had never really looked at her as a human being until then. We had never exchanged ten words, except in the form of orders given and taken. But now I began to talk to her, and asked her about herself. She told me that she was from China. Her father had been a poor working man who could not make ends meet. He was an honest man, she said, but one night, not wanting to see his children starve, he had tried to steal some scrap metal; but on a bridge over the Soochow Creek, an English sentry had shot him in the back. I asked her what sentry. She said: "I do not know. My brothers and my mother died of hunger, and I only live because I was a pretty girl, and a merchant took me away."

And you are talking to me about how things end or begin! Why, mug that you are, no man on earth knows the beginning or the end of anything that he does. The only thing you can do, pal, is what you think is right, and hope for the best.

The Conqueror Worm

I met Dempsey first in Stockholm. He was one of those pulpy personalities in which it is difficult to find anything definite. He was honest because he was afraid of the consequences of dishonesty; nobody quarrelled with him because he agreed with everything anybody said. His pale and insipid soul was dotted with silly little prejudices and principles, as feeble as the vestigial seeds of a banana. There was one particle which, hardened by pure fear, stuck in the middle of his brain—the fact that he had never done anything illegal. Other men base their pride on achievement or endurance: "I built a business," "I survived the

War." Dempsey's self-respect centred round the thought: "I have never done anything like that." He stuck to me, like discarded chewing-gum to the sole of a boot, and would not be shaken off, until that memorable night when we found ourselves stranded in Nyevinossi-Novgorod.

Oh, that town, that miserable ice-bound town of Nyevinossi-Novgorod! There are no lamps in its streets. Why should there be, since nobody goes out after dark? And who wants to go out, since there is nowhere to go? It is a coal town, clinging to the mouths of the Nyevinossi Pits; bi-sected by the line of the Arctic Circle, it skulks, freezing, under the slate-coloured sky of the Kola Peninsula—black with smoke, grey with fog, rasped by the icy teeth of the bitter White Sea; redolent of dead fish, and utterly permeated with gritty coal-dust. The streets twist and turn, as if they had writhed with cold before being frozen stiff by the wind—the paralysing wind of the Arctic, which carries with it the unbearable desolation of the northern wastes and the heart-breaking melancholy of the Eastern tundras.

We were lost there. It was nearly midnight. Every window was dark, and the roads were treacherous.

"We can get the ferry to Izbaborg at six in the morning," I said.

"But what are we going to do till then?" asked Dempsey.

"Find lodging."

"But where?"

"Oh, I don't know. We'll have to ask somebody."

"But we can't speak a word of Russian——"

"Oh, shut up."

I knocked at the nearest door, but nobody answered. You would have thought that the town was dead. We walked on. Wind began to whistle through the narrow, deserted street.

"Somebody's coming!" said Dempsey.

A man was approaching, carrying a lantern. I called him: "Hoi!" He stopped, and we went up to him. As he held up the lantern to look at us, I caught a glimpse of his face. He was a Jew, very small, closely wrapped in a wolf-skin coat, with a fur cap pulled down over his ears. His face was as narrow as if it had been pressed between two boards; marked with small-pox, and contorted in an anxious, mechanical grin, such as you see on the face of a man squinting against strong sunlight. I addressed him in German:

"Can you help us find a place to sleep?"

He replied in Yiddish: "Sleep? Can you pay?"

"Yes."

"Well, there's a hotel."

"Is there? Where?"

"Well, you go straight along until you come to Batko's; then turn to the left by the——"

"But how can we find our way in the dark? We're strangers here."

"Hum. All right. I'll show you. You come with me."

"I don't like the look of him," whispered Dempsey.

We followed the man with the lantern. The streets grew narrower, winding like snakes. We were lost in a maze of black tunnels, through which the rising wind rushed, roaring, flinging into our faces gritty fragments of ice. Dempsey took my arm, and clung to it. We came to the deep centre of the town, to a street so narrow that two men could not have walked abreast through it. Our guide stopped at an ancient and filthy wooden house which leaned over at an angle of sixty degrees on to three huge wooden props, which alone prevented it from falling down.

"Here you are, gentlemen! A hotel. Yak's. It's all right, I tell you!" The Jew knocked at the door.

"We can't go in here," said Dempsey.

"We've got to go somewhere," I said.

"I'd rather spend the night in the streets. I've got a feeling——"

"Ssh!"

The door swung open, and the entire opening was blocked by the immense bulk of a man. The light was behind him. We could see only his black silhouette. He stepped back.

"Come in," said our guide.

I pushed Dempsey in front of me, into the house. The man closed the door, and then, as he turned and faced us, I started back and put my hand on my revolver. I have never seen such a man. His bulk, alone, was terrifying: stripped, he must have weighed twenty-two stone. His colossal torso was muffled in a great bearskin coat—he seemed larger than an elephant; yet even so, his head was too big for his body. His face appeared to have been twisted out of shape by some fantastic disease, until it bore a distinct resemblance to the head of a rhinoceros: it had the same scalloped mouth, bestial forehead, and ponderous jowl. His nose was smashed flat. An ancient scar, which must have laid open the whole left side of his face, twitched up a corner of his mouth in a perpetual snarl. His flat skull was covered with coarse white bristles, and under his lower lip hung a tuft like a shaving-brush. Our guide whispered to him: they both laughed. The anxious, grinning little face turned towards me, as he said:

"This is Yak. You'll be comfortable here. Such a bed! You'll never want to get up again. Good night! Sleep well!" The door closed on him. We were alone with Yak.

"Let's get out of here," whispered Dempsey, shaking like a leaf; but it seemed ridiculous, now, to go back into the streets. If I have one English trait, it is that I would face death rather than do something that seems ridiculous. Moreover, I had my revolver.

I said to Yak, in German: "We want a bed."

He shook his head. He did not understand; and all the time, he looked at us with one wicked little red eye.

"What's Russian for 'bed', Dempsey?"

"I don't know. Oh, please, please, let's get out of here!"

"And freeze to death?"

Yak moved, pushing us before him. He steered us upstairs, to the first floor, struck a match, and lit a lamp. The flame popped and spread. We were in a tiny bedroom containing a great old bed, and no other furniture. The windows, I noticed, had been firmly boarded up. I turned again to Yak, and said in a tone of authority:

"We must be called at five o'clock."

He shook his head.

I made gestures. I pointed to him; then to Dempsey and myself: indicated an imaginary clock; conveyed, in pantomime, sleeping and waking up, and spread out five fingers.

"What's Russian for 'five o'clock'?" I asked.

"Something like 'pyet chessov'," said Dempsey.

"Pyet chessov!" I said, very loudly.

Yak nodded, and then, with a grin that made my blood run cold, said: "Pyet chessov."

He went out. Something went *click*.

"He's locked the door!" cried Dempsey.

I tried the door. It was locked. I knocked. There was no answer.

"My God!" exclaimed Dempsey. "This is terrible. I didn't want to come here. It's all your fault. You insisted. Now see what a mess we're in. I had a feeling that something was going to happen. Now we're caught, like rats in a trap. Oh, God, what are we going to do?"

"Perhaps it's only a custom here, in case a lodger runs away without paying his rent."

"He would have asked us to pay in advance," said Dempsey, "but he knows there's no need to. He'll get all we've got without asking. We'll never see daylight. We're finished."

"I've got a revolver."

"My God, my God!" whispered Dempsey.

"We can lie down, and keep warm," I said, "I'm freezing, and I'm dead beat. I'm going to lie down."

I did so, covering myself with the malodorous bedclothes— the greasy matting, and the mangy bearskin rug. Dempsey leapt into bed beside me, and sat bolt upright, tense with terror, and shivering so that the bed shook.

"Relax," I said.

"I can't."

"Take your boots off."

"I can't."

"Lie down."

"I can't. I've got a premonition. My premonitions are always right. I'm psychic. You might get out of this, I never shall. I tell you, I know I shan't get out of here alive. Listen. You've been my friend, my only friend. Take my papers and my—open your eyes, please, open your eyes and listen to me. I shall die here. Something tells me ... I *know*. There's death in this house—*what's that?*"

It was a shuffling noise. In the middle of the room looking at us with sickening curiosity, sat two large black rats. I waved a hand at them, to drive them away; they did not move.

"They're waiting for us," said Dempsey, "they *know*. Rats know."

A blast of wind struck the house. A piece of ice, dislodged from the roof, slid down with a grating noise and fell into the street. Dempsey's teeth were chattering like castanets. I laid my revolver between us, and propped myself up against the headboard of the bed. There seemed to be two weights pressing down upon my eyelids. I struggled against sleep, but vast waves of weariness were running through my body.

"*What's that?*" whispered Dempsey. Something was scratching at the door. I looked, with the big revolver poised for a snap-shot. It was another rat.

"Keep quiet," I said, "let me get a few minutes' rest."

Nothing, nothing in the world could have kept me awake. Consciousness was slipping away from me ... down and down and down an infinite precipice of smooth black glass....

Then I was asleep, and I remember that I was involved in a bizarre and meaningless dream ... I was being led out into a yard, and a voice was saying to me: "You are to impersonate the Emperor Napoleon ..." I saw the rings of a thousand rifle-muzzles. There was a terrific explosion. I was blown away, head over heels, roaring with laughter, over a tremendous black landscape, soaring like a bird. Then I looked up, and saw hovering over me a gigantic machine bristling with hooks. It descended, caught me. I struggled to free myself, and heard a voice whisper: "Wake up! For God's sake! Wake up!"

I opened my eyes with a groan, and saw the terrified face of Dempsey. "Look!" he said, "oh, God, look!"

The door was opening. In the widening black oblong, I saw the revolting face of Yak, moving as silently as the ghost of an evil passion, indescribably hideous in the ghastly lamplight. He entered the room. Dempsey screamed, and then, drowning the scream, came the stunning bang of the heavy revolver, with the stinging smell of cordite. Yak dropped a vast hand to his chest, fell back against the wall, and sat down, his legs spread out in front of him. I leapt out of bed. Yak's right hand came slowly away from his breast, wet with blood, as he spread it out like a fan in front of us, stared, with utter astonishment, and said, in a fading whisper:

"Pyet ... chessov ..."

At that moment, the bell of a church boomed the first stroke of five.

"Idiot!" I said, as I snatched the revolver out of Dempsey's hand, "he was only coming to wake us up!"

We caught the first ferry-boat. Within a week, we had put five hundred miles between ourselves and Nyevinossi-Novgorod. Dempsey began to recover from the shock. At first, he said: "How was I to know? It was excusable." Then: "How do you know he was only coming to wake us up?" Then: "I'm not at all sure that I didn't save both our lives"; and finally: "I'm absolutely certain that I caught him in the act. Thank God, I didn't lose my presence of mind!"

He grew quite aggressive. In Oslo, he reprimanded a barber. In Berlin, he swore at a waiter. I left him in Paris. That was in 1920. I hear that he is married since then. He treats his wife with extraordinary severity, and was heard calling her a "sickening idiot" in the presence of strangers. He still finds it difficult to stand a direct look, but he is a roaring lion with subordinates, and has cultivated a quite terrifying manner of handing his hat to cloakroom attendants.

He is acquiring something of the reputation of a man of iron.

The Woman and the Fire

Not even the police touch the people on the benches near the Dogs' Cemetery. Dirt is their armour; lice are their watchdogs. Wash them and they die. Every morning, pink disinfectant is scattered over the places where they have rested. The disinfectant is dust which the wind blows away. By nightfall the Untouchable People are back, dragging behind them all they ever possessed—their shadows. You hear nothing from them: there is nothing they want to say. They don't even beg—to beg is to hope, and they have no hope. Nothing is known of their lives. After sunrise they seem to disappear from the earth like mist. The fact is, that nobody looks at them: everybody looks away from them because they are disgusting, like sores. There are more things to be seen than men care to look at. Once—only once—I saw a man approach these frightful men and women of the dustbins. He was a young priest, and it was at midnight. He put his left arm about the shoulders of one of the most atrocious of them all—a woman—and raised to her lips a can of soup.

She shook her head and, with an incoherent spluttering cry, spat out the mouthful of soup. Then she disappeared into her rags with a wriggle like a startled earwig.

Years later I heard that same woman talk. Everybody in West London has seen her. She used to come out after twilight in Mortimer Street, where the dustbins of the gown-manufacturers lie. She contrived to comb a few saleable handfuls of silk-cuttings out of the rubbish. Speaking of her, a Corsican who owned a coffee-shop said: "She is not Gloria Swanson, but she is a person: she does not live in the Ritz Hotel, but she gets along." He used to leave a sandwich for her on the lid of his ash-can every night. Was it Christian charity? Or was he laying offerings upon a dusty altar after dark, in obedience to dim forebodings? She was like a witch in a Transylvanian folk-tale. You could see nothing of her face but a nose, one tooth, a chin, a pair of red-rimmed eyes. A wolfish mat of hair hid the rest. On her head she wore a straw boater with an old Etonian ribbon; on her feet, rubber slippers. Each foot resembled a sockful of walnuts. Her skirt was made of two old coats fastened together with pins: I was haunted by a dread that one day it might fall off in my presence. But it never did. She wore, also, half a dozen jerseys and pullovers, a pea-jacket, and an ancient Army greatcoat blackleaded like a stove with accumulated dirt. Everybody was afraid of her. She might not be able to cast spells or look at you with the Evil Eye; but she could do worse—touch you. That would be too horrible.

It happened on the night of the first great air-raid over London. It was a bad night, that one: we remembered all we had ever read about high-explosive and the annihilation of cities. The bombs came down and the fires climbed up; London was burning and the red sky pulsated like a wound. I was trying to get home. In Holborn a man dragged me into a doorway just as a big bomb fell on a block of offices. Several hundreds of tons of masonry seemed to hiccup; then burst open and subsided in thunder, while a great twist of dark orange flame threw itself up out of the ruins. "Does your mother know you're out?" asked the man, with irony. A hot wind was blowing, and above the noise of the blitz there rose the quick, clear ringing of fire-bells. Incendiary bombs were falling: they fell with a hiss, struck with a little crack and let out a blinding light ... a devouring white light that ate into things. I went on, hugging the doorways. Near Gray's Inn Road, a tobacco-shop had been torn apart like a Christmas cracker: there must have been twenty thousand cigarettes on the pavement. But two men were standing there, pushing the packets aside with their feet and fumbling in their pockets by the cigarette-machine. One of them stopped me and said: "Got change for two shillings?" I had no change. The man who had stopped me said: "I could do with a smoke, too ..." We looked down at the cigarettes on the pavement. "No, play the game," said the other man, spurning them with an angry foot.

We all walked away, and I knew then that whoever won this War, the English could never lose it. The bombs were still falling. I heard a fireman saying: "The Docks've gone up in smoke." Everybody moved in a nightmarish tangle of flickering shadows. I heard the throb of another raider and the scream of another bomb; dived into another doorway. The blast picked me up and threw me down a flight of stairs, having flung down half a dozen firemen for me to fall upon. We picked ourselves up. One of them said: "My brother got buried under a wall down East this evening." "Good God!" I said. He added: "A red-hot wall."

I waited in the doorway, trying to spit out the vile taste of age-old plaster-dust mixed with the fumes of high explosive. And there I saw the old woman of the Untouchable People.

She was crouching there with her sack, and her face looked bright and ruddy in the glare of the burning city. The fireman who had lost his brother asked her if she was all right. She did not answer: she did not even look up at him.

"You go and get in a shelter," he said.

She waved a hand in a gesture which said: *Mind your own business; leave me alone.*

"Jerry!" shouted somebody, shouldering in among us. Again we heard the dive of the enemy and the rush of the bomb, and felt the concussion of the explosion like a punch in the head as we threw ourselves down. After that a shower of fire-bombs fell. One of them dropped on the pavement a yard or two away from our doorway, and spat splashes of whiteness like an acetylene-welder as it burnt itself out. The firemen were gone to their work. I was watching the old woman. She was looking at the fire-bomb on the pavement. The brilliance of its burning had faded. She glanced furtively from left to right; put down her sack of rags; shuffled out into the street and, crouching over the dying red glow, warmed her hands.

It was then that I heard her speak. She said, in a clear thin voice: "I haven't had a fire of my own for fifty years."

Even as she spoke the glow went out.

The raiders passed. London lay under the smoke of its burning and listened to the tolling of the fire-bells. I never saw the old woman again.

The Fortunes of the Pryskys

In the winter of the year 1809, a baker named Jan Prysky crouched behind a dough-trough and watched his apprentice, a thin little boy named Wladislaw, who was loitering near a tray of rolls. Jan Prysky held his breath. Wladislaw edged closer to the tray. The steam of the hot bread seemed to intoxicate him like wine. He gulped, looked furtively to the right and the left, and then, exactly fulfilling Prysky's expectation, snatched a roll and bit a great mouthful out of it.

"What!" shouted Jan Prysky, leaping up, "have I caught you at last?—bandit and robber!——" He was a huge man with fierce moustaches. The apprentice dropped the roll and cringed. The baker swung a heavy hand. Wladislaw ducked his head, threw himself to the floor, slipped between his master's legs, and ran away, never to return. Prysky's hand grazed itself against the brass top of a little triangular weighing-machine.

When Prysky's fury had abated a little, he sucked his injured hand, and picked up the bitten roll and ate it. He was a man who abhorred waste. Then he went to dinner.

Three days later his hand swelled. Four days later a lump swelled under his arm, and his whole body throbbed. The surgeon said: "Come, sir, be brave. On the battlefield we can take off an arm like this in ten seconds." He removed Prysky's arm in two minutes thirty seconds: but that, he swore, was the fault of Prysky, who struggled during the operation.

Jan Prysky had to employ an assistant. The assistant, having made himself familiar with most of Prysky's customers, opened a bakery of his own in the same street.

Prysky was ruined. He did not know where to turn for a meal and a bed. One evening, in a main thoroughfare of Warsaw, he stopped a likely-looking pedestrian, and, showing his empty sleeve, said: "Spare a coin for an old soldier." His extended hand received a piece of silver. It was easy. Prysky had found his vocation. Later, he described himself as Jan Prysky, late of Poniatowski's Lancers, and wore a faded uniform. Times were hard: Napoleon had overcrowded the beggary profession. Nevertheless, Prysky, who was a fine figure of a man, did well. He married a girl named Etelka, daughter of a begging-letter-writer named Polacek. They lived in ditches and cellars, whining their way across Europe, instructing their little boy Janko in the tricks of their trade.

"Hang on to every *grosch*," said Prysky. "Always take. Spend nothing. Men are fools: women are worse. Crawl, and they give with both hands. Nobody refuses food to a hungry man. Buy nothing, not even bread, and stick your takings in your belt."

Etelka died in Prague. Jan died in a doss-house in Hamburg. Janko, searching his clothes, found ten thousand francs in gold and securities. He, having thoroughly digested his father's teaching, left Jan's body to be buried by the burghers; wrapped the money about his lean waist; slunk into the street, marked the kind face of a decent housewife in a group near a sausage-shop, and whispered: "*Gnädige Frau*, for the love of God, a copper . . ."

"Poor boy, how thin you are," said the housewife.

Janko remembered that, and thenceforth ate as little as possible. By 1835, when his son Karl was born, he was known in the doss-house as "The Skull". His appearance was corpse-like, and hideous. Karl was a hunchback. "Dear God, I thank you," said Janko. "That hump will be worth its weight in gold."

It was. Karl grew up shameless, quick-witted, and cunning. Janko was proud of him. Wretchedly weeping, the little hunchback led him by the hand through the market places of Middle Europe, crying: "For my dying father, spare one coin, one copper coin! Have pity!" His pathos wrung crusts from starving artisans. Once, in Dresden, a thin woman with red spots on her cheek-bones took off her shawl, although the day was bitterly cold, and said: "Your need is greater, poor child. God bless you!" Janko boasted about this, saying: "My father was clever, and I am no fool, but this boy could put us both in a sack and tie us up."

Janko died in 1870, leaving forty thousand marks. More valuable still, he left a paralysed widow. Karl wheeled her from town to town in a crazy old barrow. What she thought of it all, God knows, for she could not talk. She managed to keep alive for ten years after Janko's death. Karl milked a hundred charities on her behalf, and was very sorry to leave her corpse in Chemnitz. He had wheeled it from door to door for three days, weeping hideously, asking for the wherewithal to give it decent burial. He was compelled to abandon it in a doorway after that. The weather was hot. All the better for sleeping out.

Karl was lucky. In a remote East German village he found a female freak. Her head and body were of normal size, but her arms and legs were scarcely twelve inches long. He wooed and won her. She went away with him. It was perfectly in order: there was nothing about the union that might have offended the most censorious soul in the world. He married her legally. The village, in a rush of sentiment, gave them a wedding-party. A Graf von Felsenmühle tossed the bride a hundred marks, "for lingerie".

Their son Johann was born in 1879. By this time Karl had to change his money into banknotes. Unbelievably ragged, indescribably dirty, inhumanly squalid, he concealed about his untouchable person the sum of a hundred and thirty-five thousand marks—something like six or seven thousand pounds, which Johann was to inherit.

Karl spared no pains in Johann's education. He taught him tricks of voice and facial expression; how to express abject humility with one twitch of the shoulders; how to make real tears run down the face. Johann was not deformed; only he looked strange. He had a little body and a large head, a mournful little mouth and huge brown eyes. Johann had the air of a youth in the grip of some devastating secret sorrow. This, Karl decided, was good. "People get tired of other people's hunger. People get fed up with other people's humps and amputations. But a mysterious, miserable look such as this brat Johann puts on —*Himmelherrgottkreutzmillionendonnerwetter!*" he exclaimed, employing Bismarck's favourite oath, "they never get tired of that!"

There was money in Johann's big head, with its heavy brow and lambent eyes. He touched the learned societies, the religious benevolent funds—even a Fund for the Relief of Impecunious Men of Letters. Johann extracted two hundred marks in gold from this well-meaning charity, over the head of a fat old poor philosopher with a Life Work in seventeen volumes. Karl died, leaving two hundred thousand marks. When the Great War came, Johann found himself in Amsterdam. Business, there, was far from brisk. He ate, it is true, and talked a poor old woman into trusting him to pay rent on a basement. He was happy when the war ended, and he got himself deported, free of charge, over the German border, back to the old, familiar soil and the old, familiar speech.

The countryside was impoverished. Johann crept to Berlin. The state of affairs in that great city was truly deplorable. There was scarcely any food to be bought, let alone to be given away. Johann Prysky was starving. He grew smaller, thinner, weaker: his eyes grew larger: he looked, more than ever, like a sorrowing philosopher. And at last, unable to endure the horrible pains in his stomach, and the profound lassitude of extreme hunger, he unrolled his secreted money-belt. He had two hundred and twenty thousand marks. Out of this hoard he extracted a one hundred-mark note, which he took to a baker's shop.

The shelves were almost empty when Johann, having waited for three hours in the queue, staggered into the shop. He said: "A one-pound loaf," and, reluctantly fondling it, slowly letting it go as a woman relinquishes the hand of a beloved child who is leaving her for a remote corner of the world, dropped his hundred-mark note upon the counter.

"What kind of a joke is this?" asked the baker.

"A loaf . . ."

"And where have you been that you don't know the price of bread to-day?"

"This is a hundred-mark note, sir."

"A one-pound loaf costs two hundred thousand marks."

"Eh?"

"Get out of my shop."

The bread-queue took hold of Johann like a conveyor-belt. He found himself in the street. He looked at the hundred-mark note, and smoothed it.

He walked until he found a bench, and then sat down. At last he rose, and walked back to the baker's shop. "I will take the loaf," he said, and took off his money-belt.

"Bread's up. One-pound loaf costs a million."

"I have two hundred and twenty thousand marks," said Johann.

"You could have a small roll for that," said the baker.

"I will take it," said Johann.

The Sailor's Farewell to his Horse

We had been talking about food as it is served in restaurants. One man said: "I'd sooner eat horse than pig when I come to consider their personal habits." And then an old Merchant seaman said: "Eat horse? Why, I'd eat anything rather than a horse. Eating a horse is like eating a man—you just can't do it, you mustn't do such things."

There was profound distaste in his tone. The very idea horrified him. I looked at him with a certain curiosity. One does not expect a sailor to feel deeply about horses: they are not his business. But this little man was scowling at the very suggestion of horse-flesh as food for men. He was, I clearly remember, a short, burly man of about sixty, with tiny gold rings in his ears. These gold rings with his blue uniform and grizzled moustache gave him an air of outlandish recklessness: they made his face arresting. But when you looked away from them and considered the man without the ear-rings you saw an ordinary, chubby, round-faced person who could not have been anything but a plain Englishman. He went on:

I was brought up on a farm. I'm a Bedfordshire man. My family have been farmers in Bedfordshire for five hundred years. My father married again. My mother died when I was born. My father was very keen on her and he couldn't bear the sight of me after she died. He didn't treat me badly, didn't knock me about or starve me; just didn't *want* me. He married again when I was about ten, a woman twenty years younger than himself. She didn't like me either. She used to smack hell out of me. She was a little, quiet-looking, mousy, timid-seeming gel, but as soon as she was alone with me she used to make me pay for all the pushing-about she ever got, for she never dared answer my father back. All in all, I had a rotten time when I was a kid. There was nobody for me to play with. Kids ought to have somebody to play with or talk to. I got into the habit of talking to animals. And I kind of made friends with a young horse we had on the farm. His name was Lightning, not because he was fast, but because there was a sort of ziggy-zaggy white splash like a fork of lightning on his chest: the rest of him was black. I kind of fell in love with that horse, if I may say so without seeming silly. He was my pal. He understood every word I said to him. He was the only thing that saved me from going melancholy-mad. I've always been sorry for lonely children ever since. This was when I was about eleven. Lightning, then, was about two years old.

Yes, I was turned eleven, when I made up my mind not to stand it any more. I ran away, to go to sea. I slipped away in the night. The only thing I said good-bye to was Lightning. I had taught him to shake hands: he'd raise a hoof and let me shake it. He did so then, and he knew that I was going away because he whinnied as if he was trying to speak. It nearly broke my heart.

But I went, and the rest is a long and dead ordinary story. I got a ship, worked like a dog as you used to when there was sail, beat about the world, and saw lots of strange countries and got more kicks than shillings. It was a rough life. A cabin-boy was less than a dog: everybody might cuff his head or kick his backside. I hardened up, got older, passed the usual milestones ... got drunk for the first time (it was in Hong Kong), learned to take care of meself in general, and banished home from my mind. I didn't want to think about it. I'd been too miserable there. As a matter of fact I've never seen the place since: and never want to. When my father died and left me the place I sold it to a neighbour by post, and blew-in the proceeds in a couple of months.

Well, I was saying, years passed and I was about twenty years old when I got a job on one of those posh little Channel boats. This, remember, was many years ago. I forget exactly when, but it was before nineteen-ten; good old days, but in some ways not so good. Those were the days of the horse-trade. The Belgians used to eat a lot of horse-flesh, and we used to ship old horses that had been worked out and were not fit to live any more. They would be sent to Belgium for meat. But what used to happen was this: when they landed these horses they would decide that there was another few months' work to be got out of them, and so they would work them, the poor old horses, until they fell dead ... and then eat them.

It was my first trip on this boat. There was a cargo of old horses. When I saw them I felt sick inside. It's not fair. Nobody has got a right to do it—to ill-treat a horse, which is the strongest and the decentest thing that God ever made. It's wickedness! I couldn't bear to look at these poor, broken-down, trembling old hacks that had worked so patiently all those years only to be sold off like this in the end. There is a special hole in Hell for people who get their money like that!

We started. The horses had never been on the water before, and they were terrified. A storm—or rather, a bit of a wind blew up. The horses were plunging and kicking. I was told to see to them. I swallowed my gall and went. I tried to soothe them. They know when a man likes them and they respond to it. And all of a sudden, looking at them, I saw one that seemed familiar.

There was a lightning-shaped splash on his chest. Yes, it was old Lightning—but how he had changed! He had been a proud and beautiful animal, but now he was humble and wretched and broken. The tears came to my eyes when I looked at him. I said to him: "What, Lightning, Lightning my old pal, has it come to this?"

He recognised my voice and looked up. He wasn't quite certain. I said: "Why, Lightning, my old playmate, don't you remember all the long talks we used to have, and the time when I told you the story of Jack the Giant Killer? You used to let me ride on your back. I used to read *Dick Turpin* to you. We're both a bit past that now, aren't we? What, Lightning," I said, "won't you shake hands with me?" He remembered, and lifted up one of his poor old shapeless hoofs, and I shook it, and he whinnied. The wind was rising. We were out of sight of land. I looked at him, and I cried like a child.

Then I made my mind up. I said to him: "You was my pal. I never had any pal except you. And now they're going to take you over there and make you work till you die and eat you, and turn your lovely old skin into leather, and the rest of you into filthy glue. But you've still got one pal left in this terrible old world, Lightning. Do you remember when I went away in the night, and you were sorry to see me go? Are you listening? Do you still understand me?" He whinnied. I got out my knife and cut him loose, and I said to him: "One good turn deserves another. Go on, good old Lightning, make a clean end of it."

He understood. He put up his hoof for me to shake. He put his muzzle on my shoulder for a second. I cut the other horses loose too. And old Lightning stood up stiff and straight, like a two-year-old again, and threw his head back and let out a neigh that sounded like a gale in the rigging, and he went galloping out, and the others followed him. They went stampeding across the deck. And then Lightning gathered himself, took a last jump, and went into the water. Just like men will follow a good leader, so the other horses tried to follow him, and three of them made it. I saw their heads bobbing for a second or two in the rough sea, and then they were gone....

And then I looked away, and my eyes were like windows

when it is raining . . . and I saw a first-class passenger, a nasty old man of eighty who, I'd heard, had made a fortune renting slum houses. He was in a fur coat, and two men-servants were holding him up and walking him to and fro to keep away sea-sickness . . . I don't know why I've remembered that.

Then they collared me and I got hell. I paid dear, but I'd do it again. But what was I saying? Horse-flesh. Eat horse-flesh? I'd sooner eat my own brother if I had one.

Envy

Dorothy could see only the back of the fair young woman, but even about that back, she decided, there was something not quite respectable. The small white hat must have cost too much money; and in the colour of the hair beneath it was concentrated all the genius of Hanover Square. How many fittings had gone to form that dull green two-piece? How had she come by the sable tie? No, she carried herself with too much assurance: it was unnecessarily obvious that she had not a care in the world. Upon the third finger of her right hand shone an emerald as big as a farthing—an emerald such as no young woman can achieve by mere honesty. . . .

At the same time, a little voice in Dorothy's head said: *Some women are lucky!*

It was at this moment that the fair woman turned her head, displaying a pale and perfect profile.

"Charlotte!" cried Dorothy.

"Good heavens, Dorothy!" said the blonde young woman, "this is a surprise! Fancy seeing you here! Come over to my table."

The same old Charlotte, thought Dorothy. *She wouldn't come over to me; no. I have to come to her. Still playing the great lady. . . .* Nevertheless, she picked up her parcels, and went over to Charlotte's table. There was a silence. Then Charlotte said:

"Well . . . you're a nice sister. Why don't I ever hear from you?"

"Oh . . . I don't know. I . . ."

"And what are you doing so far from home?"

Dorothy indicated her parcels. "Just shopping."

"And how's Harold?"

"Oh, fine, thanks."

"Doing well?"

"Oh, yes, wonderfully well. They've made him chief of a department. And you?"

The emerald flashed as Charlotte played with a spoon. "Oh, I jog along, you know. I've just come back from America."

"Not really? What were you doing there?" asked Dorothy, with a qualm of envy.

"Oh, I just went for a holiday. We made a tour—New York, California, all over the place."

"Did you go with friends?"

"With ... a friend."

There was another pause. *She would go to America!* thought Dorothy. She said: "And did you like it?"

"Well, it wasn't bad. Too much excitement, really; but the men are awfully courteous. But one got no sleep at all. Theatres, cabarets, clubs—there was so much to do. I slept nearly all the journey back. I was so exhausted. We came back on the *Queen Mary*.... But, my dear, the shops!"

Instinctively, Dorothy looked at her parcels—the green carrier which contained two pairs of two-and-elevenpenny stockings; the small flat package which enclosed a pair of woollen pants; the other trivial purchases on which she had spent so much thoughtful calculation. She said:

"Yes ... I've heard there are some wonderful shops in America."

"Listen," said Charlotte, "are you in a terrible hurry?"

"Well, no, I've still got an hour or so before I get my train."

"Then come back to my hotel and I'll show you some of my things."

Still showing off, thought Dorothy: but all the same, she said: "I'd love to."

Charlotte paid the bill from a roll of green notes. Dorothy caught a glimpse of a gold compact, a platinum cigarette-case, and a cheque-book.

"Taxi!" cried Charlotte. The doorman shouted: "Taxi!" Charlotte gave him a two-shilling piece. In spite of her resentment, Dorothy could not help glowing in her sister's glory as the taxi moved away.

Charlotte occupied a suite in the Hôtel Pegasus, near Pall Mall—two silent, square rooms decorated in pale blue and gold. *My miserable little brown and burnt-orange drawing-room*, thought Dorothy.

"Cocktail," said Charlotte, "Sidecar? Manhattan? White Lady? Yes, White Lady——"

That's right—don't give me a chance to choose; have it all your own way....

"—I'm good at White Ladies. Once, a man wanted to marry me, simply on account of my White Ladies."

Ice rattled in the shaker. Dorothy looked at her nails, and thought: *Harold wanted to marry me for myself alone.... White Ladies! Showing off!*

"Well, cheers," said Charlotte. The sisters drank. It seemed to Dorothy that Charlotte swilled her drink like a navvy; but in order not to appear provincial, she, also, emptied her glass in two swallows, and then went so far as to accept a fat Egyptian cigarette.

Charlotte opened a vast wardrobe trunk, covered with a patchwork of gaudy labels—"Hôtel Bristol, Cairo"; "The Magnifique, Paris"; "The Mastodon, Berlin"—and began to pull out clothes.

"I got this from Lulu—an exclusive model, my dear. And you see this night-dress? That was made, originally, for a queen; only I absolutely insisted—well, no, not exactly a queen, but a king's mistress. That's even better than a queen, eh? Ha, ha! Undies by Sikorsky ... hats. Look, do you like this hat? I got it at Boadicea's, in Hollywood. It was made for Joan Crawford. I bought it because I simply *had* to have it. And then, well, I simply couldn't wear it. Isn't that funny? Try it on."

"Oh ... Oh! Isn't it lovely?" cried Dorothy.

"You can have it."

"Oh no, I wouldn't dream——"

"Don't be stupid, Dorothy; I insist."

Just like Charlotte; just because she doesn't want it, she offers it to

*me, so as to look big and generous . . . and then she'll go about saying I
wear her cast-off hats. . . .*

"Well . . . it's awfully sweet of you, but . . . well, it must have
cost an awful lot of money."

"*I* didn't pay for it."

"Harold would wonder where I got it."

"You know, Dorothy, you're a fool. You let Harold arrange
your life for you. You've thrown yourself away on a poor man,
and now you simply sink yourself in all this domestic business.
And what do you get out of it? Nothing. And yet you could have
made so much of yourself. You always were the better-looking
of us two, yet you seemed to have no ambition—no life in you.
Honestly, Dorothy, I think you're crazy. Soon, you'll be having
children——"

"I've got one already."

"No! . . . Don't tell me I'm an aunt!"

"Yes, I assure you!"

"Yet you seem to have kept your figure so well! A boy?"

"No, a girl. Geraldine."

"How sweet. . . . But, Dorothy, is it worth it?"

"Why not?"

"Now I ask you, what can you *do*, tied up with children?"

"Oh," said Dorothy, trying to force a cheerful and contented
ring into her voice, "there's plenty to do."

"But what?"

"Well, in the morning, there's Harold's breakfast to get, and
then——"

"Oh, I know, all this domesticity. How grim!"

"There's nothing grim about it," said Dorothy, with rising
annoyance. "I like it."

"But, Dorothy darling; how on earth do you amuse yourself?"

"Well, I don't have to amuse myself much. I find it all quite
interesting. And I can go to the cinema. . . . Besides, Harold and I
come up to Town quite often, and go to a show, and have dinner."

"What do you call 'often'?"

"Well . . . once in . . . every little while. But what do *you* do?"

"Oh, I have quite an amusing time. I travel an awful lot. Next
month we're going to Jamaica. And after that——"

"We?"

Charlotte shrugged, and said, definitely: "Yes, we. Myself, and a friend. And if you want to know, a man friend. He's a duke's son, and enormously rich, and really quite sweet. Well? What is there to stare at? If I didn't somebody else would: and I can assure you, my dear, that I don't lose anything by it."

"Don't you?"

"If you're talking about 'A dearer thing than life', I may as well tell you, I don't believe in it. I'm determined not to be a dowdy little *Hausfrau*, having to work my fingers to the bone, and scrape and struggle for every new hat and dress, and stagnate in some stupid suburb with some perfectly dull and boring husband and a house full of shrieking children . . ."

"Oh? And neither do I. Harold is perfectly marvellous, and Geraldine does *not* scream, and I don't work my fingers to the bone. And I can assure you that I'm quite happy, and I think you're the fool, having to rush about all over the face of the earth looking for something to amuse you."

Charlotte laughed; but there was anger at the back of her voice. "We both started poor," she said, "and I reasoned with you a thousand times. Now tell me; where d'you think all this married stuff is going to get you?"

"Where should it get me? Where is what you're doing going to get you?"

Charlotte replied: "I shall have plenty of money, and be able to do what I like, and go where I like, and buy what I like, and if I pass a shop and see something in the window that I happen to take a fancy to, I can walk straight in and have it. If I want to take a trip round the world, I shall be able to do so as soon as the impulse strikes me———" *Got her there!* she thought. *Poor Dolly; she's always had a longing to travel*—"And in other words, I shall be *free!*"

"Free from what?"

"Free . . . from domestic slavery, from poverty."

"And free *for* what?"

Thirty seconds passed before Charlotte said: "Free to do as I like."

"And for how long?"

"What do you mean?"

"Well, you're nearly thirty now. In another ten or fifteen years, what then?"

Charlotte tore her cigarette to pieces. "And you? What about you? You're thirty yourself. In another few years' time, your husband will be fed up with you, and start running around after younger women."

"I don't see why."

"No, you wouldn't. But I know men."

"Only unhappy men."

"All men are alike."

"Besides," said Dorothy, "in another fifteen years, Geraldine will be seventeen, and I shall probably have some more children growing up, and there'll be plenty to occupy my life."

"I wouldn't have a daughter, not for the world," said Charlotte. "Just think ... Besides, the time comes when they all clear out, sons and daughters; and there you are, a miserable old woman, worn out, all alone, and nothing to look back upon ..."

"Oh, don't let's quarrel, Charlotte."

"*I* didn't start anything, my dear."

"You did, Charlotte!"

"Pardon me, Dorothy, I did *not*."

There was silence. Dorothy looked at the clock, and said: "I must catch my train."

The sisters kissed as they said good-bye.

When Dorothy was gone, Charlotte paced her bedroom. *She's contented!* she thought. *The little fool; what right has she to be contented, when I ...* She looked in the mirror, examining her face closely. Was this the beginning of a wrinkle at the side of her nose? She picked up a pot containing some turtle-oil preparation, and began to massage her face, then she walked round the room again, savagely kicking at a pair of shoes which stood in her path....

By this time, Dorothy was twenty miles away. She thought: *She has a lovely time and beautiful things. Harold will never earn enough to give me things like that.*

She opened the bag, and took out the hat which Charlotte had given her—the exquisite American hat. She looked at this for a long time. Then the idea came to her: *What will Harold say?*

He'll know I couldn't have bought it. And he'd be terribly annoyed if he knew I got it from Charlotte. The window was open. She acted upon the impulse, and dropped the hat out. The wind caught it, and spun it away. She saw it fall in a field, and leaned out to watch it, until it was out of sight.

Then, a thousand annoyances and a thousand little discontents burst their way to the surface of her mind, and she sat back in the empty compartment, weeping into her handkerchief. *Some women have all the luck....*

Tread Lightly

"Once upon a time there was a time when there was no one but God," said the old woman; and she proceeded to tell a tale that was old when Darius was young—a rambling, twisted Persian tale of demons and princes.

But the baby on her knees was too young to understand. He blinked his enormous brown eyes and sucked his thumbs. "Once upon a time there was a King without a Kingdom ..."

Meanwhile the people at the loom worked steadily. There were five of them, all moving with a kind of feverish patience over a half-finished carpet of a design as colourful, intricate, and ancient as the grandmother's story.

"Now this King without a Kingdom had three sons, two of whom were dead. The third did not exist ..."

"Agoo," said the baby.

"Observe her," said the leader of the weavers. "She is seventy years old. She is blind. She has woven her eyes into the carpets. I am eighty years old. My eyes are fading. You, my son; and you, my daughter-in-law; and you, my grandson and my granddaughter; you, also, shall weave your eyes into the carpets. Work! Work while you have the light!"

He was a tall old man, with an outstretched neck and knotted eyebrows. Time and the loom had bent him like a bow. But there was a tensile strength in the curve of his coffee-coloured back, with its spine like a whangee cane and its muscles like jumping piano-wires.

"Work on!" he shouted. "Work well, and thank God! Work, my son! In six months we shall be finished. It will be a fine carpet." He paused over some tiny detail, some infinitesimal speck of red wool; stretched himself, rubbed his forehead, blinked a dozen times, and said: "They walk on your father's eyes."

The old woman murmured: "Now the Prince who had no existence took a knife without a blade and cut . . ."

The loom clacked. The wool rustled.

"It is good work," said the son.

"For which thank God," said the old man.

The baby began to cry. "Wait, wait," said the wife, and completed another row.

Seven months passed. They finished the carpet. Fantastic yet harmonious, brilliant but delicate, bold and subtle in its multiplicity of colours and patterns, it lay on the ground at the feet of the dealer. The weavers stood by.

"No good," said the dealer.

"Turn my face towards him," said the old man. He had become blind. "You say no good? For a thousand years my fathers . . ."

"I know," said the dealer. "I know all about that. For a thousand years your fathers made carpets. Of course. And you, and your sons and daughters have worked day and night for a year. Or is it eighteen months? But look at it!"

"Shahs have sat on such carpets," said the old man.

"I'm not saying the work is bad: far from it," said the dealer. "But the size! Six hundred square feet! Nobody has such floors these days. Take it away."

"Take it away? Take it away? Where shall I take it, in the name of God? And look—I am blind! This is my last carpet. I shall never see another carpet. By God and by God, I am selling you these two eyes! Take it away, you say?"

"May I never be a father to my children if I lie," said the dealer. "May I go to Hell and burn for ever. By God and the Prophet. I shall lose by it if I buy. I don't want it, Omar, not at any price. In fact, I'd rather not have it as a gift. Spit upon my father's grave if what I tell you is not the purest truth. I shan't know what to do with it. Well, I don't want to see you starve. This is my last offer. May I burn in Hell for ever ..."

Ten minutes later, the dealer walked away grinning. He had bought the carpet for something like four pounds.

Speaking to the exporter a week later, he said: "It is a gem and a masterpiece. Talk to me of Tehran? I spit on Tehran. I spit on Ispahan. This Kirman carpet is fit for the palace of the King of France. It is one of Omar's. His family has worked for my family for ten generations. I spit on all other carpets in the world."

They finished the deal over coffee. The exporter got the carpet for eight pounds. "May my sons' sons be born with no eyes," said the dealer. "I lose by this. It cost me more. Still, I don't want to lose your friendship. And since this masterpiece goes with the rest. All right. God forgive you. And may I, also, be forgiven for robbing my children."

"It is I who lose, Abdallah," said the exporter. "I take this carpet so as to keep alive the memories of old times. Upon the head of my father it is so. By the honour of my mother and my daughters, I lose on the deal. Let me rot in purgatory for eleven million years—me, and my father, and my father's father—if what I say is not true. Ai-yah, fool that I am!"

He sold the carpet to a Bond-street firm for £42. Mr. Roget ticketed it as a museum-piece, and sold it to Sir Morgan Tremorgan for a hundred and sixty guineas.

And so the carpet lay in Sir Morgan's library for five years, until the chaos of the Rubber Slump. Men blew out their brains. Sir Morgan died of a broken heart. And his creditors took over his effects, and the carpet came under the hammer at Hodgson's in the Strand. . . .

It was rolled up with three other vast carpets and labelled: "LOT 69—FOUR VERY FINE ANTIQUE PERSIAN CARPETS." A Mr. Garabed Mamoulian acquired the lot for sixteen pounds, unrolled them in his shop in the Haymarket; kicked the others aside while he lingered over Omar's work, and walked away grinning.

He had bought the carpet for something like four pounds.

But he sold it, the following year, to the press-lord of Illinois, Johnson Williams Oliver, for seven hundred guineas, guaranteeing it to be the favourite carpet of Omar Khayyám.

Oliver refused an offer of ten thousand dollars for it in California.

The old blind carpet-maker, meanwhile, sat by the side of his old blind wife.

The son, thinner and older, paused from time to time to rub his sore eyes.

"Once upon a time there was a time when there was no one but God," droned the old woman. But the baby, having achieved the age of eight years, was too busy at the loom to listen.

The Naked Man

In the forest things grew nightmarishly. Tree jostled tree. Weed strangled weed. Grabbing and sucking at the soil, vast plants raced leaf-to-leaf up towards the sun. Sometimes a great tree fell; the germs of decay that flourished in the wet heat ate it up, and the shoots of other trees wrestled for space in the place that was left. Staring blossoms of sickly scent coquetted with pollen-bearing insects in the steamy greenish shadows. Everything that had voice chattered, gibbered, roared, or sang; everything that had colour opened and blazed. Vitality ran loose—the gluttonous vitality of the forest. Ravenous birds snapped up beetles that flew like blue sparks. Sometimes, crashing and snarling, a big cat dragged down something that squealed. Fungi hid under roots, but wild swine dug them out. Even flowers turned themselves into death-traps and caught flies. One seed in a billion might germinate; one life in a million might survive birth; but that was still too much. Life ate life. To live, it was necessary to stay out of the reach of things. At least two creatures had discovered this: the louse that lived between the shoulders of the tiger; and the ape that swung in the high branches of the tree.

The apes were new creatures. Nature was still making experiments, building and breaking things, making each animal in its way perfect. She had formed pterodactyls, birds with teeth, impossible lizards taller than trees, impracticable cattle with too many horns; but all these monstrosities had been rubbed back into the mud from which they had come. But new things were being born of the struggle. The defenceless beasts of the plain beyond the forest developed strength and speed. Springy power and lithe beauty were rising out of the terror and weakness of the antelope that bounded beyond the claws of the hunting cats. The shocks and worries of existence were changing the face of life. Species were becoming stabilized.

But still there occurred strange accidents.

A grey, primeval ape of nondescript form, mating with a big red she-monkey, begot strange twins. They were born one night in a tree-top. The one that died was grey like its father. The other, a male, lived. His colour was carrot-red; his fur widespread but sparse. His face was different; there was more of it above the eyes. Fed on insects and fruit, he grew slowly, but survived his perilous infancy and became big and strong. There was about this creature something that distinguished him from his fellows. He was either more, or less, than the things that swung, gibbering, from the branches. His hands were larger. Like the apes, he wandered purposelessly in blind curiosity, but he possessed a strange faculty for imitation. Seeing wild swine rooting, he would root. Seeing the tiger lie in wait, he also waited. He ate everything, cramming his mouth with fruit, flowers, bark, beetles, and carrion.

And all the time he fought. Running with the apes, he nevertheless kept aloof from them, tolerating no companionship. In the season, he fought the bachelors for mates; but having won them, he drove them away, producing no offspring. He was at once intrepid and cowardly, shy and audacious, ferocious and treacherous. The apes hated him; he was of the wrong size and shape; an unmatchable freak; an accident.

One day they drove him away. The battle was short and furious. He was outnumbered. Soon he disappeared in the trees and hid, licking his wounds. One sleek little female followed him, plaintively chattering. He sent her screaming with a red gash across her neck; turned, snarling and grunting, and swung away. He travelled steadily, hurling himself from branch to branch, sending burst blossoms and startled birds fluttering into the shadows. He ate as he travelled, snatching fruit, eggs, spiders, and on one occasion a gurgling green bird with a red crest.

While the light lasted he went on, and slept briefly and suspiciously on a branch. Sunrise followed sunrise. Something was driving him. He grew thinner, but travelled faster. The trees became wider-spaced. He dropped to the ground and ran uncouthly, sometimes on his hind legs and sometimes on all-fours, skirting the steaming river and the black mud where crocodiles snapped and sank and rotting logs drifted. There was no more fruit. He ate bark and twigs. Once, smelling pig, he hung on a high branch and dropped to fight desperately with a small wild boar, which he killed with his hands and teeth as a child demolishes a toy—breaking legs, tearing hair. So he ate and slouched on his way.

The river grew wilder. The air was cooler, and a breeze blew. The sounds of the forest faded, giving place to a murmuring, and unending sighing. He passed the last tree. There was silence, dreadful and immeasurable. He roared. Echo roared back. The sun sank. It was profoundly dark in the sand-dunes. He lay in a hollow, covering his face with his arms and slept. And then it seemed that he was again in the forest, sleeping high in the branches of a tree … and something was cracking, and he was falling. Instinctively, he reached out a groping hand to clutch a bough; found nothing; cried out despairingly, threshed wildly and awoke with his hands full of sand. The trees were far behind him, and he was sitting on a wide, sloping beach. He looked about him. The sun was rising. It burst over the horizon. Miles behind him the jungle stirred, shrieking and twittering. Before him lay the end of the world. It ended in green water, sparkling and heaving, running forward, drawing back.

And as he looked, there flashed into his soul a strange pang: a pang of terror mixed with exaltation; a yearning to advance combined with an impulse to go back; a ferocious anger; a misery. He rose erect on the dune, blinking at the dazzling water; sucked into his ponderous chest a vast draught of salty air, pounded his bosom, and roared with all his might at the shining, empty silence.

He knew, then, that somewhere before him or behind him there was a mate. Meanwhile, he was thirsty. He ran down to the water, waited for a wave, and filled his mouth; spluttered, grimaced, and spat. He growled in his bewilderment. The water was bitter.

He was the first man.

Time passed. There were hot days and cold nights. Mountains became boulders. Boulders split in the frosts, and the wind ground them to sand. Grain against grain the sand milled itself to dust, and the wind drifted the dust into dark, waving heaps. There was no means whereby a man could find his way, for the face of the earth altered with every breath of breeze; hills became valleys, and even as one looked the valleys became lakes of rippling dust.

In the middle of a dry hell of dust-dunes that shifted, murmuring, like a landscape in an evil dream—across the wilderness under a dreadful liver-coloured sky, a creature staggered while the light lasted. It was a male, covered from head to foot with shaggy hair, the colour of which was lost under a caked coating of grey dust. He might have been an ape, but there was something about him which made him either more, or less, than an ape. He walked almost upright. Above his reddened eyes there was a protuberance like a forehead. He was hungry; the skin hung from him in dry folds. Thirsty: his black tongue lolled, swollen, between big, prominent teeth. Something was driving him. He ploughed, reeling, between the singing dust-heaps, sometimes looking up at the huge red sun that hung low in the western sky. Suddenly it sank. There was no more light. The night was impenetrable and cold. He dared not rest, but lurched on in silence.

The night passed. The last moment of endurance passed. He found that he had fallen, exhausted and without hope. The reddened eyes closed. And then there came into his soul a new terror, one which he could not understand. It seemed that he was in a high place, and was falling with inconceivable speed through empty space. Instinctively, he threw up a hand to clutch something; found nothing; tried to cry out, and awoke with his hands full of powdery dust.

The dunes were drifting again. He was almost buried. He rose and went on. Then he saw a redness, and felt a whiff of sickly heat. It was the dawn. He watched it. The sun sailed up, swollen and blood-coloured. Below, under a sky blackened with floating dust, lay something that heaved. As he looked, the heaving thing cracked in a zigzag like a lightning-flash, and the red light of the dawn shone on the water. The man ran down, ploughing through the dunes; felt his feet sink into warm, wet mud; wallowed forward; touched the edge of the water, and, with a great sweep of his arms, drove aside the piled dust that floated upon it. He plunged his mouth into a wave; recoiled, coughing and gasping.

The water was bitter.

He sat down in the mud and looked over the grey, heaving waste. The crack slowly closed. The dust covered everything. He was dying. He knew that. But at the back of his head something seemed to seethe and struggle. Soon he would sleep, and let the dust cover him; and then there would be nothing but the lurid sun in the sky above, the bitter waters in the sea below, and the murmuring dunes in the wilderness of dust behind him. A strange madness came upon him. With his last strength he rose, stared up at the blank, tumid disc of the sun, filled his lungs, beat his chest with his skinny fists, and uttered one little croak of defiance and despair.

He was the last man.

Gomez

I got this story from Crump, who had it straight from the lips of Gomez. And very strange lips they must be—knocked out of shape; cracked here and there; divided in two places by old white scars.

Scars. If you could strip Gomez you would discover a complete history of violent accidents carved upon his knotty little body. Life has chiselled some queer hieroglyphics in the flesh of that abnormally tough Mexican.

Looking at him, you would say that he had got caught in

the cogs of some monstrous machine. His skull is battered and dented like an old aluminium saucepan. His ears have been man-handled so that they resemble those bulbous red fungi that grow on old trees in dark forests.

One eye is darkened for ever; the other has the brightness of two. The butt of a rifle has made a sinister ruin of his nose. The line of his jaw has some peculiar lumps where it was broken and badly set. Yet, by some miracle of chance, he has never lost a tooth and flashes a great smile that seems to be made of peeled almonds set in coral.

He limps. His shoulders, under the white jacket, look as fragile as a coat-hanger. A bulge at the left armpit betrays the presence of a big revolver, worn in the American style. He talks gravely, and with punctilious observation of all the courtesies; drinks little, eats less, smokes much, and loiters to this day in the cafés of Mexico City.

There he sits, smoking black cigarette after black cigarette, and taking tiny sips of tequila—that desperate liquor which the Mexicans distil from the cactus and which rasps the throat like prickles and leaves an arid flavour of the desert. . . .

Gomez had a political education. That is to say, he was in a revolt or two in the good old days when bullets were dear and life was cheap and Pancho Villa steeped himself to the elbows in blood. Then, since Gomez was younger, and had both his eyes, he could shoot the pips out of the six of spades in six shots at twenty paces. (Now he can manage only five out of six.)

One day a company of soldiers surrounded the farmhouse in which Gomez and seven of his comrades were hiding. It was a lively little siege, while the cartridges lasted, and there seems to have been some very pretty hand-to-hand fighting in the last few minutes.

But in the end Gomez was captured. He was the sole survivor, and had been wounded during the battle. Nothing much: a ball in the lung. The enemy captain dragged him out, and slapped his face, and burnt him with a cigar-end for good measure, and told him to say his prayers.

Then Gomez was propped up against the white wall and shot. He counted the firing-squad: seven. His last thought was that he wished he had the Mannlicher rifle of the second man on the left.

These are the bare facts. Gomez was sentenced to death, executed, shot seven times in the chest, and has the scars to prove it. He fell. The captain gave him a finishing shot in the head, and the soldiers rode away leaving him to the vultures. Night fell. Day broke. A couple of peons passed, and saw a redness which seemed to move. It was Gomez. He was not dead. The captain's bullet had passed between the skull and the brain; the soldiers' bullets had punctured no immediately vital spot.

The peons bandaged him up. He recovered and went on his way. A year or two later he joined the forces of law and order and became a policeman, married, settled down, begot daughters. There were little incidents, of course. Once a criminal broke his skull with a hammer. He recovered.

Another time he was shot in the back. The bullet missed his spine by a sixteenth of an inch, scraped his heart, perforated a lung and came out at his armpit, just grazing the great artery. He got better. Two men threw him from the roof of a four-storey building, through a glass fanlight. He lay with eleven broken bones for a whole night before he was found. But everything healed up quite nicely.

Then the authorities sent him after a bandit—some desperado who had shot a cashier in a restaurant and taken to the hills. Gomez loaded his guns and set out. But the word went before him and the bandit was waiting. He had a very particular desire to kill Gomez, just because no man had ever done so before. He was a methodical fellow, this bandit. Having notched the noses of six big bullets, he sat behind a rock until Gomez came within point-blank range, then opened fire.

Two of his bullets hit Gomez in the abdomen, the rest struck higher up. Gomez found time to fire one shot, which killed the bandit, and then fell flat.

An ambulance picked them up next morning. It was impossible that Gomez could still be alive. They took him fifty miles up the bumpy road and put him on a slab in the mortuary refrigerator. The good wife of Gomez came to look at him. She screamed: "My husband! He lives! He moves!" And so he did.

He was not quite dead. The cold of the refrigerator had kept away peritonitis: the miracle was that he had escaped pneumonia —quite apart from the extraordinary gravity of his wounds.

After a few months in hospital, Gomez walked again, and went about his business. He still covered the underworld. Black-browed assassins found a new hobby: trying to kill Gomez. It became a craze, a foible, like Squaring the Circle or Perpetual Motion.

He was shot again, twice. Then somebody decided that the knife was surer: you knew what you were doing when you had a blade in your fist. So the doctors of Mexico City were confronted with new freaks of human survival. Gomez was cut to ribbons. He lived on. He survived stabs in the liver, the stomach, the throat. He is one of the few people whose hearts have been stitched, and who live to boast of it.

He touched nothing without getting hurt. Once he was thrown through the windscreen of a car. Once he was in a lorry with four other men. The lorry went over a precipice. The four men were killed. Gomez was unhurt, except for a broken leg. And as late as 1938 he was attacked in a café by three bad men, and stabbed seventeen times. He was sewn up: the men were buried.

So you still see him, sitting placidly over a little glass of tequila, politely acknowledging the salutes of the awestruck customers: always refusing three times before accepting a drink, in accordance with the dictates of Mexican etiquette; smoking tobacco strong enough to choke the devil, and exchanging light conversation.

And he is afraid. That is the extraordinary thing—the really incredible thing. At the back of his mind there is one little nagging fear.

"I fear," he says, "that God is preserving me for something terrible."

The Ruined Wall

You would have longed for rain to wash and night to bandage
the sore eye of the sun. There was a tenseness. The world felt
like a time-bomb. It was the heat—that and the dust, together
with a certain electricity in the air which made every hair feel
as if it ought to be standing on end, and sent imaginary insects
crawling from shoulder-blade to shoulder-blade. The horizon,
beyond those abominable plains, was vague. It vacillated. A
queer, weaving shadow flitted across it. The Rumanians have
a legend about that trick of the dying sunlight: it is Larra the
Deathless, running alone and desolate, worn down to nothing
but a shadow. He hunts for death, but he cannot die: nothing
can kill Larra. He was too proud—the son of a princess and an
eagle. He became a murderer, and so he wanders for ever in the
twilight and the dust. Such is his destiny. One day God may
forgive him; but not yet. So he runs: a devil, a poor devil.

I stopped at a cottage and asked for a drink. A very old
woman, brown and wrinkled as a tobacco-leaf, said: "Ah, but ..."
She looked at my clothes, and said: "A drink of what?" You may
rest assured that I slapped my pocket and let a jingle be heard
before I replied: "Of anything that flows." Some travellers swear
by South French hospitality. But some claim to have seen the
Indian Rope Trick.

"It is going to thunder," I said.

"Perhaps," said the old woman. She was giving nothing away;
not even an opinion.

With a certain ostentation I took a cigarette out of a silver
case. She said: "Wine is dear, but water is almost dearer. Please
come in."

"What a charming little house," I said.

She replied, as one who stated a simple reason: "I have lived
here seventy-two years."

"So long, madame?"

"I was born here."

"Is it true?"

"I assure you," she said, "that it is true."

I drank, and said: "I should not have believed you to be more than forty-seven or at the most forty-eight."

"All the same, I am seventy-two," she said. "My father was born here, too."

"Not possible!"

She smiled. "But yes. I left here only once, to stay with my sister at Arles. Only once, for a month. Never again. Never, never, never again in my life."

"You don't like Arles?"

"Oh ... for that I don't say yes or no."

"Then why never again?"

"Look," she said, and pointed. One of the flat white walls was hideously smeared. The plaster had been scraped and lime-washed. But under a chalky film, there were visible scars; deep scratches and raised cicatrices. Her voice was angry as she muttered: "Félix promised to plaster it over. But that was thirty years ago, and it is still as you see it."

"What happened, then?"

"Miserable sinner that I am," she said, "I went to Arles because my sister wanted me to go, because her husband was dead and she was alone. I always was too generous and silly like that, me; that is my character; I am like that; it is stronger than me, so what can one do then? So I went to Arles. My judgment said: 'Do not go.' But my heart, my stupid soft heart said: 'Go for a little while.' Besides, my sister's husband had been an ironmonger in a comfortable way of business. Even so I might not have gone, but she said: 'You are all I have in the world, sister; and be sure that I shall see you don't lose by coming to see me. I have fifteen thousand francs,' she said. Eh, well! Blood is thicker than water. I went. Fool that I was! She married again five years afterwards, and much I saw of those fifteen thousand francs. She gave me two hundred for coming to stay with her, and even then I had to fight to get it. She wanted to give me a hundred, but I sat down on the doorstep of the shop and said: 'Two hundred or I don't budge.' Oh, no, no, no—never again do I leave this house of mine.

"Now before I left there came along a woman from the village. I have never spoken to her from that day to this. She said: 'Marthe, for how long do you stay away?' And I said: 'Three weeks, four weeks perhaps.' She said: 'Jacques Tubois is looking after the chickens, I hear.' I said it was so, Tubois and I had an arrangement: he owed me a good turn because seven years before I had done him a good turn. I am like that: it is my character, sir. I sat up all one night with his mother who was dying, and took no payment for it."

"Madame, you are too good."

"I have a tender heart. I can't help it. It is stronger than I, my heart. So; this woman said: 'There is a rich fool from Paris who is looking for a place to stay; an artist, a painter. He wants to live here for two weeks. He would pay well, I think.'

"So I see this fellow: a fool, skinny and dirty. I hate dirtiness, me. It is stronger than I am. I love cleanliness. I have, safely put away, copper pans which I have never even used, and also linen. You may examine this house, sir, through a glass, and not find a speck of dirt. He was dirty and little and foolish, what is more. Wrong up here, sir; he wept as he talked and looked at me in a funny way. He talked about religion, in a blasphemous way. He picked up my hands and said: 'Jesus liked hands like this. They are beautiful.' I said to him: 'I am not here to be insulted, or to be cursed and sworn at. Language like that brings bad luck. If you want to stay in my house it will cost you thirty francs for the month.' I would have been glad to take twenty, for I am weak and silly; but he pulled out his money. He only had forty francs altogether. He put the thirty francs in my hand, and another five. He was mad, mad, sir, *fada*.

"So I went to Arles, but not before I had quarrelled with the woman from the village, who asked for five francs for sending me that little man. Well, the end of it was, I gave her the five francs on condition that she kept the place clean every day. Of course, I hid away all my little valuables; my copper pots and my linen, and a silver spoon more than a hundred years old, and a printed picture of the Virgin Mary that had cost me sixty sous and was as good as a photograph. I said to the artist: 'What is there here for you to paint?' And he said: 'Why, all that,' and pointed out of the window there, to—nothing at all! Some trees, some sky, some hills! So I said: 'That is your affair,' and went to see my sister, and things happened as I told you. She died ten years ago, leaving fifty thousand francs in money, and a business, all to her sons. And to me five hundred francs. She was no sister of mine, and I'm glad I had nothing more to do with her after that trip. You know Arles? A Sodom and Gomorrah. Men and women drink in cafés. At nine o'clock at night people are still prowling about the streets. Filthiness!

"I stayed nearly a month. And then something—a voice inside me, here—told me to go home. I had a feeling of danger. God told me to return, and I did, and ah, God was right!

"As soon as I set foot inside here I felt that something was wrong. The painter was gone. The place was empty. It had been swept and cleaned, yes. But my wall! You see for yourself, that wall. And after forty-five years it is still dirty. The stuff soaked into the plaster, deep. It has been scraped a hundred times. Ah, the tears I have shed over that unhappy wall. Judge, sir, my horror and anger! The painter had painted pictures all over there. I am an old woman and may tell you frankly what he had painted. A woman without clothes on—only a skirt, working in a field among men stark naked except for shoes and trousers, with all kinds of vegetables and trees growing. It was a mad picture. There was a thing with wheels and clouds of smoke, too, and men with pickaxes on their shoulders, all black, and half-naked too. And worst of all—there were three or four filthy urchins with dirty noses and muddy faces playing with some pebbles, and standing by them, almost joining in, was ... no, it was too strong! The Lord, smiling like a schoolboy.

"Tubois said he knew nothing of it; also the accursed woman. But I believe she put him up to it, that dirty little artist. I scraped the picture off, but I could not get the wall clean. And plastering is dear, sir, and I am poor. I complained to the police. 'Find him and bring him back, the malefactor,' I said. 'A little slice of a man with a carroty head and blue eyes, smelling of tobacco and wine,' I said. 'Some kind of a Prussian; Von Gugg, Vincent Von Gork.

A spy, no doubt,' I said. 'Van Gogh, yes, that's it. Where is the law, where is the justice in the world if men like this can go about the earth wrecking houses with their filthiness and their swin-ishnesses?'

"But they never found him, and nobody has heard anything of him from that day to this, though somebody is supposed to have seen him in Arles. And my beautiful clean wall! Ah, I have suffered, sir, I have suffered . . . and I am a poor, lonely woman . . . imposed upon by all the world. . . ."

The Dungeon

"The dungeons are down here," said the jailer. "Take care how you go. The steps are worn. We are below the level of the moat. It is very damp. Don't touch the walls. A sort of mushroomy thing grows all over the stone. It won't hurt you, it won't hurt a bit; only it soils the clothes. . . . Yes, the dungeons are empty now. I hear they built a new prison, what they call a hygienic, up-to-date prison, over at Kalvarea. What I say is, a prison should *be* a prison. Good men don't go to prison; so why should a prison be just so? . . . As long as they can't get out of it. . . . Now this place is eight hundred years old, and as good as new. It was built, gentlemen, by Count Manolescu in the twelfth century. And until ten years ago it was in constant use. Do you want to see the dungeons, or would you rather go straight on to the torture-chamber? The dungeons. Very well, only there isn't much to see . . ."

The jailer pushed open a heavy iron door, and held his lantern as high above his head as his rheumatic right hand could reach. The dungeon was a dreadful place; ten feet square, ten feet high, stinking of dampness, sickeningly oppressive, cold as death, hopeless.

One of our party said: "Bring that lamp over here. I seem to see some carving on this wall."

"Carving, sir?" said the jailer. "God bless you, all four walls are covered with it. Here, sir, the light falls better this way . . ."

We crowded about the sprawling rectangle of yellow light

that fell on the North wall. Somebody had carved the stone in a crowded and elaborate bas-relief, representing scenes from the life of Christ. Here was the Crucifixion. The artist had made the stone writhe. There was something terribly poignant in the patient suffering carved into the face of the Jesus.

"If you look closely," said the jailer, "you will see that these are not old carvings. They were done by the last prisoner here. He died . . . I forget exactly when; about ten years back. I forget his name. It was John something-or-other. I don't remember what he was here for. It was something to do with politics. He was condemned to perpetual solitary confinement. He was a young man of very good family. I was jailer here when they first brought him in. 'Jan,' they said to me, 'Jan, this one's for the Black Hole.' (That's what they called this cell, gentlemen, The Black Hole.) 'This one's for the Black Hole,' they said. 'No communications. Life imprisonment. Lock him up.' So I said: 'He won't be out of this in a hurry,' I said. 'I've always done my duty, thank God.' And so I have, gentlemen.

"Well, at first he said nothing. You could see he was a proper gentleman. He would look at me as if I was dirt when I brought him his meals. But I said to myself: 'You wait, my fine sir: you'll be glad enough to talk to me sooner or later.' And so he was.

"After a month of it, he said to me, one morning: 'What day is it?' Now *no communications* means no conversation, so I said nothing and went out.

"Next day he said: 'For the love of God, what day is it? Have I been here a year yet?' I couldn't help laughing. A year! And he hadn't been here five weeks.

"By the end of the second month he would have given anything for a chat. Yes, gentlemen, I'm only a humble warder of a jail, but I've had the nobility on their knees before me in my time.

"He went and fell on his knees, and said: 'For the love of God, talk to me!' I shook my head. Duty is duty. And I used to hear him laughing and crying. Cruel, sir? Maybe so. But if I'm employed to keep a man without communications, I keep a man without communications.

"After three months he was offering me fortunes. 'Be human,' he'd say. 'Be kind. Talk, and I'll pay you well. I'm innocent, I swear! I'll pay you thousands. I'll pay you a thousand for a word, one word.' But I'm incorruptible. Besides, where would he get thousands from? Well, gentlemen, after that he raved and shouted a bit; and in the end he shut up again.

"You understand, I was told that if he wanted to do away with himself, that was quite all right. He had a knife, fork, spoon, and so on. One morning he asked for a new knife. I looked at the old one, and saw it was worn right down to the handle. Aha, I thought. He's trying to cut a way out; and I laughed a bit, for these walls are solid granite, fourteen feet thick, with a moat above them.

"I flashed my light around, and saw that he had been trying to scratch a face on the wall; it was quite lifelike. He was occupying his mind, as the saying goes. So I asked for instructions, for I had no orders about new knives, and at last I got him one, and he kept quiet again.

"Mind you, every week or so he'd burst out with: 'Have I been here ten years yet?' and 'Have I been here twenty years yet?' and 'Is my hair white yet?' but that got less and less as time went on. He went on scratching his little pictures on the walls, just like you see; face after face, figure after figure. It's quite a novelty, really, seeing as he did every stroke of it in the dark, for we didn't let him have a light. I had no instructions about that.

"But the carving kept his mind occupied. He started to wear out too many knives, so we gave him wooden knives to eat with and old nails and screws to play about with. Many's the bushel he must have worn out on these walls, gentlemen, in the thirty years he was here."

We looked around us at the damp walls of impregnable stone. We felt, already, a frightful sensation of halted time. The tomb-like smell of the place seemed to stick to the roofs of our mouths. The dank air got through our overcoats and clung to our skin.

"Thirty years," I said. "God have mercy!"

"Thirty-seven," said the jailer. "I remember now, thirty-seven, because he came here on my little girl's tenth birthday.

"He filled up all four walls. And do you know what? When we had instructions to remove him to the Infirmary ten years ago—you'll laugh at this bit—he kicked and struggled. He bruised my knee, he did. And do you know what he said? He said: 'Go away! Can't you leave me in peace for five minutes?' He died on the road. It's my belief the air killed him.

"Now, gentlemen, if you're ready, we'll go along to the torture-chamber ..."